The Glass Ar

Sometimes it seemed more like a school or training camp for cadets than a brothel for soldiers on leave. It was only on weekends when the men arrived that the atmosphere changed. Friday was the great metamorphosis, the hinge of each week when the dormitories were transformed into the backstage area of a cabaret. Sports equipment was chucked aside in favor of rhinestone stockings and elaborate makeup.

Michael found bizarre the idea of these sudden shifts from well-regimented boyhood to orgiastic enthusiasm. But they assured him that once one learned to accept the game and to adhere to the guidelines, it could actually be enjoyable. So what if they lay with men. It would be a lot more interesting than going to school. Besides, the champagne was good, the food was delicious and most of the men were not unkind. Some of them could be almost tender. . . .

THE GLASS ARCADE

Adrian Brooks

PUBLISHED BY POCKET BOOKS NEW YORK

Another *Original* publication of POCKET BOOKS

POCKET BOOKS, a Simon & Schuster division of
GULF & WESTERN CORPORATION
1230 Avenue of the Americas, New York, N.Y 10020

Copyright © 1980 by Adrian Brooks and Elsboy Incorporated

All rights reserved, including the right to reproduce
this book or portions thereof in any form whatsoever.
For information address Pocket Books, 1230 Avenue
of the Americas, New York, N.Y. 10020

ISBN: 0-671-82916-5

First Pocket Books printing July, 1980

10 9 8 7 6 5 4 3 2

POCKET and colophon are trademarks of Simon & Schuster.

Printed in the U.S.A.

After hearing the testimony of witnesses at the trial of Adolf Eichmann, Paul Aaron wrote the story upon which this novel is based. It could not have been written without his aid and inspiration.

PART I
1934

Chapter One

When Michael let the screen door slam, the baby began to cry. He crossed the porch and went down three wooden steps. As he hurried across the garden he could hear his father's words over the infant's wailing.

"What is it?" Michael's father sounded annoyed.

"Oh, nothing," his mother replied. "The front door . . ."

The boy started for the forest that bordered their meadow. Although the trees were only thirty yards from the house, the refuge they offered seemed far distant. At any moment he expected to hear a summons, a call to stand shamefaced and mute as his parents lectured him about waking the baby again. But there was no sound.

The forest was cool and silent. It was a welcome relief from the midafternoon heat of the house and the open field. This was sanctuary!

His favorite spot was a stand of linden trees surrounding a small pond. He often came here to while away the hours when the midday sun made it too hot to do chores. And, although he hadn't braved the water this season, today would be a good day for a swim. June the first! The beginning of another unknown summer!

Michael stood by the pond and stared down. He could see leaves at the bottom, resting like scraps of colored paper captured by the wind and dropped there to dissolve. From where he stood he could see the greens and pale yellows turning to brown in the muddy depths . . . or he could concentrate on the glassy surface and see the towering trees reflected on the water; they loomed above him like the vaulted arches of a cathedral. Beyond them, a uniformly blue sky. Nearby, his own image. He backed up so that he couldn't see the image of his pale hair and slender body. Now, perfectly mirrored in the enclosure, he could observe heaven and earth and the darkness below.

For some reason the complexity of nature was depressing to him. It hadn't always been so but in recent months, ever since his fourteenth birthday, he'd begun to feel more and more isolated, more and more cut off from a world he'd always perceived as personal and welcoming. Now even a butterfly or a certain view of the moon seemed utterly oppressive.

Not to mention the new baby. Michael shed his cotton shirt and short pants and paused for a moment. The narrow shafts of sun which pierced the glade made his body dappled and flecked with leaf patterns and shadows cast by distant branches. He smiled as he gazed at the golden light which enveloped his body. And, for a moment, he forgot the melancholia caused by the outside world of grown-ups and their problems. It was summer and he was on the edge of a million discoveries!

Without further ado, he plunged into the pool. Almost at once he surfaced, gasping and sputtering, kicking out and groping for the nearest land mass. Too cold, too cold! And he hadn't thought to bring a towel! Oh, what a mistake!

He clutched the bank and tossed a shock of wet hair from his face. Just as he gathered himself for a leap into the welcome sunlight, he heard footsteps.

As they approached, coming closer and closer, the boy shivered despite himself. Of course, he knew whom to expect. Still, there was no way to escape. And yet, the water was so cold!

Instinctively, he dived back into the pond, immersing

himself and swimming about in the half-light of the amber water. As he swam, he tried to accept the coldness and plan his course of action.

Of course, he *could* get out and pretend that there was nothing amiss. That seemed wrong, however, despite the cold water. It was too embarrassing. In recent weeks, tiny blond hairs had begun to enfold his sex. While he realized that such growth was inevitable, natural or not, he was alarmed. His body would change. It had already begun! Life, which had always been so orderly, would overwhelm him and end his childhood. The worst thing was the way it all came so fast with no time to prepare. In some awful way, he felt that his years of bliss, or ignorance and innocence, were ensnared by these tiny hairs and the arrival of his unwelcome younger brother. Somehow they both proved that he was perishable, that nothing was his and that whatever he claimed, he would lose. Puberty had come and with it tides of humiliation and depression.

His lips were blue and he was shivering uncontrollably. He had no other options; he came up in waist-deep water. His father was waiting on the bank.

For a brief moment, father and son regarded one another in silence. Michael had always thought of his father as aged, but such was not the case. Thirty-five years hadn't obliterated all traces of youth from the man. Oh, the farmwork had made him lined and strangely quiet, to be sure, but his eyes were open and clear. Now, as he held out a hand, Michael wished that he could permit himself the luxury of being drawn up and engulfed by the strong arms. But the embarrassment made it impossible. He shook his head.

There was something else! Something which seemed to strangle his true voice, making everything artificial and so, doubly offensive. He wanted to blurt out something awful to make the man go away. He wanted to disappear into the water and stay there. After all, he'd come out here to be by himself! Now, once again, the choices were not his. The most he could do was to refuse the proffered hand and remain standing in the safe depths.

"You must be cold." His father's tone was difficult to read. Was he angry? No. If he was he'd sound different. But, if he wasn't upset, why was he here? Couldn't he go back to the house and leave everything as it had been?

"At first it was," the boy replied, turning his eyes from his father's steady gaze, feigning interest in the way his hands made sweeping arcs beneath the water's surface, camouflaging his nakedness. "It gets better," he added.

"Lunch is almost ready."

"I know." Still, he made no effort to move. Perhaps, if he was lucky, his father would sense his discomfort and give him time to dry off, alone, in the sun. Then he could dress in peace and return to the house in time for the midday meal. But the man showed no sensitivity to his son's plight. In fact, he seemed quite prepared to have a lengthy chat for he selected a stick to use as a pointer.

"Michael, why don't you obey us?" he asked very quietly as he traced a small circle in the dirt.

"I *do* obey."

"You woke your brother just now," his father said, pausing a moment, then dividing the circle in half. "You slammed the door again."

"I try to remember."

How could he argue? Of course, he was guilty. Now if his father would only go away . . .

"You forgot this morning," his father interjected. "And last night."

"Well, it's hard to remember everything. That's all." Michael felt distinctly uncomfortable. He made faster arcs in the water, pretending to be entranced by the small waves he raised as his brown hands skimmed across the pond. "I'll try harder from now on, I promise."

His father spoke quietly. "Just try to be more considerate."

"I said I'll do better," Michael insisted, making larger waves than he'd intended. The water splashed onto the bank close to his father's foot. The man looked surprised, then nodded.

"All right. Let's not get this effort off to a bad start. Your mother is waiting."

Michael closed his eyes. If I stand very still and wish for death with all my heart and my soul, he thought to himself, then I'll die and everything will be over and I won't have to move; he won't see me.

"Come on son, we'd better go in."

There was no use arguing. Whenever his father used the word "son" things were hopeless. That was the last polite step before a command. And recently, commands had been followed by arguments, lectures and punishments. The outstretched hand was unavoidable.

He accepted it and was pulled from the dark water, light brown and helpless, exposed. . . .

For an instant he paused, embarrassed to be revealed in an adolescence he sensed but couldn't adapt to. Perhaps his father would perceive the cause of his shame and avert his eyes. But the man behaved as if nothing were amiss as Michael turned to his clothes. Still tension was evident as he dried himself with the pale yellow shirt, careful to keep his back to the man. When he'd donned the short pants and pushed the yellow hair away from his eyes, he turned to face his father. The man smiled and rose.

"I know it's not easy for you to have a rival, Michael," he said as they walked back to the wood-frame house. "But try not to let it upset you."

"I don't."

"Good. Anyway, you're no longer a child."

"But I'm still young!" Michael insisted.

"Yes, but fourteen is fourteen. You're already becoming a man."

So he *had* noticed. The boy felt ashamed. He was

"becoming a man" so he shouldn't be jealous of his new brother! And he shouldn't mind being displaced and overlooked and ordered about and lectured for not being perfect? Oh, sometimes he wished he could go live somewhere else. But just as suddenly, he feared any separation and wanted to be assured of their protection and his place in their home. *His* home.

The table was covered with plates of liver and sausage, potatoes, fresh bread and cheese. There was a bowl of apples, pitchers of milk and beer, and a pot of mustard. At the center of the table was a small jar of wildflowers he'd brought home the preceding day.

They ate in silence.

To Michael, his new brother looked exactly like a boiled tomato. Once every few minutes, he stole a glance at the finely veined face of the baby. But this only served to increase the stress. He looked away.

Outside, the sun was just beginning its long decline from mid-sky. Long shafts of light pierced the open windows, striking the bright sides of copper pots, illuminating the warm reds, oranges and browns of the room. It was so quiet now, so still. This was the way it had been when it had just been the three of them.

"Stop it, Michael." His father's tone was automatic.

"What?"

"Don't toy with your food."

"Oh . . ."

They were quiet again.

Across the room, the boy could hear the even tick of the tall clock in its immaculate cabinet of polished wood. As a child, he'd had a dream in which the gleaming case was a coffin. For days he'd studiously avoided the front room until his parents had taken the time to discover the source of his irrational fear. He would never forget how calm they had been when he'd explained. And, though he was terrified when they led him into the hall, they'd shown him the inside of the clock and proved that there were no skeletons inside.

It had always been like that, the boy thought. Every task was approached and handled as effortlessly as possible. His father moved through his house and barn, attending to his chores in a gentle and unhurried way. And his mother, with even rhythm, sent him off to school, took care of her house, her goats, her vegetables and flower garden. Each day followed the next without drama or disruption. Sundays were also predictable. They always drove to church in their old truck. His father behind the wheel, his mother at the window with Michael in between on the way to town and in the back on the way home. Then it didn't matter if he got a little dusty as they drove the six miles between the town and their farm. Six miles through the woods and neighboring villages to sit in their pew, and listen to the pastor, the choir, the endless warnings of sin and the possibility of future salvation. Michael was glad they'd missed the past two services.

Grown-ups were unbelievably weird, he assured himself as his mother leaned over the baby's bassinet.

"He's so quiet," she remarked, with a small smile, to no one in particular.

"Just wait," his father said knowingly. She nodded and shrugged and lifted the babe up to her breast.

"Did I make noise when I was little?" Michael asked.

"All babies do," his mother replied, unfastening the top button of her blouse.

"Did I cry a lot?"

"Only when you were hungry," she said, continuing to undo the small white buttons. "But in general, you were very good. Much better than most."

"Better than him?" the boy asked, and immediately regretted his words, for both parents looked at him strangely.

His mother broke the silence. "What do you mean?"

"Nothing." His face was flushed. How he wished he hadn't said anything!

"No, Michael, tell me," she pressed him, not taking her eyes from his face as she withdrew one swollen breast and held it to the baby who wiggled his fingers very slightly as he began sucking on the brown nipple. It embarrassed Michael to see this. Had *he* ever done that?

"I don't know. . . ."

His mother glanced at the baby and smiled an enigmatic smile before raising her head. "You were always a joy to both of us," she said.

"But not any more, right?" Michael said.

"Don't be silly! Oh, darling, come here!" she urged, extending her free arm.

"I don't want to."

"Please?"

He went to her with an awful feeling that, by exposing his doubt he'd obligated both parents to prove their devotion was unchanged. Even though it wasn't really true.

Although his mother's arm was tender, he couldn't meet her eyes. Instead, he stared at the hand which held the baby. It was red and looked far older than her thirty-four years. One thumbnail was yellowish and cracked down the middle.

"Can't you feel how much we love you?" she asked very softly. And he looked down, not wanting to meet her level gaze . . . her dark blue eyes which always seemed able to probe the deepest recesses of his troubled heart. They made him want to throw his arms around her and be treated as a baby again. Simultaneously, there was something inside which forced him to control his feelings. He shook his head to clear his mind.

Misunderstanding his movement, she drew him even closer. Her body smelled warm and sweet. It went to his heart, that most familiar of all scents.

"Michael, nothing, no one in the world could possibly replace what you are to us," she said, patting him very slightly as she spoke. "Not this baby, not anyone. That's one reason we decided to have another child. You'll be all grown up soon. Too soon . . ." Her voice was a little wistful and she rocked him as she spoke.

"Try to understand," his mother said. "You'll grow up, make your own life and we'll need another child in the house to keep us young."

"But you are young, aren't you?"

"For the moment," she replied, arching a brow at the man and giving him a wry look.

"Uh, when you say you love me . . . what does that mean?" Michael asked.

Both parents looked at him, but for once, it wasn't too awful or embarrassing. Even he knew his question wasn't foolish and, the way he'd said it, it was just impersonal enough to be spoken aloud.

"Well, it means that you're essential to us," his mother answered simply. "You are part of who we are, who we will be. No matter how life changes."

"But what could change?"

"Everything," his father said as he stood up. "Everything changes and moves along. And with that in mind, I think I'll finish writing my speech for tonight's meeting."

"Are you sure?" his mother asked. Michael heard the worry in her voice.

"Absolutely," he answered.

"I wish you wouldn't go." She sounded sad.

"I realize that."

She sighed. "Do what you have to do."

"I don't have any choice." He stretched, sighed and looked about.

The woman sensed his thoughts, for without raising her head from the baby, she murmured, "On the mantle."

"The mantle? Oh, yes! Of course!" he muttered and, gathering his pipe and tobacco tin and matches, he left the room.

For a moment it was silent again. Michael pulled away from his mother and watched the infant who was still sucking at her breast. She smiled at him and inclined her head. For an instant he felt totally calm, totally peaceful as he watched the baby.

"Your father is an obstinate man."

"Obstinate?"

She nodded. "Stubborn. Tell him not to do something and he'll do it just because he doesn't like to follow orders."

"What 'orders'?"

"No . . . not *orders*," she corrected herself, lowering her head again. "But he's preparing another speech to read at the town meeting. I just wish he wouldn't stick his neck out."

"Is that bad?"

"No, not really . . ."

"Then why do you want him to stop?"

She looked up, and for a moment, the boy thought she had nothing to say. "Because we are so . . . . unimportant."

"Well, if we're so unimportant then what he says doesn't really matter," Michael reasoned, surprising himself with his own logic.

She smiled. "I hope you're right, Michael. I really hope you're right."

The baby had fallen asleep. She started to fasten the buttons on her blouse, moving as smoothly as possible. As she leaned over the sleeping infant, the sunlight struck her fair hair, bringing out the gold, which had darkened in recent years. For an instant, she seemed younger.

His mother mystified him. In her youth, she had been beautiful, so beautiful that people still mentioned it when they went in to town for fairs or to church. People teased her about the days when she'd been the reigning beauty in their region. Sometimes they told her that she'd only improved with time but Michael sensed his mother knew they were only saying this out of kindness. Sixteen years of marriage and life on their farm had replaced girlhood charm with strength and an attractive manner. And, though she was no longer beautiful, she had a good face, even-featured and gentle. Her clear blue eyes were mild. Occasionally, the boy pictured her as a woman of the town in a smart dress and a fashionable hat. But, as she lay her baby to her breast, she bore more resemblance to a madonna than to any city woman.

And they hadn't been to town for a church service in weeks.

"Why don't we go to church anymore?" he asked.

For a moment, she regarded him without expression. And when she answered, her tone was strange. It was as if she was concealing something from him, holding back a secret. "We have different beliefs than some of the others."

"Then why did we go in the first place?"

She looked uncomfortable and Michael feared he'd asked the wrong question. But she didn't appear angry as she draped her shawl around her shoulders and, when she spoke, her voice was very gentle. But there was something about the way she was talking which alarmed him.

"Your father and I feel it is very wrong for people to injure others," she said, keeping her voice low. "But our pastor . . ."

"Grunewald?"

"Yes, Grunewald refuses to speak out against it. Your father called him a hypocrite and so that's why we stopped going."

"But I don't understand," the boy said. "Are they against us?"

"No, not exactly," his mother replied, glancing toward the front room where his father had gone to finish his speech. "It's mainly the Jews."

"But we're not Jewish!"

"But they're people, just like us."

"The Jews?"

"Yes, the Jews. And the Catholics and the liberals. All of them. Like us. The same, only . . ."

"Only what?"

"Some people, the Grunewalds for example, don't think so. If you look behind their words you see that they have no principles at all. They'd do whatever they have to do, just to get by."

These words came as a surprise. Of course, he knew his parents didn't support the Hereditary Farm Act which made it illegal for any person with a trace of Jewish blood to remain on German soil. Anyone with that stain was supposed to quit their farms and, though no one had yet enforced it in their township, only last week he'd heard his father telling the Muellers that it was wrong, that as a result of the bill, innocent people would be displaced and made homeless. The next day, his father had gone into town and not returned until evening. When he'd come in, he'd told his mother that he'd given a speech before the town hall, denouncing the Nazis and the Farm Act. His parents had argued and his father had gone out for a walk. And that was the second week they'd missed church. Now, he began to understand why they'd been staying at home more often.

"But what about the others? The Mayor? The town council? Or anyone who hears father talking? Won't they be angry?"

She stood up and touched one shoulder before answering. From long observation, the boy knew that when she did this, she was choosing her words with great care.

"Michael, there will always be some people who will be angry with you if you say what you feel or speak the truth. Especially if it's not what they want to hear. But the important thing to remember is that the only way we can remain satisfied with our lives is to be true to ourselves. To remain firm in our beliefs and to hold to them. Even if that means that others will be upset. Their opinions cannot matter."

"But what will they do?"

"They'll do what they've done," she replied. "Most of our friends won't dare agree with us, although they

feel the same way we do. And some others will say
unkind things and make it difficult for us to sell our
produce or find help for the farm. But we'll get by. We
always do."

"Will we?"

"We have each other." She smiled.

"Doesn't it bother you?"

"You mean if people say bad things?"

He nodded; she shrugged.

"So it's going to be all right?"

She came close to him and wrapped her arms around
his shoulders. "Yes, it's going to be all right. Now, help
me clear the table *without* waking your brother."

They carried the plates into the kitchen and for the
first time in several weeks, Michael felt comfortable.
Something had been appeased. He felt that no matter
what outsiders might think, his family would go on.
They would stay together and help each other and
never be lonely or . . .

"Oh no!"

"What is it?" he asked.

"There's no water."

"I'll get it."

Once again, he felt an unaffected joy in the sense of
his world. Everything went so well at times like this. It
was all so sensible and clear.

Chapter Two

He slipped out the back door with two wooden buckets and started toward the little pump at the far end of the garden. Sometimes, simple tasks were challenging. He liked to see how well he could accomplish a perfectly mundane chore. So, he made up his mind to fill these buckets to the very brim. And return to the house without spilling a single drop.

Michael sat by the pump and filled the buckets more slowly than usual. He enjoyed watching each spurt of water as it leaped from the spigot into the wooden pails.

"*Michael!*"

His mother! A cry! A scream! The boy wheeled to see her standing at the back door, waving her arm wildly, beckoning. "Come quickly, run. Run!"

His first thought was of fire. They'd need water! He seized both pails and started forward.

"Leave the water!" she screamed.

He spilled, he slipped, he stumbled. He picked himself up and ran toward the house.

"*Hurry!*" his mother hissed.

As he crossed the garden, Michael saw his father dash around the far side of the house. The boy reached the house and faced both his parents. He saw at once that his mother had his coat.

"Why are you . . ." he began, but his father hushed him up at once. The man looked into his eyes and took him by the shoulders; his face was pale.

"Soldiers," he said as his mother stuffed a parcel into the boy's coat. *"Don't talk, Michael, listen. Listen."*

He was frightened. He could see the desperate concern on his parents' pale faces.

"Run. Down the outhouse hill and into the trees. Don't turn around and don't come out until they've gone. *No matter what happens!* Do you understand?"

Yes. He must have said yes, or given them a sign of some sort. But of that there was no memory. Just the quick kiss of each parent and frenzied arms, pushing him away.

"Go now! Run! Run! *Run!*" As he turned, he heard engines.

Michael ran; he slid down the steep hill and headed for the woods. Behind him soldiers were emerging from a truck. He could hear some of the men shouting as he reached the trees and threw himself down.

What was happening? What did this mean? And when had it begun? It seemed hours since he'd looked for a clue in the faces of his mother, his father. But nothing was clear. Just those sudden, terrifying words: *"Don't turn around and don't come out until they've gone! No matter what happens!"*

He moved through the trees, keeping as low to the ground as possible until, from where he lay, he could see the front of the wood-frame house. As if from another world, he saw the garden his mother tended with such care. A car was parked directly on top of one of the rosebushes.

There were half a dozen storm troopers beside the truck. But Michael's attention was riveted on an officer who stood on the porch talking with his father. It was much too far away to overhear conversation but the boy had an unobstructed view as his father stepped back and allowed the stranger into their house.

Everything became perfectly still. The silence was eerie. It was as if the soldiers were dark marionettes, figments of his own imagination. But no! This was real! This was happening! To him! To others! To all of them!

The wind changed direction, blowing the long grasses away from the house, toward his hiding place. A cloud passed beneath the sun and the yard was temporarily in shadows. Then, it was bright again.

He could hear the men speaking in low voices. From where he lay, the boy could see them emerge from the house. His mother held the baby; his father carried a suitcase. Behind them, that officer, tapping a small book with a pen. Before them, the soldiers.

Where were they going? Would they leave without him and not come back? How would he ever know where to find them? One of the soldiers opened the rear doors of the empty truck. His father put the suitcase in, but his mother turned and glanced at the woods. What was it? Did she want him to come out?

For a moment, the boy thought they were waiting for him. Of course, they'd never go anywhere and leave him behind! He stood up before remembering their instructions. No! He had to stay where he was! His mother was saying a final goodbye to her husband. They were taking him away. . . .

When it happened, it all happened so suddenly. The boy couldn't fit the pieces together. It was as if the sounds had been separated from what he saw.

One of the Brown Shirts touched his mother! She turned, jumped back, and his father was there, his deep voice clearly audible. "Take your hands off her, you swine!"

His father shoved the soldier away. The soldier picked himself up from the ground as the others turned and watched. He drew his gun.

Later, Michael wondered if it was fact or if his confused mind could actually isolate the sounds in the wind which encompassed him. For soon, too soon, the air was a braid of shots, an odd echo of screams.

"Oh my God! Oh no! Oh no!"

Still clutching the infant, the woman threw herself on top of the dead man, wailing his name. The sounds of her lamentation were punctuated with fragments of an argument and the baby's shrill cries. And then the last sounds, words from the major who seemed disturbed by the unexpected trouble. "Shoot them. It'll be easier this way."

The machine guns came up in a smooth line. The woman rose, wrapping the squalling infant tighter in her arms as the soldiers looked to the major. For an eerie moment, it was perfectly silent as his mother backed away from the men, inching toward the house, gathering herself to run, turning, picking up speed . . . she could make it! It wasn't far! She could climb the stairs, get inside!

And then, the shots. She fell, spilling her baby as bullets splattered her flesh. She lay motionless, shuddered, jerked her head, spit blood and was still.

Now the wind carried the sound of engines and the smell of gasoline. Smoke from exhaust pipes belched into the well-kept garden as the vehicles moved away. The car was followed by the truck as it drove down their long lane, slowing near potholes as they descended toward the paved county road.

Once again, Michael was running. He slipped out from the woods and ran toward the house. He told himself this was all a nightmare; that when he reached them the dreams would end. They would still be alive! All would be as it was!

The bodies lay ten or eleven feet apart. They appeared to be asleep but there were dark stains seeping into the dust, wide patches of blood oozing through their clothes. These wounds where punctured flesh let life escape! How had his baby brother been driven from his mother's arms? Were bullets so strong?

Michael stared, too stunned to weep. He told himself it was not real. He could not let himself think it was. No, if he just stood still and held his breath and did not let go of his certainty that it was a dream, it would *have* to be a dream.

Slowly, he looked up from the dead bodies. He saw that the scene was repeating; the car and truck came up the dirt road for a second time. It was happening again, it was real. He stood still until one of the men shouted something at him. And then, he wheeled and ran for the trees.

A shot! A second, third, fourth, fifth and sixth whipped through the trees and summer grass. For a second time, he was running along well-known ground, into the shadows of pine, along paths he'd explored all the years of his life. Keeping low, he ran until he found the small stream and moved along the shallow bed, half-buried in ferns, covering his tracks in the water.

A bullet slammed into a branch less than two feet from his head but it was a shot fired at random; they didn't know where he was.

Far away, he heard voices urging him to come out and give himself up. They assured that, if he obeyed, nothing would happen to him. This would be his only hope. If they had to come after him, he would regret it. Their calls became faint as he raced deeper into the dense undergrowth.

Finally he stopped. He threw himself onto a cool sheet of pine needles and stared up at the darkening sky. He was sweating but his feet were cold. He removed his shoes and dried his feet as best he could, using his coat. He tried to assess his situation.

It was the first day of June, in 1934, and he, Michael Kurtz, was being hunted as if he were a criminal or a felon. He was fourteen years into a life which would probably be over in another few hours. Or days. Or a week, perhaps. But no matter when they captured him, it would end after ending. Maybe, he could cheat the devil and remain dead among the living.

As day fell into evening, he remained numb and incapable of tears. He sat motionless for hours and stared and stared at his hands. His mind wouldn't abandon the theory that it was all a dream, a shocking dream which had blossomed into nightmare. Come morning, he'd realize he'd been asleep. Come morning, he'd be safe again. Yes. It had to be.

An owl sounded and the woods were still. It was a place of wind and water and the last vestiges of his childhood. One mile away, the cool flesh of his family turned blue beneath the summer moon, but Michael kept still and tried to think of nothing.

In the morning, they came back with dogs.

Michael heard the barking; even to his dazed and bewildered mind it was obvious that they were no more than three or four hundred yards off. He gazed up into the cloudless sky until confusion gave way to awareness and fear.

He raced through familiar meadows, deeper and deeper into the trees, ignoring low-lying branches, brambles and thorns. Nettles stung his face; he stumbled, fell, got up and continued.

If only he could get to the road, to the turnoff which led to the train station or town! If he could, he'd be safe! He might stay the night with the stationmaster of the farmer's depot and then he would decide what to do. Perhaps he could ride a freight train into the city. Once there, he might find work or investigate a way out of Germany, one that required no papers or money. Switzerland wasn't that far away! But could he really leave his home? And, if he did, could he ever find his way back?

There was no time to wonder, or plan his own uncertain future. The road was over two miles away. Perhaps three. In the forest it was impossible to judge. He'd explored these paths so many times, trails leading through thick stands of trees into sudden open patches of wild weeds and flowers. Familiar meadows and hillsides, blackberry patches and places to climb rocks. Places to picnic. Places he'd discovered with . . . the dead ones.

He stopped to wipe the sweat from his face. Now, there was no sound of the dogs. Surely they couldn't have followed his scent through the stream? But in obedience to instinct and fear, the boy kept running.

The county road wound through woods wet with morning mist. Trees muffled vehicular noise; they rose above the Tarmac remote and aloof.

If he listened very carefully he could be absolutely certain there were no cars approaching the fork where the ways diverged; the road on the right led to town where the soldiers were quartered. The left led toward the old railway depot which was used by local farmers.

Although it was a relief to lie in the thick ferns which crowded the paved road, Michael told himself he couldn't remain there. It was still too dangerous. He had to cross the main thoroughfare and find a safe place along the old depot road.

He crawled out from the ferns and trotted past the turnoff to town. A few hundred feet along the winding road, there was an enormous boulder which was clearly visible from any direction. Many times he'd seen people stand there, hoping for a ride from a passer-by. His father invariably stopped so Michael knew it was a good place to rest up, catch his breath and wait. And, if worse came to worst and he couldn't get a lift from any of the local farmers, he could proceed on foot.

The boy climbed onto the pale red boulder and sat, staring down at the road and trying not to think of the last time he'd come this way. It had been earlier in the week. He and his father had driven to the depot hoping to pick up some equipment for the farm. The delivery had been delayed. His father had sent Michael out to wait in the truck and when he'd come out of the stationhouse a few minutes later, he'd been unusually quiet. He hadn't said more than a few words all the way home. Michael hadn't understood. Only now was he beginning to see clearly. His father had not been so unimportant after all. Opposing the National Socialists had been a fatal mistake.

The sun cleared the treetops and warmed the rock where he sat. He removed his coat, conscious of the tears which welled up as he lay back. But there was an unpleasant bulge, a hard lump in his coat. Reaching into the pockets, he discovered the small packet his mother had given him, the leather bag she'd pushed into his hands before he'd run into the woods. He loosened the draw strings and emptied the contents into his upturned palm.

Gold. Coins caught the sunlight and reflected radiance onto his face. His hand was filled with the precious metal. Why? Had they known, or expected trouble? Why would his father and mother have to give him all their money?

A clear image of the preceding day returned to him. He saw the faces in the dust and the dark blood on his mother's chin. Oh no, no . . .

He shook his head, trying to reject the image but a dozen images of his parents occupied him simultaneously. His father tending the animals, chopping wood or walking out into the fields just as the sun set, his favorite time. His mother sitting on the porch swing, knitting or singing in a soft voice as she did the mending, honey-colored hair covering her face. Or sometimes when they were all together and the touch of their hands on his shoulders was . . .

No, no . . . His eyes grew blurry and he knew that, at last, he could grieve. He could release his tears now.

The sound of an approaching vehicle interrupted his grief. Michael forced himself to stand. He must not permit strangers to witness his agony. He must master his feelings and think of all this later . . . later . . .

But his tears were not so easily dispelled. The automobile was just around the nearest bend as Michael wiped his eyes with the sleeve of his coat, momentarily blotting out the sun. He blinked a few times to be sure he was in control before looking at the approaching vehicle.

As it neared him, it slowed down and came to a stop. Michael stood still; movement was impossible for his stare hooked into the man's confident face.

The major gestured with a pistol. "Get in the car."

decided. It was so logical... sharp, getting rest and
his friend our drinking. Then... momentum. At its time to

PART II

1964

Chapter Three

Seven-fifteen. His alarm ended the memory. He tried to bury his head beneath the warm pillow, but the ruthless noise continued. It was time to get up. Outside, rain . . .

"*Gott*," he murmured before correcting himself. "God."

He extended a pale hand and fumbled with the horrible alarm clock, jabbing at all the levers until the insidious clang stopped. Hillary was already out of bed. Downstairs, probably, making breakfast.

He couldn't focus his eyes. For a moment he tried, but the room looked foreign, a dream on this side of the nightmare. He retreated into darkness, drew the quilt over his head and breathed against the silky fabric. Better . . .

When things were so insular and comforting, nightmares seemed impossible and memories unbelievable. He turned into his pillow but there was a damp spot where his head had lain. Tears? He pushed the pillow away.

Seven-sixteen. If he didn't get up soon, she'd come check on him and ask if he was feeling all right. Although she usually ignored his nights of tossing and turning, he knew that if he stayed in bed Hillary would confront him. It was impossible to forget that she was right there, witnessing his torment. Sometimes, when he woke up crying or feeling that he couldn't breathe, he was afraid that he'd called out a name or said something that she'd think was wrong in some way.

Two nights ago, he'd dreamed of the dogs again. He was chased by them through that strange forest where all the trees had been stripped of their leaves. The earth had been burned and as he raced across the charred fields, running as he'd run when he was young, smoke or steam rose up from the scarred ground. He was enveloped by the mist and couldn't see more than a few feet in front of him. The dogs were behind him. Then, suddenly, he came into a clearing, something which had never happened before. There was a Christmas tree, but, in place of decorations, the boughs were festooned with bones and human flesh.

He'd cried out and sat up, trembling and bathed in sweat. And that night neither he nor Hillary had bothered to pretend that it was "just another one"; she'd held him in her arms, cradling him as if he were a frightened child as she assured him that everything would be all right. But each of them knew it was comfort without conviction. Finally, after an hour of shared anguish, he managed to fall into a fitful sleep.

In the morning they made a great effort to ignore the previous night and the wrenching memories his dreams revived. They had become well-practiced in domestic rituals which seemed to forestall any need to confront the source of his terrors. The deception was part of their formula for order and marital harmony. And if it seemed like enforced sanity, at least it allowed them to move through their respective routines without disrupting the fragile truce they'd maintained between his personal agonies and their twenty-year union. Each knew there were things too painful to be shared, too frightening to be exposed.

A few days before his dream about the dogs, Hillary had allowed that most of their friends were seeing, or considering seeing, psychiatrists. He hadn't replied. He'd expected her to let the "helpful hint" pass. But for the first time in their married life, Hillary had come right out and asked him if he didn't think that a qualified doctor couldn't help him resolve his pain. He'd promised her that he'd think about it and then let the matter drop.

He forced himself out of the high-backed bed, stretched and winced as he endured the cold floorboards on his way to the frigid tiles of the bathroom. There, an electric bulb effectively shattered remaining traces of night. For a moment he wished he could turn off the light and shave in the dark.

"I can't do this," he muttered, leaning over the sink. He turned on the hot water but, as he stood there, he felt like a cow waiting for slaughter.

Why did he have to have those dreams? He'd told his family everything he thought they ought to know. It had taken him years and years to learn to trust, to begin again. He'd come to a new country and learned a new language as well as the ways of a new people. He'd buried the past. When he first met Hillary, it was easy to avoid going back. The war was still on; there was no question about returning. It was true, however, that when it ended he had considered a trip back to Germany. He might be able to find someone, or succeed in locating a strand or a lead, anything to connect him to the love and care he'd finally found and . . . no . . . ! Stop!

He had not gone back. He had stayed and made his life with her and the children, a boy and a girl. Life had been good. They had been safe, well-fed. They had the good things, no fear. They belonged.

Until recently, it had been enough. It was more than satisfying to be the father and the husband, the provider and the head of the household. He knew he was needed and loved and cared for.

But in recent weeks there had been changes. How could he explain the shift? It wasn't anything external, except that the kids were away for the summer. That wasn't it; they'd gone off before. No, it was in him. It was as if he'd always forced himself to look forward, to a brighter tomorrow, to the future which America

promised its refugees. Now, for some reason which
mystified him, he sensed he had staggered in the
well-orchestrated progression. He'd lost footing in
some inexplicable way. Without falling, he'd slipped
and found himself wedged between nightmares and a
suspicion that life as he'd constructed it was becoming
breakable.

He moaned and pressed his temples with the palms
of his hands. Another dizzy spell. This always happened whenever he thought about *that*. Headaches,
dizziness. Maybe these *were* reasons to consult a
specialist. Maybe there *was* something physically wrong
with him. For the first time in twenty years, he was
aware that he wasn't able to risk including Hillary in his
life. When she asked questions or tried to probe for the
truth, he pleaded ignorance or confusion. And when he
did, and she accepted him at face value, he felt a
different kind of resentment. It was as if he wanted her
to tell him that she couldn't accept his explanations; the
fact that she didn't compounded his isolation and
despair. After all, if she really knew him, she would be
able to see that he wasn't telling her everything.

Perhaps he was making a mistake thinking he could
figure it out without her help. But he didn't want to ask
her for advice. It was too dangerous . . . too frightening to reveal so much doubt about himself. Especially
in *that* way. How could he reveal his huge fear and
confess to so much guilt? He knew that, when they had
met, long ago, it was partly his air of self-assurance
which Hillary had been attracted to. Despite the
underlying perishability, even the mirror had said, *You
can trust this young man in his three-piece suit; even
though he's German (by birth) you can have confidence
in his deep eyes, straight nose, firm jaw and wide, even
brow. Nothing about him is unproven or untested.* The
mirror lied.

He shook his head as he thought about who he was
and how he first appeared to those staid New En-
glanders, Hillary's family. For he was a perpetual

outsider, an orphan who came into their lives with no past. At least Hillary had a beginning, and connections that would not disappear or be lost. He hailed from disaster; a truncated clan which had been destroyed, spitting him out in the process as a homeless, unwanted thing.

He returned to the bedroom and dressed in silence. At the end of all his thoughts, at the end of the endless series of transparent cubicles which formed the trail from his boyhood into present tenses, there was a residual fear of death, of the Nazis, of terror materializing from nothing. All innocence had ended in murder. It was the child who had undergone shock. It was the child who remained numb and stricken with horror. It was the child, mute, soundless and still hidden who plagued him. And this child was his legacy, his bleak inheritance. He stood at the bedroom window and stared out at the rain. It was easing up.

Chapter Four

"Michael?"

Hillary was calling from the kitchen.

"What?"

"It's getting late."

He took a deep breath and went down. The kitchen was warm and filled with smells of breakfast. As Michael entered, Hillary turned to greet him.

His wife was tall and still slender and had dark hair and blue eyes, diamond-shaped when she smiled. This morning she was wearing her dark green sweater, a plaid skirt and galoshes. Her hair, held in place by tortoise-shell barrettes, was slightly damp. For a moment Michael didn't understand. Then glancing at his place, he saw the rain-soaked newspaper.

"Did you go out . . .?" he began, gesturing toward the paper.

"Sure did," she chirped, pinching a piece of toast from the toaster.

"You're the best."

"Ah, flatterer . . ." She laughed but when she turned to smile at him he saw that she looked tired. Beneath her even brows, her eyes were strained. No doubt about it. She was putting on a good show but she was worn out. Still, the hand that grabbed his sleeve was firm. She leaned her cheek to him for a kiss.

As he kissed her smooth cheek, he inhaled a little, loving the way she smelled.

"I thought you'd sleep late," she said, stroking his shoulder as she checked the eggs.

"Oh?" He crossed to the table and sat down.

"You okay?" She sounded noncommittal, as if there were no special meaning to the words.

"Sure," he paused. "I woke up all alone though . . ."

"You know me," she chuckled. "Up with the first excuse." She sounded convincing until she yawned and gave him a baleful look, and then a smile.

He returned her smile.

"Mind if I turn on the radio?"

"Be my guest."

She flicked on the radio and returned with his scrambled eggs but, as soon as the music entered the kitchen, Michael felt more tense. Maybe it was just lack of sleep. But there was something annoying about the smooth, inane lyrics. It was too early for the "you and me baby" or the mellifluous commercial messages.

"Well, it looks as if the rain will let up anytime now," Hillary observed, making conversation.

He nodded and continued eating as Hillary poured a cup of coffee, and then glanced out the kitchen window.

"Oh, its Jersey!"

Their milkman was on his way up the drive. Hillary hurried out the back door. "Hi, Jersey!"

"Mornin' Mrs. Kurtz," he replied. "Two bottles today?"

"Just one. We've got some left over. You know the kids are gone and things are out of whack around here."

"How they doin'?"

"Just great. We got a call from Susan last night. She's found a place with two other friends."

"Sounds real nice."

"I know," Hillary confided. "I'm green with envy if you want to know."

The milkman sounded enthusiastic when he talked with Hillary. Of course, she did have a way with people, Michael thought. Just five minutes and she could charm the socks off anyone. Now, as he listened to her cheerful voice, he wondered how she managed to stay in such good spirits when he was such a nervous wreck all the time. As they conversed, the radio began playing another spoony tune, and Michael reached out and switched it off. The room was quiet again and the voices audible.

"I gotta go now, Mrs. Kurtz. Say hi to Mr. Kurtz."

"Will do, bye!" Hillary sang and reentered the kitchen with one bottle of milk. As she put it in the refrigerator, she turned to Michael.

"Oh, Michael, guess what?"

"What?"

"I ran into Margery when I went out to get the paper."

"Who?"

"Margery Nicholson. They bought the blue house."

"Oh, right."

"I told you about them. Her husband's some kind of engineer and she plays the piano. We've talked about duets."

"I remember."

"Well," said Hillary, trying to stay positive, "she invited us over for bridge some night this week."

"Oh."

"So . . .?"

"Did you say yes?"

"Of course!"

"Oh."

"You don't sound very interested."

"I guess I'm not, really."

"Why? They seem like very nice people."

"It doesn't matter to me."

Hillary sighed. "It matters to me."

"Then you go."

"But I need you there."

"Why?"

"Because that's how people are. And we need four for bridge."

"I don't want to play cards with strangers."

Hillary looked unhappy and he felt himself getting upset.

"Hey, honey?"

"What?"

"I'm worried about you."

"It's nothing to do with you."

"I know that but I want to help. Michael, I'm Hillary. Not some stranger . . ."

"I don't know what to say," he muttered, hating himself for not being able to meet her halfway, but sensing that if he gave in at this point, he would have to tell her everything. And that would be too dangerous.

"You're being tortured by something," Hillary blurted out. "I've known it for a long time. Until now, it never seemed to have very much to do with us or the kids. I always thought that it was better if I didn't ask you about it. But it's affecting everything in our lives. What we do in the morning, here. What we do at night, in bed. You work all day and come home tired and instead of getting any rest or being comforted by me, you spend another night twisting and turning and crying out or waking up all covered with sweat. You're terrified by something and Michael, I can't stand not knowing what it is! I can't bear feeling that I'm not helping you!"

"You do help me," he said slowly, but still avoiding her eyes.

"If I do, it's only because I care so much. But I feel like I'm improvising because I don't know what to do or say. I don't even know what the problem is!"

"There's no one thing . . . no one problem. . . ."

"Okay, then, tell me! Take it piece by piece. Let me know," Hillary implored, her voice cracking a little. "I know about the day the soldiers came to your house and . . ."

"Don't . . ."

"I know what they did. And you were there and . . ."

"Please . . ."

"You ran away and they came after you and you were captured. Then? What? What happened next?"

"Hillary, *stop it!*" He almost shouted the words but, not out of anger. He was dizzy and, if he didn't stop her, he'd have to go back and say it in words. Suddenly it seemed that he might be able to articulate the experience. The thoughts and memories were clear. The faces, the countryside pushed back into silence, back into memory . . .

"Michael." Her voice was soft and her tone was calm. It's choking me . . . It's like being strangled by something that I've always known was there, but can't recognize or fight. I feel as if I've failed you in some terrible way."

"You haven't failed me." Michael reached out and pulled her close to him.

"Michael, I can't . . ."

"Just trust me, please?"

She sighed and gave his shoulder five quick pats. It was passing. The tension broke. She took a deep breath. "Hey, it's eight o'clock. You'd better get going."

"Let me finish this." He waved his coffee cup.

"I'll get your things." She hurried into the hall as he downed his coffee and exhaled a long jet of air. He put his cup in the sink and turned as she reentered with his coat and briefcase. Michael put the coat over his shoulder and walked toward the back door. She followed him, holding the leather case in her arms.

He reached out for his customary hug and kiss, but, instead of the routine embrace, she wrapped both arms around him and held him as tightly as she could. For a moment he felt a little tense but he stroked her dark hair with his free hand.

"Love, love, love . . ." she whispered.

"Love, love," he repeated.

He kissed the top of her head but she didn't release him. Instead she lay her cheek against his chest and murmured: "I know it's not easy, Michael. It's always been painful for you. But I never cared because it never kept us from being close. I want you to be happy."

"I love you."

"I know. But, Michael, I don't want us to lose what we have."

He kissed her gently. At last it was spoken. He should have known that, when it was no longer avoidable, Hillary would be the one to say it out loud.

He hurried out into the backyard. It was drizzling. As he sat in the car, allowing the engine to warm up, he felt lonely again, and uncertain.

Chapter Five

He left his house and began his drive into the city. The daily commute from the quiet lanes of surburban Wesbury into the jagged canyons of New York had become a strange part of his life. For in his car, he felt suspended between worlds. Now, as he drove past the attractive houses of his neighbors, he paid little attention to the handsome colonial architecture or the well-tended lawns. All so familiar that nothing held any surprise or mystery for him.

The rain had almost stopped. Michael turned off his windshield wipers and drove along in silence. Two children in yellow slickers marched along the pavement. Michael watched them as they crossed a street. They seemed like small invaders from outer space.

Michael muttered: "I don't know what I need. I don't know what I'm missing. Another afternoon of important engagements and appointments and the same four walls and the same faces and telephone calls. Christ! Why am I doing this? If it's not making sense to me, what's it for?"

A red light silenced his musing. As he came to a stop, the sun appeared for the first time and Michael rolled down his window. There was a wrought-iron gate on the far side of the road. And although he couldn't see the house, the presence of bulldozers and wrecking equipment told him that yet another mansion was being demolished to make room for smaller, more cost-efficient housing.

Michael stared at the elaborate gates. He knew he was on the perimeter of what had once been a beautiful estate. It was one of the places which had been open to the public a few days every year. People used to go through on tour while the family was away.

A horn cut into his thoughts and he came to his senses. The light was green; he pressed the accelerator and drove on. But, as he did, he became more and more agitated. There was something about those gates and the demolition of the hidden mansion which disturbed him and reminded him of . . . And there, seeming to appear out of nowhere, standing too far out in the road, a hitchhiker with his thumb extended and an expectant smile on his sunbrowned face.

"*Damn!*"

Michael jerked the steering wheel and swerved to avoid the young man; the car swayed wildly as it careened by the solitary figure but, as he passed, Michael realized that the kid hadn't budged. Instead he'd turned and smiled. There was a momentary flash of dark eyes, dark skin and white teeth.

"Idiot!" Michael screamed to himself.

He glanced into the rear view mirror. The hitchhiker was still standing out in the middle of the road, but this time, he was staring after Michael's car; no doubt about it.

"It's almost as if he expects me to pick him up! It's as if I'm supposed to give him a lift!" he muttered to himself.

He hadn't picked up a passenger in years. Not since he'd gotten his first automobile and felt so guilty about it that he'd sworn to give needy people rides. That resolution had lasted about one week or one dull conversation too many. Since then, for whatever reason, he'd always avoided contact with strangers. But everything was different today. "But maybe he'll think I'm after something if I go back now. It'd be too embarrassing! If I'd stopped when I saw him, all well and good. But I didn't. How can I explain turning

around and going back to pick up some kid I don't
know? He'd think I was nuts!"

Another two or three hundred yards down the road
there was a gas station. Then a movie theater and a
church where he slowed down and, finally, came to a
stop.

He took a deep breath and lay his head against the
steering wheel. His underarms were sticky and his
stomach felt tight. "Company would be nice. Just some
conversation. Just some talk with a stranger whom I'd
never have to see again."

He turned and went back.

"Where are you going?"
The kid grinned; he seemed a bit unsteady but his
voice betrayed nothing.
"Anywhere."

He had dark eyes and was very tanned for so early in
the summer. Beneath a beat-up leather jacket, his navy
blue T-shirt was more or less clean as were his tight
jeans.

"I'm going into the city."
"That's fine by me."
"Hop in."

He had a paper bag in his hand. As he got into the
car, Michael saw that, for such a broad-shouldered kid,
he was surprisingly lean. Of course, the scarred boots
added a few inches to his height. He was probably six
feet.

As they started forward, he leaned toward Michael
and nodded his head as he spoke.

"Thanks for picking me up."
There was liquor on his breath.
"Don't mention it," Michael replied, checking the
rear view mirror.

"Going to work?" the curly-haired youth inquired.
Michael nodded. "What about you?"
"I don't care."
"What's that?"

"I just want to get out of Mineola."

Michael looked surprised. The youth took a swig from his bottle and went on. "Me and my old man just had a fight. He threw me out of the house."

"How come?"

"Ah, he says I oughtta go to college in the fall and get an education."

"That's not such a bad idea," said Michael, who had told his own children the same thing.

"I don't want to spend four years sitting on my ass," the boy said.

"Education is very important," said Michael, not wanting to provoke an argument but glad to have something to talk about.

"Not for me," the kid shot back.

"I see. . . ."

"Besides, I already have a job."

"What do you do?"

"I paint houses most of the time."

"Oh."

"And sometimes I drive a delivery van. Or do hauling."

So that explained the big chest and shoulders.

"How come you're not working today?" Michael asked. The youth shrugged.

"No jobs. Anyway, I made enough money already this week. Don't have to do too much until I run out."

Michael nodded. There was some sense to this logic. Seeing him nod, the kid stuck out his hand.

"My name's Scott. Scott Perkins."

"Scott, I'm Michael Kurtz."

"Pleased to know you."

"Thanks."

"Thank *you* for the ride."

"Don't mention it. Actually," Michael started before he knew what he wanted to say, "I was worried about the way you were standing."

"Yeah, well, I had to get a ride before my old man came out of the house and saw me. He took away the car keys so I decided to hitch. But the drivers around here have all got their heads up their snobby assholes. Excuse me. . . ."

"That's okay," said Michael, more than a bit amused by the kid's description of the commuters.

"Just a lot of paranoid turkeys with lists of things to do," Scott muttered, taking another swig from his bottle. "So I have to stand out in the street whenever I need a ride."

"You do this often?"

"Whenever the old man and I have a fight. It's the best way to get out of the house."

"Where do you go?"

"Ah," the kid waved a hand. "I just stick out my thumb and go wherever the driver's going. I've got money on me—enough to get a bus back. Usually I just take off for a day or two. It's all right. I meet a lot of nice people. You'd be surprised."

Michael was intrigued by the idea that Scott was free to roam, free to drift away from his life and drift back.

"Mind if I smoke?"

"Suit yourself."

Scott produced a pack of Camels and offered one to Michael who shook his head but watched out of the corner of his eye as the young man struck a match, inhaled and extinguished the flame with one brisk shake.

"Whenever you feel like it, you just take off for a couple of days?" Michael asked.

"Sure," the kid said, sounding surprised by Michael's interest. "It's better than staying around listening to my old man gripe.

The kid slouched down in his seat a little and thrust his crotch up a bit as he took another swig.

Michael frowned a little and kept his eyes on the road. Was this some kind of invitation? Or was it only adolescent ease?

"Sure glad you came along when you did," the boy put in.

"How's that?"

"Well, I'd been waiting for twenty minutes." The kid frowned and took another swallow of the bottle.

"Hey, isn't it a little early to be drinking?"

"Early?"

"Scott, it's only eight-fifteen."

"It's not early, it's late."

"What time do you get up?"

"I haven't been asleep."

"Not at all?"

"Not at all," the kid echoed. "I was up all night with a friend of mine."

"Oh . . .?"

"Yeah, we were talking," Scott drawled.

"Talking?"

"Yeah, about hitching out to California. Have you been there?"

"Only on business."

"Well, it'd be kicks," the kid suggested, "probably."

"I'm sure you can have fun just about anywhere you go."

"Sure. I don't care what's happening as long as people are having a good time." He yawned.

"Tired?" Michael asked.

"A little."

"Feel free to stretch out."

"Thanks but I'll wait until later. So you, uh, live out here and work in the city?"

"That's right."

"I can tell. I can tell a lot about people."

"Perceptive?"

"Pretty much. Like, I can tell you're not from around here."

For the first time, Michael felt uncomfortable. There had been too many years of people remarking that he wasn't "from around here." Too many years of feeling guilty about his origins. Of course, once people knew what had happened, they didn't suspect him of being a "bad German," but he hated having to explain or "sell" himself. He shifted uneasily. Scott noticed nothing.

"Oh, yes? How's that?"

"Well, you don't sound American."

Michael raised a brow and bit his lower lip. "Oh."

"You're not from here, are you?"

"No," said Michael. "Not originally."

Had the youth been sober, he'd have heard the slight edge to Michael's voice. As it was, he blundered on. "I didn't think so. You have an accent but I can't tell where it's from."

"I grew up in Germany," said Michael, glancing into the rear-view mirror although there hadn't been any traffic behind him for several minutes. "I spent my first fifteen years there."

"Were you in the war?"

"I got out before the fighting."

"Did your whole family come over?"

"No. Just me."

"How come you left?"

"It was dangerous for me at the time."

"Are you Jewish?"

"No."

"Huh," Scott exclaimed. "I thought it was only dangerous for the Jews. I mean, I thought that Hitler only went after . . ."

"The Nazis killed everyone who caused them any trouble," Michael cut in. "Jews, liberals, Communists, Poles, artists, priests, journalists . . . everyone, any-one."

"I never heard about that."

"Read up on it some time, or go to school," Michael said, sounding a bit more blunt than he'd intended. But the kid didn't take offense.

"Yeah, maybe I will," he said. "I sort of liked history when I took it. It was just like hearing a lot of old stories all about the wars and the explorers." Scott took another swallow and offered the bag with the bottle in it to Michael who shook his head.

"You sure?" Scott asked.

"Sure am," Michael replied. "What is it anyway?"

"Rum," Scott said. "That's all he had left."

"Who?"

"My friend." Scott paused, and then spoke. "We started out with a few six packs of beer, but that ran out. So, then we finished off the bourbon. And then, this . . ."

"You'd better watch yourself," Michael admonished. But Scott ignored the warning.

"I know, I know," he said. "But we've been working a lot in the past two weeks painting a house and doing some deliveries. We haven't had a binge for at least eleven days." He hit the bottle again and offered it to Michael.

Michael laughed and shook his head. "Getting to work late is one thing, but coming in smashed is something else."

"What do you do?"

"I'm an investment counselor."

Scott took a quick glance at Michael's suit and shoes. "Are you rich?"

"Not rich," Michael replied. "We get by."

"We?"

"My wife and I."

"Right, you're married."

"Very much so."

"How long have you been married?"

"Twenty years."

"Wow! And you're still in love?"

"In love? Well, not the same way but, loving? Yes. Sure."

"Twenty years. That's eternity," Scott pronounced. Michael couldn't help smiling.

"I guess it all depends on how you look at things. What about you?"

"What about me?" asked Scott.

"Do you have a girlfriend?"

"No way."

"Really? Why not?"

"I don't want to be tied down. I'm a lone wolf," Scott claimed.

"Have you ever had a girlfriend?"

"Sure. I've had lots of . . . all kinds of . . . you know."

"Sure," said Michael, who had no idea of what Scott meant.

"But it's just not what I want right now."

"Love can be scary the first time around."

"Sure," said Scott. "Love."

"Still, everyone's different."

"Especially about things like *that*."

"Excuse me?"

"What we're talking about," replied Scott pointedly. "Love. Marriage. *Sex*."

"Oh, right."

Michael's anxiety was becoming more generalized. There was a little too much probing. A little too much investigation. Now, he was afraid of slipping backward. For a few moments, he was in present tenses. Even if it was only a fantasy, he wanted to feel that he could share this young boy's experience and know how it was to be growing up now.

"Tell me more about yourself."

"What about me?"

"Oh, anything. Anything at all."

At eighteen years old, Scott Perkins was only too happy to oblige. Buoyed by the drink and the pleasures of a free ride, he sat up and stretched in that provocative way and launched into a story of his young life. Of his parents and his summers at the shore. Of odd jobs after high school and the buddies who got together to drink beer and ride around in their souped-up cars. Of plans to live in the woods and of his Labrador retriever.

But nowhere was there any mention of any important friend—male or female. Despite his suntanned bravado, there was more than a trace of loneliness about him.

And Scott talked and got lost and kept drinking. And his eyes got a bit bloodshot as he lost the thread of his narrative and mercifully relocated the skein. This time it was a dream of the future in which he and several buddies would go up to Canada into the Northwest Territories where they could get some land in the wilderness and homestead. Maybe they'd build one huge log cabin and go hunting or trapping to make a living.

As Scott finished this part of his story, he yawned and settled back into his seat. When Michael glanced at him, the boy smiled and confessed, "I must be boring you to death."

"Not at all," Michael replied truthfully. "I like your plan."

"Really?" Scott sounded hopeful. Michael smiled.

"It sounds good to me if that's what you want."

"Maybe it is. I don't know. But you know what?"

"What?"

"I like talking to you!"

"I like talking to you too," said Michael.

"I mean it. Most grown-ups are really stupid. I don't mean that personally but they all say the same thing: grow up, go to school, get a job, get ahead. They don't even think of kids as people. Just because they think they've got what they need, they think they know what's good for everyone else."

"That's strange."

"What is?" asked Scott at once.

"All day, ever since I woke up, I've been wondering what *I* need."

"I thought you had everything."

"In some ways I do."

"Then how come you don't know?"

Without realizing it, Michael slowed down. "I used to think I knew. But now . . ."

"You don't." Scott filled in the blank; Michael nodded.

"I'm tired of just surviving."

"Is that all you're doing?"

"Sometimes it feels that way. Today it does."

"That's what I don't want to happen to me."

"I hope it doesn't."

"I hope not too. But . . ."

"What?"

"Just that it seems that if you know what you want you can get it. But if you don't know . . ."

"Then what?"

"You'd better find out before it's too late," said the boy.

He and Michael exchanged a different kind of glance.

"I think you're right," Michael said. Scott yawned and nodded and took another swig. "Hey, you'd better go easy on that stuff," Michael added.

"Hell," Scott chortled, "it's the end of a long night."

A few minutes later, they were approaching the entrance to the highway which connected suburban lanes to city streets.

"Hey, Scott?"

"What?" The young man had closed his eyes and had leaned back in the seat.

"We're about to get on the highway. Do you want out here or in the city?"

"Sure." Scott was bleary-eyed.

"Does that mean the city?"

"I hadn't had anything to drink in ten days," Scott assured him and closed his eyes again.

"Okay, okay, just take it easy," said Michael as he continued onto the entrance ramp. Scott would be all right no matter where he wound up.

Scott's snores began as soft sounds. Glancing at him, Michael thought that with the sun on his dark hair and his bronzed skin, the boy was almost beautiful. Seen from this perspective, he seemed almost innocent, despite his strong features.

Sure, Michael thought to himself. He'll make out all right in New York; he can get a room and rest up. Or take the bus home whenever he feels like it. He's free.

Chapter Six

Signs marked the city-bound lanes: NEW YORK, KEEP LEFT. UPSTATE: RIGHT LANES ONLY.

As he watched the cars crowding into one another as they approached the turnoff, maneuvering for faster lanes through the upcoming toll booths which led into Manhattan, they suddenly looked like metallic bugs being fed into an enormous machine. One after another would disappear through appropriate stalls and be funneled into the monster.

The thought bothered Michael; he switched lanes and came over a rise in the last hill before the expressway severed city-bound traffic from the last chance at the countryside.

For the first time in years, he acted spontaneously without considering the consequences as he jerked the steering wheel to the right. His car seemed to leap not one, but two lanes through a chorus of squealing brakes and outraged horns, as he crossed into the lanes marked UPSTATE. Then, just as suddenly, his sense of responsibility softened his sense of freedom. Anxiety and exultation warred for conquest of his conscious mind. For an instant he wavered, but excitement and a certain amazement won out.

"What the hell difference does it make?" Michael exclaimed. "For once, I'm doing something for myself! And no one else!"

Scott stirred and opened his eyes halfway; they were bleary and red. "Whaa . . .?" he stammered.

"Nothing," Michael assured him. "Go to sleep."

"Where are we?"

"Just driving."

Scott muttered something and closed his eyes. And Michael drove on. He drove; he took a turnoff and for the first time in his life, he didn't read the road signs. Anywhere would be good enough as long as he was moving! He turned on the radio and switched the dials around until he found a Vivaldi violin concerto. Perfect. No. Too crazy. He flipped the radio off and drove in silence.

Scott was snoring again; Michael glanced at the boy. He felt as if he were surfacing from an interminable period under water. Each breath was a first, each sight remarkable. He felt he was cutting away from every nightmare, every echo of an unendurable past. Now, for the first time, he was on his own, out on the road with no one to demand an explanation or lay claim to the time. He had a full tank of gas and freedom!

He drove; he stopped; he took off his coat, got in the car and kept driving. Hours passed. Scott was still asleep and snoring intermittently. The tank was three-quarters full. Michael watched the scenery become wide open, pastoral. Fields transfixed him.

A fourteen-year-old German boy was still running across a brown field. He had passed the baton to the man who drove his car away from his home, away from his wife, his children, all that was certain. Now, he drove away from a pale man who'd pushed him off in time to save his life.

"Don't come back. No matter what happens. Do you understand?"

Yes, he must have said yes. The boy acquiesced, the man nodded and pressed on the accelerator. The car shot forward. Poles and signs and fields flew by as he sped past cars and trucks. Faster and faster. Sixty. Sixty-five. Seventy. Seventy-five. Eighty. Eighty-five. Scott woke. "Michael . . .?"

Michael took his foot off the accelerator.

"I . . . uh . . ."

"Are you all right?"

"Sure, sure I am."

Seventy. Sixty-five.

"You're driving awfully fast."

Sixty. Fifty-nine, -eight, -seven, -six, -five.

"It's okay now."

"Good." Scott yawned.

"Go back to sleep."

Scott grunted and closed his eyes. Michael wiped his forehead and shook his head slowly. Christ, what the hell was he trying to prove? If Scott hadn't awakened . . .

"Don't be an ass," he muttered to himself.

At fifty miles an hour the car ran more comfortably. He refocused on the wide road. No, it wasn't about death. He could forestall that longing and concentrate on the present. Anyway, if he had to go, it'd be better to go alone—without taking an innocent person with him. There had been enough slaughter, enough bloodshed.

He wiped the sweat from his forehead without even stopping to consider what it would do to his clean cotton shirt. A thin stream of sweat trickled from his underarms down his ribcage. He took a quick glance at his watch; it was almost noon. By now the office had phoned home and Hillary would have phoned the highway patrol. Perhaps they'd suspect an accident or a kidnapping? Well, no reports would involve his car in an accident. At least, not yet. Not as long as he had Scott in the car. But maybe he should take a less obvious route just to be sure he wasn't pulled over by an "all points" bulletin.

He got off the highway and took another road, continuing north. Past flagpoles, libraries, post offices and markets. Past suburban communities not unlike his own. It was all very sensible and somehow reinforced his sense of dread.

Chapter Seven

"Hey, uh . . ." Scott's voice was shaky.

"What?"

"Can we stop? I think I'm gonna be sick."

"Oh, Jesus!"

Michael pulled onto the shoulder of the road and ran to Scott's side of the car. But he barely had time to open the door and reach in when the white-faced boy leaned forward and puked. It all happened so quickly, Michael barely had enough time to get out of the line of fire. He was only partially successful for a dozen specks wound up on his shirtsleeves.

"Goddammit!"

"Oh . . ." Scott groaned.

"Hey, you okay?"

The red-eyed Scott nodded.

"I'm sorry. I . . ."

"That's all right."

"No, I'm really sorry to . . ."

"I said it's all right."

"Look at me. I'm a mess."

He was not exaggerating. While he'd been more or less successful in aiming for the road, there was one patch of vomit on his pants and another on his T-shirt. The backs of his hands were spattered and his face was changing from tan to a pale shade of green.

"What a disgusting mess," he muttered.

"Don't worry about that now," said Michael who was inclined to agree with this assessment. He wondered why he'd been saddled with the baggage. He couldn't entirely overlook the inconvenience which the youth represented. "Just sit there until you feel better."

A few minutes and a small series of spits later, Scott wiped the most obvious stains from his clothes and said that he felt well enough to go on. But his miserable expression and soiled clothes were an unspoken plea for attention.

Michael drove along and tried to reason with himself as he considered his options. Of course, it'd be ludicrous to go out of his way for this stranger. Still, the kid could use some help, at least getting his laundry taken care of. But why should he have to go out of his way to see that it got done? Well, it would look pretty ridiculous—Scott standing in some laundromat in his underwear, if he even wore any! And anyway, Michael's own shirt needed washing.

They would have to go to some motel, one with a laundry service. But wouldn't it look suspicious? An older man and a young boy checking into a motel in the middle of the day? No reasonable explanation aside from Scott's condition. Of course, he could explain that the guy was sick and that he was an old friend. But no one would believe that, even if it were the truth. Which it was, up to a point. What the hell difference did it make what anyone else thought?

But what was the truth? And why did he have to make up some excuse to do what he wanted to do? There was no denying the fact that Scott was a handsome creature. Even with a blanched face, there was a curious kind of beauty about his face and the way his strong features fit together. His nose was chiseled and his upper lip was just a bit more pronounced than the lower. It made the red mouth look even more ripe.

Michael looked back at the road and lectured himself into a rational state of mind. It could be easy, he decided. It was so logical, after all. A young man and his friend out drinking. Then, an accident. Who should

think it strange that they'd need to get cleaned up?
Even if it was the middle of the day. They could just get
a room, spend a few hours together, get their clothes
cleaned and later, check out. Nothing to it. Unless one
wanted to see it from another point of view.

He thought to himself: "Look, Michael, it's just you
and yourself so why waste time pretending? After all,
no one can hear your thoughts. He's young, he's
beautiful and you could have him if you tried! No? Yes?
Maybe."

Then: "No, this is too crazy! I can't let myself think
this way! Well, why not? Haven't you ever looked at a
man and thought he was attractive? Of course, but it's
not the same thing. The same as what? Well, the same
as *wanting* it. Or *needing* it. Who said anything about
anybody *needing* anything? Isn't being curious needing? Well, is it? Is it for you? Look! He's young and
new and beautiful. Couldn't you let yourself if he
wanted to? If you're curious, why not try? Because I'm
not that way! But you *are* curious! Well, so is everyone,
at least sometimes! Are you sure? Sure I am. And
anyway I put all those thoughts aside, a long time ago.
Ah, now we're getting closer! But I thought I had,
when I was a kid. Ah, closer still! Keep going Michael.
Come on! Tell the truth. Are you sure you never
wanted to explore that part of yourself? You know it's
there; it's there in everyone but you have your own
special reasons for temptation."

"Scott?"

"Huh?"

"What do you say we go and get cleaned up?"

"Sure, whatever you say."

"I think it's a good idea. You've got to get out of
those clothes and I've got to get this shirt washed."

"Right. Christ, I'm so disgusted with myself."

"Let's concentrate on finding a place to wash up. Is a
motel room all right with you?"

"Sure."

There it was! It sounded so easy. But, as Michael drove that familiar acidic knot in his stomach became more and more pronounced.

"Why did I come north with him if I was going to back out? What the hell am I doing with this day if I can't face whatever comes as an opportunity rather than as something to be denied or put off? Is this how I want to live? Is this how I'm going to deal with opportunities to indulge my curiosities?"

There were signs to the Sleepy Hollow Motel. Four miles on the left. Three miles. Two, one. Five hundred yards . . . Vacancy. Office. Manager. Please ring.

There was a small bell on the counter under a picture calendar of "Autumn Leaves." Orange and red; oaks and maples.

He rang again; a door flew open and the manager marched in. She was gray-haired and wizened, booted and plaid-jacketed with a suspicious face.

"What can I do for you?" she barked.

"I'd like a room," Michael replied.

"Eh, what's that?" she snapped.

"A *room*," he said, thinking, "I wonder if I sound foreign?"

"Single with single, or single with double?"

"There are two of us," he said, gesturing with one hand toward the parking lot where Scott sat in the car.

"Does the lady want her own bed?"

"It's not a lady," Michael answered.

"Oh," she grunted.

"But one room with a single bed will be fine."

"Planning to stay the night?"

"I don't know. Just let's have a single room with two big beds instead, all right?"

"That's twenty dollars."

"Fine."

"In advance." Michael paid.

"By the way, do you have a laundry service?"

"How much do you need washed?"

"Just a few things."

"I'll send the girl."

"Thanks."

"Room twelve. Fourth door on the left. Come with me."

As they went out, he let the screen door slam. She turned and glared at him. She forgave nothing.

The room was beige with two single beds, a night-stand, desk and chair. There was a beige rug, beige lamp, and two beige bureaus. Still, despite its lack of charm it was scrupulously clean and functional.

"Bathroom's through there," the old woman cut in. "There's lots of hot water. Be sure to let it warm up. It takes time so don't call me to complain."

"Thank you."

"If you want your bags, give me the keys to your car and I'll have them brought in."

"We don't have any luggage," said Michael, feeling uncomfortable and wishing he'd just said it wasn't necessary.

"I see," she said, letting the unspoken insinuation slither out into the open air.

Just then, the red-eyed Scott stumbled in. He was still ashen despite his tan. The old woman wrinkled her nose and stared first at Scott and then at Michael who felt satisfied, giving her a knowing look.

"High spirits," Michael explained.

"Oh," she grunted, deciding in Scott's favor.

"Well, we'll have the wash ready for you in five minutes," said Michael, pushing the screen door open.

"Check out time's ten-thirty A.M."

"Thank you."

As soon as she was gone, Scott began to strip. Michael locked the door. The old wraith's flinty manner had unnerved him. He peeked out the window but she'd disappeared.

"What a lousy mess," said Scott, dropping his leather jacket on the beige rug.

"They do laundry," Michael volunteered.

Still standing at the window, Michael didn't know where to look, or where to position himself. Should he examine the room, or stare out the window, or go out for coffee, or just stand there and pretend to be relaxed while Scott unbuttoned his pants?

"Well, I'm glad to hear that," said Scott, removing his shirt and allowing his eyes to meet Michael's.

"I'll check the bathroom." As soon as he said it, he felt stupid and chastised himself. What a ridiculous thing to say! But now, he'd have to "check the bathroom"!

He walked into the next room and switched on the light. It was clean, ordinary, functional. No surprises.

"Christ, I stink," he heard Scott exclaim.

Michael reached into the shower and turned on the hot water. Then he turned and called, "It'll heat up in a minute or two."

"That's music to my ears," said Scott, appearing at the door.

He'd stripped down to his white shorts and Michael felt embarrassed. He didn't want to turn away but didn't want to stare, or be observed staring, at the perfectly muscled brown body which stood before him. To make matters even more difficult, the way Scott stood there, so relaxed or seemingly relaxed, made observation unavoidable.

"So why don't you look, then?" Michael said to himself. "Looking is only looking. But you know there's something else, don't you? You know you're tempted to reach out and touch that bronze chest and those firm arms. Isn't that right? Is it? Or not? Well . . .?"

Words made no sense. He took a step back as Scott reached into the shower.

"Ah, *hot!*"

"I'll give the girl your things."

"Sure, thanks."

Michael walked into the bedroom. As he gathered Scott's warm clothing, he caught a glimpse of the youth, standing beside the shower stall. Michael's eyes fell to the pink-tipped sex resting in the bed of brown hair. And although he must have been aware that he'd been observed, Scott paid no attention to the man as he stepped into the shower.

Michael removed his shirt and stood in the middle of the room. The stain wasn't all that bad. Still, it had to be washed. When the doorbell rang, he was embarrassed again. He'd never answered a door without being fully dressed. He grabbed his friend's leather jacket and pulled it on. A thin young woman stood outside. She was slightly cross-eyed and had pasty skin. Pink plastic barrettes, shaped like bows, were in her hair.

"Laundry?"

"Right here," Michael stammered, trying to hand her the wash without having the coat reveal his chest and without having her hand touch the wet parts of the clothes. "I'm afraid it's messy."

"I don't mind," the girl replied, taking the soiled clothes and adding, "it'll be about an hour, an hour and a half."

"Thank you," said Michael as he closed the door and locked it.

"Hey, this is great," exulted Scott from the bathroom.

"Enjoy it," said Michael. He looked down at his palms and realized for the hundredth time that he didn't even know where the major lines on his hands were. After all these years, they were still oddly foreign.

"What?"

"I said, *Enjoy yourself*," Michael called.

"I can't hear you!" cried Scott, turning off the water.

"Doesn't matter," said Michael. He could hear Scott stepping out of the stall.

"God, I've had so much liquid today I feel like a fish," Scott said.

"You should rest."

"I hear that. Hey, you should try the shower. It's great."

"Thanks, but no thanks."

Michael turned. He'd expected that Scott would have moved directly toward the towels on the bathroom wall. But Scott just stood there, rubbing his eyes with his palms. And although there was nothing self-conscious or deliberately exhibitionistic about the way he was standing, Michael wondered if the kid really knew what he was doing. No one could stand like that, one hip thrust slightly higher arche the other, one foot slightly forward, with both hands above his head as they slicked back his hair and simultaneously exposed the rhythmic bars of rib and muscle along his torso, and *not* know how provocative the pose was! As Scott turned away from the bedroom, Michael saw that his spine was a well-defined line between his brown shoulders and the brown flesh of his small, hard buttocks.

He didn't want to dwell on it! It came too close to fear of man-to-man confrontation he'd experienced most intensely in public restrooms where he found it difficult to pee in psychic comfort, lined up side to side in that too-intimate, congested space of ceramic urinals. It came too close to the dreadful silence which inhabited such areas for it was as if all men had declared a phobic, impersonal zone where they could stand, just inches apart with one hand coddling their hidden sex.

"Well, that was just what the doctor ordered," said Scott as he sauntered into the bedroom, tying a white towel around his waist.

"Feel good?"

"I'll say!"

"I think I'll wash up," Michael said quietly.

He walked into the bathroom and closed the door for no reason except that it gave him another moment alone. Somehow, what had begun as his day had become a collision. For a moment he wanted to reclaim his solitude. He could go retrieve his shirt, make some excuse to Scott and continue driving. But where? Did it really matter, then? But anything would be better than that bedroom. No. Oh, Michael! Stop planning! Stop thinking! He leaned over the sink and washed his face, arms, neck and armpits.

When he reentered the bedroom, it was dark. Scott had drawn the Venetian blinds and the room was more shadow than sunlight. Long black bars crisscrossed the beige room, cutting space into thin sections.

Scott sat on the far bed, drying his hair with the towel he'd brought out of the bathroom. As Michael entered, the naked youth looked up and said, "It's easier on my eyes like this."

"Sure," Michael said, his voice a little strained. "No problem."

Scott said nothing but continued drying his hair.

"Say, you must be getting tired," Michael allowed.

"Maybe."

"You feel okay?"

"Much better," Scott responded. Michael sat down on the near bed and felt the knot tighten in his stomach. He was a little dizzy now.

"What now?"

"I don't know," Michael said. "Are you hungry?"

"God, no," the boy retorted, tapping his flat stomach with one hand. "Food's the last thing I want."

"Yeah, I'm not hungry either," Michael confessed, feeling that he'd pitch forward if the dizziness got any worse. He closed his eyes; there were little flashes of white light moving in the darkness.

"Where's your shirt?"

"Being washed."

"Did it get hit?"

"Just a little."

"I'm really sorry."

"It's okay." Pause. "No kidding."

"Do you do push-ups?" Scott was staring at his bare torso.

"Twenty-five a day."

"It shows," said Scott.

Pause.

"So," Michael began, pressing his hands together before realizing that he had nothing to say.

"Are you going to call home?" asked Scott, breaking the silence.

"No, I don't think so."

"Why not?"

"It's just too soon."

"I see."

"No, you don't. How could you?" Michael blurted. "I mean, I don't even know what I'm doing!"

"Oh." The voice was noncommittal.

"All I know is that I can't go back home or to work or anywhere until . . ."

"Until what?"

"Until I can just be who I am without feeling like I've got to protect myself all the time so that I won't be . . ."

"Go on."

"Wounded."

"Won't your wife help you?"

"I don't know. I haven't really given her that chance. I mean, there are times I don't know if I even know her. Maybe it's because I don't know what I need."

"Do you love her?"

"Yes, in my way."

"What way is that?"

"It's not romance. There's something missing. It's not security, because I feel so vulnerable and uncertain. It's not what I dreamed. It's not what I used to think it would be. I've given up the romantic ideal for the safety of a durable marriage. Now that that is slipping, I can't be sure of what we have. It's all changing."

"But you *had* the romantic ideal?"

"Yes! No . . . well, yes, I have! Only it was something else and so brief. How can I explain it? It's the difference between the illusion and reality. Between something I've wanted and something which happened to me in spite of me or what I intended. Does that make any sense to you?"

"I'm not sure."

He wanted to explain and have it be right but the words wouldn't come. But he had a sense of impending breakthrough. It was too volcanic not to happen even if he didn't have the ability to chart the course or predict the results. He felt dizzy and shaky and ill-at-ease. He closed his eyes and lay back; as he did a soft sigh escaped his lips.

"Hey, Michael, are you all right?"

"Dizzy, I . . ."

"Well, I know a cure for that," Scott asserted. "Here."

"What?"

He opened his eyes just as Scott rose from the other bed and leaned over him. He could smell the inexpensive motel soap on that perfect body as the youth reached down and took one leg in his hands.

"Here now," Scott said. "Just keep one foot on the floor and you won't pitch forward. It works every time."

Scott was right. With one foot on the rug, the spinning came to a halt. Michael looked up at Scott's face.

"Better?"

"Better."

It was true. The dizziness had ended but the tightness in his stomach remained and there was a pounding in his forehead.

"What is it?"

"A headache, I think."

"Here, let me help."

Scott reached out and took Michael's head between his hands. They were strong and warm. Michael let the boy turn his neck this way and that as he massaged the cranium, the back of the neck and the temples.

"I don't know what happened. I was fine one minute and then . . . My God, look, I'm shaking. My whole body is trembling."

"Looks like epidemics are going around," Scott laughed softly and quite naturally.

Michael opened his eyes; Scott's face was closer. The brown-eyed boy smiled without guile. Michael was surprised to see no strategy in the eyes.

The hands kept stroking his neck, bending his head one way and then the next. The tension seemed to be on the wane. He couldn't think, he couldn't be sure. He lay back and closed his eyes; the boy leaned even closer, rubbing his neck a little bit harder, massaging the shoulders. It felt easy enough, his fears could subside. Yes, as the moments passed, he felt better.

When Michael reached out and touched Scott's hard arm, the boy said nothing; he didn't pull away or discourage the hand. The arms were strong. Michael was surprised to touch the forearms and biceps. They were so firm; it had been a long time since he'd stroked such flesh.

It was so easy to let himself return the gentle caress. It was so easy to give up words and allow him to accept the tenderness and care. Four arms, four hands kneaded and massaged the weary muscle and bone. It was a little faster, now. A little more sure.

The shoulders were broad, the skin there a bit warmer. The sides striated muscle and the ribs, deeply indented. He let his hands move along the long lean thighs, hips and cubed stomach.

So close, so near . . .

Even with his eyes closed Michael knew that Scott

was giving himself up. The boy leaned into him with a bit more assurance; the hands were less tentative.

For the first time in weeks Michael could relax and enjoy the ease of bed and care in another person's arms. This sweetness was something he'd sacrificed to the nightmare. Now, he could draw deep breath heated from another living being. Now he could let himself be comforted, approached, known. . . .

He arched his neck and felt Scott's palms slip over his face stroking the skin with open hands, going down to his neck, chest and shoulders. He rolled his head and Scott's hands covered his ears, turning him, holding him as if his head were a fragile globe. As he let the boy's hands guide him and let his own stiff neck go limp, Michael felt himself transfer authority from his posture into the boy's capable hands. Scott could show him. Scott could position him as he willed. And then, when his head was on the pillow and the boy's head lay in his fingers, he could chart the orbit for the youth.

Without having it be part of any conscious plan, Michael drew the boy into an embrace. But as his arms closed around the youth, Scott stiffened.

"I think that's . . . uh . . . a little too much for me."

"Does it frighten you?"

"No, not really," Scott attested. "But I don't want to go too far.

"I feel so close to you," the boy confessed. "No one your age has ever really wanted to know about me. And they haven't told me about themselves or what they felt about their lives. But I don't want to . . . you know."

"That's okay," Michael said, leaning back and closing his eyes. It was that damn dizziness which bothered him. Even though the touching had stopped, he was feeling better. But now he felt an even greater urgency to explain, to have Scott understand.

"Are you sure it's okay?"

"You don't have to apologize or explain," said Michael.

"But I thought you needed . . . or wanted . . . you know."

"I don't know what I need. That's why I'm here," said Michael.

Scott looked confused.

"Maybe it will make sense to you. You . . . you're the right age, you're young. It's something that happened to me a long time ago. It's something I . . . I need to share with someone."

"Tell me then," Scott said, and his voice sounded curious and surprised by Michael's urgency. "Go on . . ."

"I'm trying. It's . . . so long and oh, Jesus, I never told anyone." A carved seal had been struck from an amethyst jar—allowing an essence to pervade his brain. It was something inescapable and wise. He closed his eyes.

He was falling deep into the gold of another age, feigning ignorance but yielding, at last, to the memory of half-forgotten touch and the rustle of silk, a light step and mystery in the air, which would have to be an afterimage of his mother. He promised himself that any thought of dark eyes, soft music and the dusky light of lamps lowered in a window would bring back the smells or sensations of his first home. The pale man would have to be his father. The man who taught him to care for the land, to tend animals and understand the subtle correspondence between earth and sky. The tall man who'd led him toward his own manhood and paid with his life for protecting the innocent. . . .

He opened his eyes, and yet he didn't see Scott. More than anything else he was aware that the room was dark. It was so easy to see it as a pattern of black stripes across the beige furniture. It was unreal and geometric. Now, he could focus on Scott. But even the boy seemed abstracted. Only his eyes were real to the man. They were so dark. So like other eyes.

Michael had to force the words up as if each one was something he'd invent or forge for the first time. The words seemed to emerge from a void out in hollow space. Still, he could hear himself begin.

"I want to tell you about a boy named Michael and what happened to him. The Nazis came and killed his family; he ran away but they found him. And they took him away forever."

PART III

1934

Chapter Eight

The major seemed well-pleased as they drove toward the depot. Then, he glanced at his pocket watch and his mood darkened; he looked at Michael once. Only once. The rest of the ride he stared out the window and tapped his fingertips against his knee.

The station had been built just before the end of the last war. Originally, there was to have been a railway connecting it with several other depots on the way to Munich, but that plan had been abandoned. Now, it was used solely for the transportation of produce, animals or farm equipment; never for passengers. They used the station in town.

As they approached the depot, Michael noticed that the station had been marked "off limits"; there were more soldiers—Brown Shirts standing at wooden barricades. As they came up the lane, he saw three trucks parked on one side of the road. Down the tracks there was a train.

Prodded by the driver, Michael got out of the car. The major seized him by the arm. Shoving the boy toward the soldiers, he snapped, "Get him inside and keep him there!"

A corporal pushed Michael toward the stationhouse, through a dark green door, into the office.

It was cool in the high-walled room. There were a pitcher of water and fresh flowers on the desk. Michael was thirsty but he didn't ask for a drink. The soldier motioned for him to sit down; he obeyed. In the brief moment which followed, he looked at the man without expression. The man blinked and, lowering his eyes, looked at the floor.

Although he knew it was rude to stare, Michael couldn't resist examining his guard. He regarded him as a specimen rather than a human being. No, he told himself, this *thing* wasn't human. He was an animal, a National Socialist—something from a zoo with his yellowish hair and skin and his pointed Adam's apple. His face was thin, slightly gaunt.

Michael looked away. The door opened and a second soldier came in. Michael shuddered and tears filled his eyes at once. *This* was the one who'd touched his mother and shot his father! This thick, coarse-featured, burly man with little pig eyes. Squatface, Michael named him to himself, as he struggled to control his tears and remain outwardly impassive.

"Why don't we . . . *you know?*" Squatface asked, leering at Michael.

"You mean *here?*"

"Why not? Schüller is busy."

Yellowface shook his boney head. "It's too risky."

"We're behind schedule," Squatface muttered.

Yellowface crossed the room and peered out the window. But when he let the curtain fall, he turned to Squatface. "Let's just wait and see what happens. Maybe later, after the train pulls out."

"They'll be loading soon." Squatface sounded half-interested.

"How many coaches did Helmut get?"

"Only two."

"They'll be crowded."

Squatface snorted. "So what?"

Michael sat on a hardwood chair, watching, waiting.

The door opened and the major entered, and sat down at his desk. Squatface had his rifle ready; Michael studied his ugly face and realized that the man would kill him if the major ordered.

The officer reached into his coat and withdrew a long

piece of paper. He placed it beside a form and murmured to himself as he leaned over the papers.

At first, the names made no sense. Michael was preoccupied with the rifle Squatface held near his head. But gradually, as the minutes passed, he let his attention wander to the desk where a silver-framed photograph showed the major shaking hands with Adolf Hitler. The two men were smiling.

"K," the major murmured. First a name, then a quiet "yes" and a check on the list. Another name, another affirmative, another check until the horror-stricken boy realized the full implication of the man's task.

At first Michael felt nauseated; he reeled in his chair. The major glanced at him briefly, then turned back to his papers.

"Kibel? . . . Yes."

Check.

"Kittelman? . . . Yes."

Check.

"Kurtz? Hmmm. Well, yes."

"*No!*"

No, the echo of the wound. *No,* a cry of loss—blood in the dirt, a dark patch over the man's heart, blood on the woman's chin—a hole in the baby's forehead. *No,* the bodies without movement, the dream not ending, the thin boy chased by bullets and dogs, captured, brought here, to this place. *No! No!*

His eyes were blurry as he stood before the desk, banging his fist on the papers, scattering a pile of reports, the vase of fresh flowers, the photograph of Hitler, the inkstand with its silver eagles, everything, anything. The office was a wet dissolve and words meant less than nothing. Only *no* against the "yes" of death or captivity. *No*—one word to bring them back to life—his father and mother and the baby. He would, he would have to . . .

The major's voice was curt. "Shut him up! I'll say it's a mental case."

Fury obscured everything, the boy told himself as he seized a handful of papers and threw them at the man. Fury would end death, shots, a cold night of fear. But not a sudden pain which descended with the rifle butt, cracking his head, smacking him down. Darkness smothered the open wound.

He was broken. From the darkness, the voices were far away, swimming throughout his dark sea. If he kept his eyes closed, maybe they would pass—electric eels or crescent fins of white sharks slicing the waves before going down where no one would know.

". . . no reason to wait."

"Get water . . . undo them . . ."

"Now?"

"No, gag him or . . ."

Darkness was his only hope. But his skull was an unwilling drum. Each heartbeat throbbed against a membrane pierced and violated by those voices. Nothing remained but pain; it had engulfed him.

The words were more clear now; he could distinguish whole sentences.

"Where's the major?"

"Outside."

"Then we have time."

"If we get started."

"You go first."

"Really?"

"Soften him up for me."

The voices were closer. A hand reached down and grabbed Michael's coat; he was jerked up but movement sharpened his pain. There were tiny white stabs of light behind his eyes. He groaned.

"He's awake. Good!"

"I want to see his eyes."

"Ha-ha."

"Hey, you!"

One hand held his collar while another slapped his cheeks. Each slap multiplied the little white lines in his head. They seemed to penetrate to the center of his brain. He felt that his head would fall apart if it continued. Slowly he opened his eyes. The pit-marked face was inches from his own. Michael stared into the bottomless eyes, trying to locate a trace of gentle feeling. Something to contact, to establish concord. The face receded into the bare room.

Michael looked about. He was lying on an old couch. Across the room, there were several wooden chairs and an iron bedstand with no mattress. No curtains. No rug.

It pained him to have his eyes open; the light was almost unbearable. But, just as he began to close them, Squatface barked an order. "Stand up!"

The boy got to his feet and stood before the pig-eyed soldier.

"Take off your clothes!"

Squatface held a knife. For a moment Michael hesitated. Which would be worse? To expose himself or to let the man kill him? And did it make any difference?

"Hurry up!"

Fear outweighed modesty. He let his pants drop to the wooden floor, unbuttoned his shirt and started to remove his shoes. But the man was too impatient. "Never mind those. Do this."

He put his arms behind his head. Michael copied him, ashamed that his own will to live had led to this. Perhaps it'd be better to die, even by that knife. It would all be over quickly, hopefully. Still, with a knife there'd be pain, more pain than bullets.

Squatface pushed Michael's shirt aside and surveyed the boy's torso. As he did, Michael noticed small beads of sweat on his upper lip.

"Turn around." Michael turned.

"Lean forward now. More . . . more . . . *more* goddammit! Ah . . . good!"

Rough hands grabbed him and pushed him onto the couch. He was turned so that he lay on his back. A hand covered his mouth. Now, the knife appeared just two inches from his wide eyes. The top of the blade traced the inside of his nostrils. The voice was soft. "Make a sound and I'll cut you from your throat to your asshole."

Squatface set the knife down and, with his free hand, opened his brown trousers; he pulled out an enormous, red-tipped shaft. Michael had never seen such a huge penis. He stared at it in horror and amazement. As he did, the soldier turned to Yellowface. "Look at him! He wants it!"

"Don't keep the lad waiting!"

"Hold his arms."

Yellowface came to the couch and grabbed the boy's wrists; he pulled them back as Squatface forced his knees in between Michael's legs. He wedged them apart.

"Go on," urged Yellowface. Above Michael, the soldier's free hand went to his mouth, obscuring the twisted smile. It emerged liquid with spit, the stubby fingers coated with the foamy froth. And then, it disappeared, down the delicate seam behind the boy's scrotum, searching out the opening.

It found the spot and pushed, jabbing at the tightened rectum, hurting him. What was he trying to do?

The hand returned to the giant mushroom-capped protuberance which loomed over his stomach. It coated the angry head with more saliva as the soldier started down, clamping his palm even more tightly over Michael's mouth as his other hand fumbled at the damp spot, the warm wet target. The boy closed his eyes.

The uniform was rough against his skin, the weight on his bones was too great! It was hurting him and then, there was pressure at his flesh, stretching him, forcing . . . no, oh, hurting now. . . .

"What is going on here!"

The voice cracked the silence. The men jumped up, Squatface looking particularly ridiculous as he stood at attention, his pants around his hairy calves, his enormous organ wilting in the air.

Turning his head, Michael saw the major at the door. Why was he here? Hadn't he ordered this?

The man sauntered into the room, slowly. "I asked you a question," he said quietly.

"Nothing," Squatface stammered. He'd shrunk to normal size.

"Nothing?"

"Well, he's nothing . . . no one," Yellowface interjected.

Michael heard fear in their voices, and guilt.

"There are rules about this sort of thing. You both know that."

"Yes, sir."

"You were supposed to watch him, not molest him."

"Yes, sir."

"What gives you the right to disobey orders?"

"Nothing, sir."

"Quite right."

"Only . . ."

"Only what? the major snapped.

"He's very pretty, for a boy, sir." The voice was only almost a suggestion. Squatface seemed very nervous. The major sat down on one of the wooden chairs and surveyed his small audience. Then, he turned and spoke to Michael.

"Stand up."

Michael paused, embarrassed, afraid.

"I said stand up!"

Michael stood.

"Turn around."

Michael turned.

"Remove your coat."

Michael obeyed.

"The shirt. And now, turn back."

Michael turned.

"Come here."

Michael went.

The man who'd presided over the butchering of his family had pale blue eyes. Looking into them, Michael sensed that they saw nothing. They were like light blue mirrors reflecting his own face, his chest, his legs. He could see himself in the man's eyes, bending around the iris.

"Not bad," the major muttered. "Not bad at all. Tell me, how old are you?"

"Fourteen," Michael replied, ashamed to have to speak even a word to the murderer. Then, as soon as he'd answered, he'd wished he'd lied and said anything but the truth. He told himself that whatever else the man asked, he'd lie. No matter what, he wouldn't ever tell the truth to a Nazi!

"Fourteen," the major echoed, speaking more to himself than anyone else. "Of course, he's a bit dirty and has that contusion on his head but with a little soap and water, he should be all right! Yes! Definitely. He will do."

Do for what, Michael thought. What was he talking about?

"You may get dressed."

As Michael got into his clothes, the major took the small notebook from his coat and withdrew a piece of paper. Without looking up, he scribbled a note and sealed it into an envelope, and passed it to Yellowface.

"Can you find it?"

"Yes, sir."

Deliver him to Lorken. Use one of the staff cars."

"Yes sir."

"But, deliver him intact! No mistakes this time!"

"Yes sir."

"He's worth a good deal to me as he is. Exactly as he is."

"Yes sir."

The major turned to Michael. "I'm sending you somewhere. If they accept you, you'll probably escape what happened to your family. It's more than you deserve coming from a family of such agitators and troublemakers, but never mind about that. You should consider yourself very fortunate to have this opportunity."

The tears which filled the boy's eyes prevented him from seeing the major's departure. But he did hear the last words.

"I want a reply."

"Yes, sir."

the furnace building with the ferrol to their
from coal-bars apparel receptacle of bottom
and dynamo mines to the gas of one another near

Chapter Nine

When Michael emerged from the stationhouse into the direct sun the light intensified the pain in his head. He was still weak; there were small spots and darts everywhere he looked. But he forced himself to show no pain and refused the impulse to touch his scalp to see how much damage Squatface's rifle butt had inflicted. The soldiers must never know how they'd hurt him; he vowed that they would know nothing!

The train had left the station. How long had it been? Ten minutes? Fifteen? Michael had no sense of time.

He turned as the car approached the spot where he and Yellowface stood. As they got in, Michael was suddenly desperate to ask questions. But he resisted the impulse to know. Let them go without asking where or why. Let there be nothing but this glaring sunlight and the wind in the trees and the smell of a summer which ended life.

He watched the station grow small from the rear window of the car as they drove down the same lane he'd traveled with his father so many times. To avoid looking at the storm troopers who sat on either side of him in the back seat, he concentrated on familiar sights: the trees, the whitewashed rocks which marked sudden twists in the road, that conspicuous boulder with its reddish hue, the fork where they split, taking other travelers into town. And now, the most familiar part of the drive: the three bumps near the turnoff to their farm. Not theirs anymore. The tree hit by lightning and, coming almost to the gate of the Mueller house, he saw Johann, the baker's oldest son on his bicycle! Johann was his friend, at least had been until their fathers had argued. Now, he was gone, a small shape disappearing over the horizon. Not a Jew. Not Catholic or Liberal or Polish or radical or Communist.

Michael turned and faced forward. Again and again he told himself that the pain must originate from the soldier's cruelty. It had to be that. It had to be! Because if it wasn't, if he felt the way he felt because of what happened yesterday, then life was over. And no matter what came next, he would not ever be able to feel anything.

Thinking was a simple thing for the moment. There was what had happened the day before *not* to think about. And there was where he was now not to think about or question. Like a barbed tuning fork, his thoughts vibrated between impossible considerations. In an odd way, he found evasive ruminations deadening to all sensation. He could be blank.

This was more or less possible as they drove along the familiar roads. There were enough associations, enough memories, to distract him. But as the moments passed, his insecurity increased. For the landscape was increasingly less personal, harder to connect with specific journey. As the car continued forward, they were leaving an area he'd known and entering places he'd used only as reference points on the perimeter of his home ground.

Finally, nothing was familiar. Everything became strange. He was out of his world.

The soldiers were obviously quite pleased with themselves. Whether it was the motor car and chauffeur or the short leave or just the afternoon, whatever the reason, they sat in the back of the car with the boy wedged between them and chatted. Their conversation was cheery and good-natured and, although Michael tried not to listen, it was difficult to avoid being sucked in now that there was no longer anything comforting about the view from the car.

Squatface was telling Otto about the night life in Berlin before the National Socialists came to power. The music and the clubs, the beer halls and gardens. For several minutes Michael listened to a variety of lurid tales, but gradually his attention shifted to the pistol which Squatface wore at his waist.

If he could grab it and shoot, first to the left and then to the right, it might be done in less than two or three seconds. If he could lean on the man's right arm and keep him from moving as he seized the gun, he might be able to kill them both and force the driver to stop. He could get out and run. Well, what did it matter what he did *afterward?* The important thing was that, before they had time to do much about it, he would have avenged the murder of his family.

As the plan ran through his mind again and again, Michael polished his moves so that they'd take the very minimum of time, and a cold rage washed over him. He was overcome with violence and a lust for revenge. He would do it! He could do it, for this is what the scriptures demanded! Equal blood for equal blood shed by killers! No matter what they did to him afterward, even if he was hunted and caught.

And it was these men who'd come to the house, grabbed his mother, shot his father and turned their thirsty pistols on the baby! It was these men who'd tracked him with dogs, forced him to stand naked as they toyed with him. They'd beaten him, contaminated his body!

He brought his hands up into his lap and closed his eyes. It was easy to pretend to fall asleep and lean back against Squatface's arm. It was easy like this, to restrict the man's freedom of movement and press against the hated body.

Give it time, give it time, he told himself as the minutes passed. Squatface was telling Otto about one night when he had three whores all to himself when Michael's fingers grazed the handle of the gun. The car came around the bend, giving him even more of an excuse to angle up against the sturdy man's side. Michael grabbed the gun and pulled it out but as he turned the man seized him by the arm.

"Wha . . .?" There was surprise and indignation in Squatface's voice. And then, retaliation.

The fist came down on the boy's thin shoulders, on his head and on his back and neck. Again and again, the blows fell, smashing his light body to the floor of the car, picking him up, battering his face and pounding his ribs until he couldn't tell if the cracks he heard were his bones or the creak of leather.

Yellowface was the one to stop it. "Don't kill him!"

"He tried to shoot me, Otto!" Squatface was outraged; Yellowface more composed.

"Remember what the major said? Don't hurt him."

"Fucking piece of shit!" A final kick.

"Stop it! Look what you've done! Now how are we going to explain this?"

"We don't have to."

"What are you talking about?"

"We can shoot him and say he tried to escape."

"I don't think so."

"Well, look at him. He's useless now."

"Thanks to you!"

"Never mind that. What do we do?"

"Let's just deliver him as he is. And let Lorken worry about it. Anyway," Yellowface decided, "it's not our problem."

They drove in silence for several minutes. Michael lay on the floor of the car, too weak to sit up, too abused to cry. He was afraid to close his eyes now. Afraid that if he did, he would die. Death which had been so welcome just a few minutes before was too possible now. He would keep his eyes open for as long as he could. Then he would know he was alive. He would stare at the gray rug, black boots, the small flecks of dust in the air. Above him, the voices continued. He could hear fragments of a story.

". . . cabaret."

"The Glass Arcade."

"When?"

"Until two years ago."

A bump in the road seemed like a bomb blast.

"And Roehm?"

"And Roehm. Of course, with Hitler. I saw him."

There were three or four flecks of dust in the air, turning slow motion somersaults around one another. It was a delicate ballet for, as close as they came, they never seemed to touch. It was good to have something to watch, something to keep his mind off the men. Yes, it was easy; he could concentrate on them.

". . . an arena?"

"Rows of boxes connected by ramps with blue lights on poles and . . ."

The back of Michael's head was damp. Without reaching up to touch it, he knew there was blood in his hair. Maybe he should try to see if . . .

No. Each movement was agony. Wave after wave of pain coursed through his bruised head and neck. He felt himself slipping, surrendering to the darkness. Maybe this was death. Yes, right before their eyes, as they talked, he would die. And then they would have to go back and tell their major what they'd done. He hoped they would be punished.

When he came to, they were in the country, driving down a wooded lane. There were many holes in the road. Each bump aggravated his pain. Still, he controlled his tears.

The car slowed down; Squatface noticed that Michael was awake. He reached down and yanked him back into the seat; Yellowface hissed in his ear: "Now don't try anything or we'll break every bone in your body!"

Michael ignored him; he sensed that the soldiers wouldn't disobey their commanding officer. The major had insisted they deliver him unharmed. Well, he *was* harmed! Tears came to his eyes but he forced them back. Still, the pain of sitting upright was fearsome and his head was aching. He reached up and touched it very gently. He'd been right. His hair was matted with blood clots and there were three huge bumps and several areas which must have been severely bruised. Squat-face saw him touch his hair, and remarked, "That's what you get for being a troublemaker, you piece of shit!"

The car came to a stop. They had reached an immense pair of wrought-iron gates. Two storm troop-ers armed with machine guns approached the automobile. Squatface rolled down his window as the men neared the car.

"We've brought something for Lorken."

A sentry peered in and glanced down at Michael. He looked surprised and turned to Squatface who hastened to add, "He gave us some trouble along the way."

The sentry stepped back and nodded; the great iron gates swung open and the car moved forward onto the smooth gravel of a wide drive. As they passed the checkpoint Michael saw one of the guards pick up a field phone and speak into it.

They drove into a forest and then out on the other side—through a wild meadow, past dark glades and well-tended lawns where symmetric ponds were framed by marble statues. In one grove of oaks a delicate bridge spanned a narrow stream before they reentered the forest. For a quarter of a mile, Michael could see nothing through the close undergrowth until, at last, the car turned around a final bend and entered an avenue of poplar trees which led toward a stately house at the end of the long drive.

They drove more slowly as they approached the cream-colored building. It was enormous. With the exception of picture books and engravings seen only in shop windows, Michael had never seen anything like it. From the even and harmonious facade of the edifice, symmetric wings extended to embrace the roundabout which encircled a great basin. At the center of this

pool, a marble Neptune, his hair wreathed and festooned with seaweed, held a struggling nymph in his
heavily muscled arms.

The chauffeur stopped at the foot of a staircase which
led from the drive to a wide terrace. As he got out of
the car, Michael saw that the tall windows and columns
ended in a maze of chimneys which towered over the
entire structure. It was a house from a fairy tale,
splendid and enchanting.

As soon as the chauffeur had helped them out of the
car, a man and two boys emerged from a door beneath
a terrace; images from another era, Michael thought.
They each were wearing gray wigs and pale yellow coats
with white breeches, stockings and black leather
pumps.

"Good afternoon," the older man said. "What can I
do for you?"

"We've brought something from Major Schüller,"
answered Squatface.

The elderly gentleman nodded and bowed very
slightly as he said, "Please follow me. I'll send for Herr
Lorken."

He whispered something to one of the boys who
disappeared immediately. The other boy, who was not
very much older than Michael, followed their strange
party as they ascended the curvilinear stairs.

It was difficult for Michael to move as quickly as the
others. His body was aching, his muscles were stiff and
he lagged a few steps behind. For a moment, when the
soldiers had already entered the immense front doors,
he paused. If he turned and tried to run, what would
the other boy do? Would he help him, at least tell him
which way to go?

Michael turned and found himself eye to eye with the
brown-eyed boy. He must have looked peculiar because
the other lad seemed taken aback by his unexpected
about-face.

"How can I get away?" Michael hissed.

The page recovered his composure but, instead of

giving Michael directions, he gestured toward the front doors.

"You'd better go in," he said quietly.

For a moment, Michael wanted to slip by him and run for the far off trees which couldn't have been more than one hundred and fifty yards from where he stood. But if this fellow gave the alarm, there would be no chance of escape. He turned and continued up the stairs.

As they passed through the tall doors, Michael forgot his vow not to be impressed. He stood still and stared. The entrance hall of the palace was a fantasy of pastel colors, tapestries and ornate columns. Cherubs, angels and carved garlands adorned the hall up to the second- and third-floor balconies which circled the perfect space beneath a painted dome at least forty-five feet above the blue- and white-checked floor.

A great staircase spiraled as it wound around an enormous chandelier which hung suspended on a thick velvet cord. Carpeted with a blue strip, the staircase seemed to be a path to the stars.

The page coughed; Michael recovered his composure and, following a wordless glance, saw the direction he was to go. He crossed the hall and entered a sitting hall. Though not as august as the entrance hall, it was astonishing to him too.

It was a large room of soft grays and yellows. All along the paneled walls painted ancient courtiers peered suspiciously at these intruders.

Why was he here? To wear a yellow coat and white leggings? To follow people with his eyes kept low? He turned to look at the page but the other boy's face revealed nothing. He had been well trained.

The chairs and couches were covered with needle-point patterns of flowers and birds. As he perched nervously on the edge of one seat cushion, Michael inspected the room more carefully.

Before him, on the table, there was a large crystal vase which held a spray of yellow roses, the same thick color as the curtains on the tall windows which overlooked the gardens. On the mantel, across the room, a pair of angels wrestled for possession of a silver globe. Was it the world? No. Looking closer, Michael saw that the engraved orb was, in fact, a clock. How different from the plain wood "coffin" which had housed his family's timepiece!

It hurt to strain his eyes. He leaned back, closed them and felt better without the little darts of light flashing before him.

It was so quiet, so very quiet in this house.

"Nice," Squatface said.

"Very," agreed Yellowface.

Michael opened his eyes just enough to see the two men sitting on a couch, examining the leaves of a leather-lined book.

"Look at *that*!"

"Uh-huh."

Michael closed his eyes.

"Wait, let's see that again."

"This?"

"Yes. Who is that?"

"That, my dear Otto, is Frederich Lorken."

"Does he really look like that?"

"How do you think he got this house?"

There was a brief pause.

"What goes on?"

"What doesn't go on?"

"The S.A.? Here?"

"And the S.S."

"And Gestapo?"

"Why not?" asked Squatface. "It's discreet."

"Does Hitler know?"

"Of course!"

"And he doesn't care?"

"Why should he?"

"But if anyone found out!"

"It's here, isn't it?"

"But for the privileged only?"

"Of course," said Squatface knowingly.

"Of course," echoed an odd voice.

Michael opened his eyes and traced the echo to a pale man who stood in the door observing him. That must be *him*, he thought, as the figure moved into the room.

"I understand you've come from Major Schüller."

Squatface cleared his throat and spoke. "Yes, he sent *that*," he said, indicating Michael.

He didn't speak to the major like that, Michael thought to himself. No, his voice had become more self-conscious and less gruff.

"I see," the strange man replied.

"And, uh, he asked me to deliver this," Squatface added, prodding Yellowface who produced the major's note.

The man in black didn't move.

Yellowface crossed the room rather awkwardly and delivered the envelope. Lorken opened it without a word and scanned the contents. As he read, Michael watched him, fascinated.

Frederich Lorken was neither beautiful nor handsome. Those wouldn't be the words. But there was something about him, not on the surface but contained within, which was utterly unique. He was wearing only black, but, nevertheless, there was an essence of the exotic about him. Like a woman only not a woman. And like a man, but not a man. He was something in between. It was as if each element of his being was counterbalanced by another component part. He was tall and big-boned but, in spite of his size, almost delicate. His features were simple. His hair was dark. He appeared gentle, yet there was something remotely calculating within him.

There had been a mysterious transfer of power as soon as Lorken had entered the room. Even the soldiers were aware of it. Before the pale man had arrived they were masters of the situation. Now, they seemed as out of place as circus elephants who'd been let loose in the great house.

Lorken tapped Major Schüller's note against his open palm. For a moment, he was absolutely motionless, then he crossed to Michael and looked into his face.

The eyes that regarded Michael were deep brown, but they betrayed no warmth, no hint of any sentiment. But, he's in there, Michael thought to himself. He's not only watching! He's feeling something! I know it!

Was it a quick flicker of pain in Lorken's eyes when he saw the cuts and bruises? For a moment there was a trace of something unexpected in them. Beneath the elegance and simplicity there had been something alive, something ticking.

Lorken crossed to a small table, sat down and drew out a sheet of cream-colored stationery. Glancing at the boy and the soldiers he paused, tapped his pen against the inkstand, wrote a few words, paused and wrote for another moment. Then, standing, he sealed the paper into an envelope and gave it to Otto. For a moment he observed each of the men. It seemed to Michael that he was about to ask a question; the mood grew apprehensive.

Why? What did he possess that silenced the vulgar soldiers? What was it that filled the yellow and gray chamber with another essence? What was it about the tall figure in black—the controlled movements—each gesture reduced to a minimum? Lorken crossed the room and spoke to the page in a low voice. Then he turned and addressed the men.

"I shall take charge. Give my reply to the major and tell him to call if he has any questions. And now, I'm sure you are eager to be on your way."

Squatface looked uncomfortable. Lorken noticed it at once.

"Well, what is it?" he asked.

Squatface blushed and muttered something about

wanting to stay. Lorken looked ambivalent, as if he was reluctant to confide in the soldier.

"I'm so sorry. We're entirely booked up for the evening."

"Can't you make an exception?" asked Squatface. "We've come a long way. . . ."

Lorken shrugged as if to imply that he was not responsible for accidents of fate. "As you know, we're on a strictly reservation basis. And now, if you don't mind . . ."

"Are you sure you can handle him?" asked Yellowface.

Lorken nodded wordlessly.

"He's a rebellious one," Squatface put in.

Lorken regarded the men without blinking. And, although his voice was soft and his tone polite, it was clear as he spoke that they were being dismissed. "It will be fine, thank you. And now, Klaus will show you to the door."

Half-bowing, half-muttering apologies they followed the page out into the great hall of angels.

Michael and Frederich Lorken were alone.

It was the first time in over twenty-four hours that Michael hadn't felt fear. As he watched the master of the house, he felt curiosity and apprehension, but not fear. The man was standing at the window, staring out toward the garden. He seemed absorbed by something.

Michael looked down at his hands; they were scratched and red from the nettles of the woods. Suddenly, he felt ashamed to have such hands in this beautiful room. They reminded him that he was a rude country boy who didn't belong in these surroundings. He put them in his coat pockets, but just as hurriedly, withdrew them. There was no reason for *him* to feel shame! No reason for him to hide *his* hands!

Rage overwhelmed him again. For a few minutes, ever since entering the palace, he'd been so surprised by the fantastic interior and the presence of Lorken that it had been easy to forget that he was another of *them!* He wasn't in uniform but, whatever his function, he was working for the same people: Adolf Hitler, General Roehm—the Nazis!

Michael glanced into the hall. There was no one in sight. Maybe if he could steal out the front door . . . if Lorken was still lost in his thoughts, there might be a chance. He could slip out of the building and run for the woods which encircled the house and lawns. The forest wasn't so far away. Perhaps only a hundred or so yards. He stood up and started for the door. Almost at once Lorken spoke, not in anger but in curiosity. "What is it?"

Michael seized the nearest object and threw it blindly. A Dresden shepherd boy flew through the air and smashed into a wall behind its startled target. Pastel fragments scattered in all directions.

For a moment they regarded one another in amazement.

"How dare you . . .?" Lorken began. Michael ran. Out into the baroque hall. Out across the marble checks toward the great doors where he grabbed unfamiliar levers and tugged at them desperately. But, too soon, Lorken was upon him.

It was no match; exhausted by the previous day, the bone-weary boy collapsed before the weight of the man, and his unexpected strength. Still, Michael fought as long as he could, trying to bite, kick, punch or scratch the impassive mask of his new captor.

Lorken shook him. "Stop! Do you want to live or die?"

But words no longer made sense; there had been too much stress and too much fear. Now, he fought, forgetting his wounds; he fought desperately and determinedly, convinced that if he gave up he would never have his own life again. They would put him in a yellow coat and make him walk with his eyes low. If he gave in, he would fall and never regain his own balance. There was blood on all of them, the blood of his family and the people crowding onto the train at the depot.

He tried to grab Lorken's face, to pull the smooth skin off the underlying skull. Lorken shook him again, this time hard enough to stun him. *"Michael! Stop it!"*

Michael stopped struggling.

"That's better."

They lay on the polished floor a moment, regaining their breath. The cool marble was soothing.

Lorken rose and pulled Michael up by the coat. The boy groaned for the pain was insurmountable. He touched his head and realized that he was bleeding again.

"Follow me."

They walked through the hall, past the wide base of the staircase, past a series of magnificent chambers and a series of closed doors as the great hall ended in a narrow passage. There was a long wall to the right; windows on the left overlooked a courtyard and terraced gardens. A man was washing out the inside of a fountain. *The same color hair as my father's*, thought Michael.

They went through a pair of swinging doors and descended a small flight of steps into the pantries and kitchens. Steel vats simmering on immaculate stoves. Michael tightened his stomach as they passed through the long room. How many hours had it been since he'd eaten? Twenty-six? Twenty-eight? He'd had no water.

Down another passage, past storerooms and a plain dining hall. Here, the long tables were set with blue and white plates and bowls. But so many places? Was this for the staff? How many servants could there be?

Up a flight of stairs carpeted with a thick brown rug, into another corridor. Only this was a back hall where dark blue doors had big locks and brass numbers on the outside.

Lorken inspected a list on the wall and walked to one

of the doors. He unlocked it, pushed the door open and beckoned for Michael to follow. Michael didn't move. Lorken grabbed him by the collar, shoved him through the door and slammed it closed. His voice was cold and impersonal.

"Sit down," he said. "I want to talk to you."

Michael scanned the room. There was a small bed, a high dresser, a wooden nightstand with a brass lamp. On the floor, a rag rug woven of many colors. The walls were light blue. The room was simple but pleasant if anything here could be.

"I said, *sit down!*"

Michael sat in the only chair. Lorken paused, drew a breath and regarded Michael in silence. The boy thought the man looked like a big bird who was about to tear a worm to bits.

"What you just did is never to happen again. Do you understand? If you ever damage anything in the house again, you'll be replaced, is that clear?"

Replaced? What did that mean? Michael stared down at his hands. Once again, they looked dirty. Lorken continued.

"I want you to understand where you are and what has happened. This is an institution for young people, many of whom are your age. You are lucky to be here. You will have opportunities to participate in games, to see films, to enjoy fresh air and good food. You will be taken care of properly, housed and clothed. *But* you will live according to our rules. Is that understood?"

Michael said nothing. Lorken went on. "For the next few days, you will rest. You look as though you need a bath and some food. Are you hungry?"

If I don't speak to him, Michael thought, he'll have to go away and leave me alone.

"I asked if you are hungry!"

I don't care if they do leave me here to die, Michael decided.

"Well, I think you *are!*" Lorken suggested. "I'll have

some food sent up when Peter comes in to look after you. But no more foolishness. Whatever has happened . . . out there . . ." he gestured with a spidery hand to indicate the outside world, "is external. In here, there is another world."

Michael closed his eyes and imagined Lorken put on the train. But no! Nothing would ever happen to this Nazi! He was one of the major's friends. He would always survive.

"In return for this privilege," Lorken continued, "you will be expected to fulfill certain functions. For now, you are to keep this room clean. Later, you will have other responsibilities."

"Any questions?"

Michael remained silent.

"No? Very well. I'll send for Peter and he'll attend to your immediate needs. We shall talk another day, you and I, and perhaps you'll tell me about yourself."

Never, Michael vowed. Not if I live to be a thousand!

After a final look at the boy's expressionless face, Lorken strode out into the narrow hall without closing the door. Michael could hear him talking on the telephone.

"Let me speak with Peter."

Lorken lowered his voice; Michael listened more attentively but couldn't make out what he was saying. His new master reappeared. Michael didn't look up. In the silence he thought to himself: He might as well wear the same uniform as the others. Even if he doesn't have the same eyes what does it matter? He's one of them! One of them! And I'll never do what he wants even if he kills me. I'll never give in to him! I hate him just as much as all the others!

When he looked up, Herr Lorken was gone. Michael was relieved.

Peter came to take care of him. He was an older man, impossible to hate. He was the man Michael had seen scrubbing out the fountain. He had a trustworthy face and looked exactly like a hunter in one of the picture books the boy had as a child.

Peter led Michael to a bath. The boy lay in the tub and marveled at the faucets which produced hot water, filling the tile bathroom with steam. At home, he'd had a simple tub which had to be filled with water heated on the stove. Here, it flowed directly from iron pipes into the porcelain basin.

He lay back and let his muscles relax. And, when Peter washed him and applied medicine to his abrasions, the boy allowed himself to realize that the man was being as gentle as possible. Still, it required a great effort not to cry out as Peter cleaned the open wounds.

Peter told him to dress in the white cotton jersey and blue pants he gave him. Michael felt like a young sailor or cadet in these new clothes. But his own were gone when he emerged from the bathroom. Only his shoes remained and Peter assured him that he'd have new ones in the morning.

The loss of his clothing disturbed him and undermined the relaxation he'd allowed as he lay in the water. They'd stolen the gold his parents had given him. They'd taken everything, except his shoes. Now nothing remained. Just an endless tear in the fabric of his young life.

When dinner arrived, he refused to eat. Peter looked disturbed at having to take the meat and dumplings to the kitchen but Michael was adamant. If I don't eat, he mused, I'll die and it'll be over. Sooner, rather than later. In any case, there's no reason to continue living. These people are my enemies. Murderers and thieves!

He didn't answer the soft knock on the door. There was no reason to talk. No reason to eat or explain. No reason to do anything they wanted. His father had died without a sound. Just one quick shot and he fell. Perhaps, if Michael wasn't helpful or useful, if he refused to put on a pale yellow coat and white leggings, perhaps, if he was fortunate, he could fall before a hail of bullets and have it be ended. Like his father.

The door opened and Herr Lorken entered. But he was not the same person whom Michael had seen in the afternoon.

He was wearing a coat and leggings of little silver disks which glistened in the light and threw reflections into every corner of the room. There were silver lights in his hair and on his face. He must have painted it for his features were no longer plain, no longer the rather ordinary features of the afternoon. Now they were alive, and something wonderfully beautiful, a marvelous illusion between man, woman and boy, without specific age or sex. Just a fantastic veil where the face had been only a few hours ago. The veil hovered, thin skin pierced by dark eyes staring out over a cascade of silver flakes which clung to his cheeks as iridescent rain. He wore a wreath of white roses and glittering stars. In his hand he held a spangled wand.

So this was Frederich Lorken, the Frederich Lorken Squatface had depicted! Now Michael understood; he was a living chandelier!

"Peter tells me you won't eat."

No answer.

"Why?"

No answer.

"Won't you talk to me?"

No answer.

"Are you sad, Michael?"

Was he *sad?* Was that the word you used if you totaled the past thirty-six hours? The murders, the beatings, gun butts, molesting, rough hands, blood in the dust and the dead hands of the baby, reaching out for nothing? Was he "sad" if he'd seen his parents slaughtered, the mother killed even as she begged for the life of her baby in soundless eloquence and he, the older child, trapped, unable to intercede, unable to do anything until it was too late? Did this make him *"sad"?*

He stopped his tears as they issued forth and drove them back into their bed of pins. Never tears before the

Nazis! Never that shame! Only pride. Silence and pride, until death.

"Michael?" The voice was calm, patient. So easy to fall into, so easy to slip into, in, easy, easy.

"I know now what happened to your family. I spoke to Major Schüller and he told me."

Through his tears, Herr Lorken seemed less like a person than a silver mirage, an incandescent blur in the blue room.

"The men who beat you have been punished, but I want you to know that I am very sorry."

Michael collapsed on the bed in helpless sobs. He wept for a long time, dimly aware of a hand on his back. He couldn't hear the words as he cried until finally, exhausted and unaware of transition, he surrendered to sleep.

Chapter Ten

When Michael woke, it was still dark. He sat up in his bed and looked at his room. "His room"? It wasn't his room; it was his cell!

The night lamp was on; it bathed everything in an amber light. Silently he slipped off the bed and went to the door. Directly across from his room, Peter was sleeping in a wooden chair, a newspaper on the floor beside him. His snoring was soft and regular. There was no one else in the hall.

Michael took a blanket from the bed and picked up his shoes. Holding his breath, he tiptoed out into the hall and crept by the sleeping man. He stared at his feet as he slipped by, believing that if he watched where he was going, the floorboards wouldn't give him away. When he reached the bottom of the steps, he peered down the passage toward the kitchen.

There was someone there! Someone was moving about! Michael could see the back of a white apron. He stiffened and pressed himself up against the wall. It wouldn't be possible to leave through the front doors.

The boy inched toward an exit door halfway down the hall and slid the latch as quietly as possible. At any moment he expected an alarm to sound or a loud voice to demand an explanation. There was nothing.

He opened the door and inhaled the cool night air. Slipping outside, he was free!

The moon was almost full. It hung over the distant trees and illuminated the long lawns of the villa. In this pale light, the many-chimneyed roof of the great house was luminous, outlined against a starry sky. Even from this angle, the building was imposing, Michael thought to himself as he knelt down to tie his shoes.

For an instant, he paused to gaze up at the moon. And then he ran.

He ran across the grass, a gravel drive and out onto the lawns. Terrified, and exhilarated, he rushed toward the front of the residence, toward the gardens which might lead him to the bumpy land and, from there, hopefully a route to the nearest town. He was dimly aware of lights at the front of the palace as he ran in the darkness, running as fast as he could, running into a sudden wet shock and splash.

He stood up and looked down.

He had reached the rim of a pond, part of the artificial canals he'd observed on his way in. Now, he could make out the water, metallic black and yellow waves leveling out, regaining frozen composure as he clambered back onto the grass.

The blanket was waterlogged and too heavy to carry. His shoes were oozing mud, no good for running. They were slippery, clammy, spongelike. He hesitated for a moment, uncertain as to what he should do next.

And, gradually, he became aware of music. It was accompanied by laughter and the sound of glasses. Sounds of a party, of corks popping and cars arriving or possibly departing.

Curiosity compelled him to investigate. Was this why Herr Lorken had appeared in a silver costume?

Michael let the soggy blanket fall and maneuvered toward the front of the palace, staying as far as possible from the patches of electric light which fell from tall windows onto the lawns. He stayed in darkness as he rounded a corner and stumbled over something lying on the lawn.

"What?" A voice came up from the blackness.

"Oh, excuse me!"

As the boy ran off, he heard laughter behind him. It

sounded intimate, warm, two voices. A man and a woman.

When he peered through the ornamental railings he saw flames, great fires from torches blazing against the night sky. They were held aloft by marble goddesses on a wide terrace which separated the palace from the garden. Inside, beyond the garden, he could see great chandeliers ablaze with lights.

There were soldiers in the garden, many of them. Officers in uniforms and sashes and medals. Officers of the Gestapo, mingled with Brown Shirts of the S.A. and the pale uniforms of the S.S. There were other people as well.

Women, fantastic women in shimmering gowns and long capes of velvet trimmed with fur. Even from a distance, Michael could see them chatting with soldiers or dancing on the terrace like incredible birds of the night, resplendent in their iridescent plumes. Some wore metallic materials accented with jewels which caught the firelight. Others wore gowns which had been cut or slashed to show a maximum of creamy backs or delicate thighs.

Little boys in greens and golds scampered across the terrace followed by young savages streaked with silver. Several older youths costumed in black and red appeared as jesters to tease a masked faun who sat at the knee of an officer. A moment later, these costumed boys ambled into the great room where the chandeliers threw rainbows against the ceiling.

The music grew louder as Michael moved closer to the garden, coming as near as he dared.

And suddenly there was Herr Lorken striding across the terrace and moving into the garden, a silver streak flanked by two black and red uniforms. He was laughing but seemed intent on escaping the men who stumbled after him. Michael strained to hear their voices and managed to pick up a few words through the din of the music and conversation.

"Always the tactician, isn't he?" Lorken exclaimed as he maneuvered across the lawn, coming close to Michael's hiding place. Now he was just on the other side of the low wall. "But really, I'm too old for such escapades! Why don't you dance with someone younger? They're much more appealing than me!"

One of the men muttered something into Lorken's ear. The boy couldn't understand a word of it but again there was laughter as the silver Lorken attempted to extricate himself from uniformed arms. It was obvious to the boy that Herr Lorken was trying to free himself as gracefully as possible.

"I'm a fool to refuse," he said very lightly as he pried one of the officer's arms from his waist. "But on my fortieth birthday I promised myself I'd never sin again."

"You're not forty," argued the taller of the two men.

"But thirty equals forty at the Glass Arcade," Lorken riposted. "Look, I'll go with you and we'll snare someone without any scruples at all. I know two people who . . ."

And they were gone. The music had slowed to a stately waltz. Now the boy couldn't see enough. He had to get closer.

He backtracked into the night, hoping to find a better view on the far side of the garden. There were a few trees on that side which would give him a good view if he could find a good perch. But, as he approached, something caught his eye.

Blue light was coming from a window at ground level. Michael held his breath and pressed against the wall. He got down on his hands and knees and forced himself to look in.

At first he saw nothing; the lights were soft and the entire room seemed to be shrouded in mist. Michael cupped his hands around his eyes. The entire room appeared to be a construction of wax, moonlight and smoke. But this blue and soft rose was broken by a spark, a flare, a brief flame sucked back into shadow. Smoke escaped through the window. Sweet, heavy smoke.

The room was filled with naked people.

They lay on couches, all of them perfectly still as if they were sculpted in living flesh and placed in an artificial stupor.

Men and their companions were alternately revealed and shrouded by the blue smoke. Still, it was possible to see that they were sucking and inhaling on long tubes connected to silver burners. Tall pipes produced part of the sweet cloud; the rest came from an enormous silver basin at the center of the room. Surrounded by great sprays of white roses which looked blue in the subterranean light.

The occupants of this room moved only to inhale on the flexible tubes. Then, they sank back onto their couches, where they made only an occasional roll, a stretch or sigh of pleasure.

Slender youths gliding through the room carried trays of steaming cups. These were distributed and collected effortlessly, noiselessly. Other boys carried the silver pipes from one divan to the next, preparing a paste, cooking it over a small lamp and offering it up to the next willing soul. It was so subtle and serene in that cloud room. So perfectly tranquil.

Only to be shattered by the barking of dogs!

Michael jerked his head back from the window, turned to see a flashlight come his way. The beam illuminated two black dogs which tugged at a leash, fairly dragging whoever it was that restrained them.

He ran out onto the lawn, away from the barking and the gruff commands of the night watchman or soldier. Out of the corner of his eye, he thought he saw Herr Lorken standing at the edge of the terraced gardens, but everything dissolved as he fled across the lawn. He was running again, away from the spell, the intoxication and fantasy. Out, out into darkness.

He slipped in his wet shoes as he switched direction. He looked back toward the flashlight, stumbled over his own feet, got up and continued his flight, no longer certain as to where he was going, only hoping that the trees would somehow offer protection.

And suddenly the night had teeth and jaws and danger. Suddenly the air was a womb of snarling dogs, which seized him, threw him down and yanked at his flesh, one paw scratching his face as he was pressed against the wet grass.

He screamed, trying to cover his torn cheek, trying to break the sharp grip of the dog on his neck. His skin was pinched between incisors, his body overwhelmed by the strange weight and muscle of creatures which pinned him as they snarled and growled, their thick frothy spit spilling onto his face. This terrible blackness from blackness was finally pierced by the beams of night watchmen.

They dragged him back to the palace, back to the room where they threw him on the bed. Peter was awake; he looked reproachful as well as guilty when he dismissed the guards.

And suddenly there was Herr Lorken; Lorken sweeping through the door. Michael took one look at the fiery eyes of his captor and lost conscious control of himself.

With a horrible cry, he rose and leaped for the man, hoping to jam his fingers into those glittering eyes, into the jewels on the painted cheeks. Nothing but the sight of blood streaming down that flawless collage would satisfy him. Lorken had wanted to know if he was sad? Well, he'd show him how he felt! He'd let him share the experience of torn skin and pain!

But it was in vain; Lorken was too quick. He sidestepped, recovered his footing and threw Michael down. The boy struggled to his feet, just in time to glimpse the fist as it fell, smacking him back from further violence. He felt as if a cold darkness rose up to suck him down forever.

A roaring heat occupied his body. Moaning, he turned and opened his eyes. It was morning. Light streamed through the curtained windows of his cell; he was wet, he was lying in a bed of sweat, freezing in damp sheets, then feverish and hot. Water fell from his brow in thick drops. His flesh was a cluster of blisters and boils. There was a dark red rash on his chest, his cheeks were too painful to touch.

He turned his head. The empty chamber was silent, but there was someone in the hall. The door opened and Herr Lorken came in with a tray. He put it down and pulled a chair closer to the narrow bed.

Michael observed the strange face as it looked into his own. At times this man could be almost impossibly beautiful. But now he seemed remote. Lorken turned to the tray and came back again. His voice was soft, coercing. "Try to eat."

The soup was warm. He allowed the spoon to enter his mouth again and again. How long had it been! He'd lost all sense of time.

He fell asleep without nightmare.

When he woke again, it was night. He lay in bed and tried to recollect his sorrows but there was only something numb where agony had prevailed. He had passed the nadir of his grief; a quota had been reached. Now he couldn't reach across the days of fever to summon resistance or the will to die. Survival had been at work within his unconscious mind; it dulled the impulse for self-destruction and repaired him as he slept.

Herr Lorken appeared with warm milk and honey; as Michael drank he looked at the impassive face without embarrassment. Herr Lorken sat quite still as the boy finished his milk. Then, he motioned for Michael to return the cup.

His hands came up from the darkness. Neither hesitant nor aggressive, they unscrewed the cap of a bottle wrapped in white paper and placed it on the nightstand. At once, the room smelled of medicine.

Lorken unbuttoned Michael's pajamas and removed the top, placing it at the end of the bed.

Michael remained as Lorken positioned him, on his stomach with his bare back exposed. He found the anticipation exciting and permitted himself to feel pleasure when the hands touched him—cooling skin with balm, massaging the tight muscles with strong fingers, kneading and caressing the back, shoulders and upper arms.

If he opened his eyes just a bit and peered out, he could see Herr Lorken's face; in the amber light it seemed much younger than it did by day. It was almost boyish, as if the man was only a few years older than he. Well, he was old, wasn't he? Forty? No, he had said thirty. Old, anyway.

Michael hoped he'd be able to detect a clue as to what the man was thinking. But it was impossible to guess.

Lorken tapped his shoulder. "Don't tighten up," he said.

The hands pressed harder and Michael closed his eyes as tightly as he could, trying not to feel any pleasure as Lorken worked on the muscles of his lower back. He told himself that if he hadn't been so pent-up in recent days, he'd not feel so stimulated. It wasn't anything that Lorken was doing. It was just that there were a few spots on his back where it was odd and exciting to be touched.

Rather than say anything aloud, he arched his back a little. Lorken stopped touching him at once and the sheets were drawn up.

As Lorken screwed the cap on the bottle, Michael kept his eyes closed and pretended that he was falling asleep. There was a slight pause before the door closed very quietly. As soon as he felt certain that he was alone, Michael opened his eyes. And that night, for the first time in days and days and days, he stroked himself until the shocking milky drops shot out onto his stomach.

Peter came in the next morning and ruined Michael's day. He had hoped to see Herr Lorken, but went unsatisfied until evening when the man came in.

For a second time, Michael was taken aback. He'd come to anticipate Lorken in his customary black sweater, but now he was wearing another sensational costume. There were hundreds of small jewels glued to his face in every shade of the rainbow; they had been applied over a mask-like application of flesh-colored paint so the face appeared to be a warm shower of glistening stones. He was wearing a coat of bright silk ribbons which danced and fluttered whenever he moved. As before, his legs were covered with tight leggings and he wore a pair of high black boots.

It seemed to Michael that Lorken had been bombarded in a hail of adhesive crystals. But he felt betrayed that this man, who despite himself he was beginning to trust, had failed to visit him in the morning. He withdrew, determined not to remark on, or approve of, the apparition.

"How are you?"

No answer.

"Do you feel better?"

Lorken reached out to touch his forehead but Michael pulled back, taking grim satisfaction in the look of surprise and hurt on that incredible face.

"I'm sorry I didn't see you this morning but I was awake until dawn."

No answer.

"Peter tells me you ate."

No answer.

"Michael, won't you talk to me?"

No answer.

Lorken sighed and Michael felt better but it was a cold and unpleasant victory. For soon, too soon, Lorken left.

In the morning there was a gentle knock on the door. Michael had been standing by the window, but when he heard the noise he jumped back into bed. The door opened and Peter came in.

Peter asked him if he felt well enough to have breakfast outside. Michael said nothing; Peter told him that Herr Lorken wanted to dine with him but only if he felt well enough to move about.

It was a warm day; Michael forced himself to dress slowly.

Chapter Eleven

They ate on a terrace outside the great dining room. Lorken had a table put beside the ornate balustrade so they would look out over the wide lawns. Across the fields, too far away to be distracting, Michael could see a group of boys playing with a soccer ball.

It was warm; Herr Lorken contented himself with coffee and a roll. Michael ate eggs, ham, potatoes, rolls with butter and jam and two glasses of milk. From time to time, he glanced at Lorken who seemed absorbed in the newspaper. Michael wanted the man's attention. Finally, he was rewarded. Lorken sensed his distress and folded the tabloid in such a way that Michael could only see part of the front page: ROEHM DECLARES S.A. IS FUTURE OF GERMANY.

"Do you ever read the news?" Lorken asked.

Michael stared at him, trying to think of something interesting or sophisticated to say in reply. He was in awe of Lorken. It was as simple as that. To Michael, Lorken was an ever-changing image. Severe one minute, then almost maternal. Austere and grave, then sensuous. It was his smile which the boy found most interesting; it flickered across his face more a shadowy run than a concrete expression.

Whatever lay behind that complicated mask, Michael would not budge from his first vow: to stay as he was and never give up to the Nazis, no matter what they wanted him to do. True, he was less frantic than he had been upon his first arrival. But that had nothing to do with his intention to resist and remain true to his family. They might punish him for all he cared. But he would be loyal.

"Why am I here?"

Lorken raised his eyebrows in surprise. "That's the first time I've heard your voice."

Michael repeated the question.

The man nodded and poured another cup of coffee from the silver pot. As he did, a strange sound came from the distant trees, an unearthly cry. But Michael didn't divert his gaze from the face before his own. He wanted the answer. They hadn't brought him here to kill him; if they had, they'd not have worked so diligently to nurse him through his illness. Something told him that it had more to do with what had happened at the train station.

"I'll tell you, Michael. Actually it's the reason I wanted to have breakfast with you."

As he spoke, he looked directly into the boy's face. His words were soft but it was clear that he was not jesting. There was a strange quality in his tone, almost a warning.

"As you know, Germany is undergoing a transformation. Whether it is a success or failure is immaterial. That has next to nothing to do with why we are here.

"You are here because you've been chosen to help other people and to save yourself at the same time. That may sound strange but it's true. I think you've seen enough to realize that there are many people here some nights. You've seen me in costume. You saw others in fantastic clothes, yes?"

Michael nodded; Lorken pointed toward the green field, toward the boys and their ordinary game.

"There they are. Those are the people you saw with the soldiers and you've been selected to be one of them. Now do you understand?"

Michael shook his head. "No."

"Very well," Lorken said, tapping his fingers on the table. "I'll explain it differently."

"This is a prison, Michael. We are both prisoners.

You are and so am I. You look surprised. Is it because I wear pretty things and sit on a terrace and have my breakfast? Don't be deceived by appearances. You must look past them to see the truth of the situation.

"We are all in danger. One mistake, one slip and we could all disappear. The soldiers who brought you here brought you from a train station. The people who board those trains go only one way; with very rare exceptions they never return. Sometimes, if they are extremely lucky, their families or friends can pay to have them released. But not often. And the same thing could happen to us, anytime.

"This is a house for pleasure. That is why we are here. We do what we do for two reasons. First, to make the men happy when they come here. Most of them are officers. All of them are powerful. They all have influence. If they don't go away well-satisfied with themselves especially, it could be very bad on all of us. So we've got to be good at our work.

"The second reason is directly related to that: if they are happy we ensure our own survival. All of us. The boys working here help each other to stay alive. If each of us does our part as best we can, regardless of personal feelings, no matter how hard it is, or how painful, then we have a chance to survive. But if we don't, those trains are ready to take us to the labor camps."

"Is Dachau a labor camp?" Michael asked in a soft voice.

"How do you know about Dachau?" Lorken asked rather sharply.

"At the station, someone said that's where the train was going."

Lorken nodded. "It's a labor camp. There are twenty-four thousand people there. I've heard stories of how they are treated. Believe me, Michael, you don't want to go there."

"What will happen to those people?" asked Michael.

"They will disappear," Lorken replied.

He paused and Michael lowered his eyes, not wanting to look at him. He didn't want to cry. Finally he raised his head and looked across the field.

The boys had started back toward the palace. Again, he heard that strange cry. It was such an odd call, almost a caw. He followed the direction of the sound. Below on the smooth lawn, a peacock approached one of the long ponds. It was about twenty-five yards from where they sat.

The bird picked his way over the grass, craning his head or undulating his iridescent neck as if it drew him forward. He turned occasionally to glare in their direction, freezing momentarily with a fierce look in its eye, and then proceeding. The great cascade of turquoise plumes swept the ground as the imperial creature strutted by, the fantail expanding and drooping as he passed, suspicious, regal.

They watched the haughty creature in silence; Michael had never seen one before. Unconsciously, he smiled at Lorken, amazed by the gorgeous beast. Lorken returned his smile and lit a cigarette, allowing another moment to pass before resuming conversation.

"For some boys, it's more difficult to make certain required adjustments. But see it this way. You are young. You must live. So, you must do whatever you must to survive. I'll tell you something if you promise not to tell the others.

"There might be a war. I don't know exactly when, but I have good reason to think it will come. Maybe in a year. Maybe two. Still, that can't make a difference to us. Here, we have to live for each day. Otherwise, it could be very, very dangerous. Disastrous, in fact. So you see, you must make living an addiction. Become an addict to life and everything will be well taken care of. But if you fail, all of us might go down with you."

They were silent for a moment.

"Herr Lorken?"

"Yes?"

"When do I have to . . ."

"Begin working?"

Michael nodded.

"As soon as you feel ready. Not until then."

"But what will I have to do?"

"Let's not talk about that now. When the time comes, I'll tell you what you need to know. And I'll see that you have an easy time of it. Some of the men are quite gentle, really. They won't hurt you. Do you understand?"

Michael nodded and looked down. So, this was the secret behind the yellow roses, the great marble urns and peacocks and palaces! Herr Lorken was a prisoner! A slave of the Nazis!

In truth Michael had no idea as to what was expected of him but he raised his head and looked into Herr Lorken's eyes and nodded very slowly.

In the next week Michael learned a little about his new life in this velvet dungeon. He was moved from his small room at the back of the house to a larger room in one of the two long halls where the other boys lived. In a wing, just off the main hall, and just across from Herr Lorken's private apartment, the seventy-five young courtesans spent their days.

The other boys all lived two or three to a room, but, like most new arrivals, Michael had to live alone. At least, until he started to work. Until then, he was still untried and untested and none of the others would risk becoming his friend. Still, they took pleasure playing Satan to Michael's virginal Christ. And he found himself listening to their tales of temptation, trying to comprehend what they had told him.

Generally the boys had time to themselves unless someone came to see one of them; this was usually arranged well in advance. Herr Lorken booked the appointments. But occasionally an officer or influential businessman would arrive unannounced. At any moment, one of them might be selected from the leather album in the front room, the album that contained their photographs. They had to be available and ready to please even the most exacting client at any hour of the day or night. Customarily, the palace was quiet until weekends when the soldiers had their leaves and came to Wiessee from wherever they happened to be stationed. Despite the fact that the notoriously homosexual General Roehm had conveyed his blessings on several other establishments, Herr Lorken was famous for the Glass Arcade, a cabaret in Berlin of exceptional notoriety. As a result, those who could were quite willing to travel to experience his house.

The palace operated smoothly, with perfect discipline and harmony. From the third floor where the tailors, craftsmen, musicians and medical staff lived, down to the ground floor which housed the cooks, pages, handymen, night watchmen and drivers, the entire residence was a self-contained system for extravagant survival.

The first floor was set aside for visitors and receptions. Here were the great salons and unspoiled chambers: the ballroom, the green and gold library, the yellow and gray sitting room, the blue salon, writing room, gallery and dining room. Behind these perfect rooms were pantries, kitchens, storerooms and the boys' dining hall. It was that room which Michael had glimpsed on the first day when he'd wondered how many servants could be employed in such a building.

Herr Lorken's office occupied a small room between the library and the arches which led into the back of the house. Here he received anyone who wished to see him for, as Michael was quickly and sternly informed, no one, absolutely no one, was permitted to enter his private apartment. Not one of the boys had ever been inside. The only person, aside from Major Christian Stauffer, Herr Lorken's protector, who had ever been known to enter those rooms was Peter.

Some said that Herr Lorken had chosen the most beautiful objects of furniture in the entire palace for his private use. Others said they were certain that his entire apartment had been imported from a villa in Italy. Johann, a black-haired boy with pale blue eyes, swore that there was nothing in those rooms, nothing at all. But, whichever theory one subscribed to, the truth was that no one knew for sure.

Upstairs at the top of the winding staircase was a seemingly endless maze of fantasy chambers and boudoirs, each concocted with a precise vision of abandon in mind. There were rooms of marble, designed to resemble ancient Roman baths. One had a lily pond beneath a bed that could easily accommodate six. There were two rooms lined with fur, one black, one white and one warm tent filled with patterned cushions and mirrored rugs from Afghanistan. There was one room with white pillows and another of blood-red velvet. In one alcove a mirrored pavilion, a glass arcade, had been constructed. Blue poles pocked with silver stars supported the ceiling. Here, one could lie on a wide bed of dark blue satin and look up into the candlelit smile of an alabaster moon.

There were other rooms as well, rooms for those whose tastes ran in a darker vein. Aside from the canvas gymnasium, the shadowy labyrinth for impersonal encounter and the room of racks, there was one room, behind the spike door, which few of the boys cared to investigate. Besides, why bother? There were so many nice things to see! They showed Michael a small cabaret with colored lights and walls covered with masks!

Here, upon occasion, Herr Lorken had been known to entertain, but only in deference to an unavoidable request. With a pianist and one small spotlight, he'd acquiesced to insistent demands for certain songs that someone might recall from his years in Berlin. He'd been legendary then. Now his performances were extremely rare; the small cabaret remained deserted most of the time for Lorken declined invitations to intimate evenings or theatricals.

Michael found himself swept into a cocoon of scarves

and spangles, of veils, capes and robes. He was drawn in to inspect the treasured chests of boys only too willing to exhibit the trophies of their bondage. Personal traumas were something no one seemed to care about; personal discussions were things to be avoided at all costs. Each of them had become part of a clan predicated on ignoring the past. Now, the tangible evidence of initiation was souvenirs of orgiastic excesses: prized collections of fawn-colored velvet or satin vests, silk tights, breeches or jade-colored caps or cloaks of Chinese brocade. He, too, could have clothes like this, they assured him. There were bolts of every imaginable material on the third floor and tailors-in-residence ready and willing to create anything any of them designed, providing it had Herr Lorken's approval.

Michael's arrival generally was welcomed with good fellowship, but he saw that there were several of the older boys who took a guarded approach to him. One of them in particular, a flamboyant adolescent named Josef, mocked his innocence and nicknamed him the Spotless One. This continued for a day or two. Then, for no apparent reason, the heckling ceased.

Michael discovered that there was next to no interaction between his peers and members of the household staff. Peter was the only one with whom the boys had any contact for it was he who supervised their sports activities and took them for walks in the woods. There were miles of bridle paths in the forest which surrounded the palace. One of their rare pleasures was to be allowed to go out exploring, with Peter along as guide, of course. Occasionally, they went to a pond and enjoyed a long swim when the water was warm enough. But as far as the members of the staff were concerned, there was an invisible barrier. Contact was prohibited.

Within a day or two, Michael learned that Peter, as well as some of the manual laborers, lived in the old servants' quarters just on one side of the deserted carriage houses and barns. That part of the estate was "off limits." It had been forbidden ever since two of the boys had fallen from high rafters and had to be "replaced." None of the boys knew exactly what happened to them. It was better not to know.

Most of the youngsters had lived in the villa for some time and, while they appeared to appreciate one another, they maintained a tangible distance at all times. It was not that they lacked a sense of comradeship, good humor or support. Each relied on the others to do his part and carry his own weight. Professionally, they were allies, but, particularly among the ones who'd been with Herr Lorken for several years, there was a distinct reluctance to become personally attached to anyone.

It was common knowledge that the S.A., over which General Roehm presided, was responsible for the immunity their villa enjoyed. Despite his public proclamations, Hitler had no reservations about the private morality or behavior of his lieutenants. In any case, Roehm was Hitler's coequal. Hadn't he walked by his side at Nuremburg? Was he not the head of the three million Brown Shirt storm troopers? And, even if something happened to Roehm, Herr Lorken's protector, Christian Stauffer, was one of the rising stars of the black Death Head Squad, of the newly created Gestapo. Therefore, they enjoyed the sponsorship of two of the three most powerful forces in the Third Reich. Hitler knew enough to leave them alone!

Despite such backing, life in the palace was a fractious union, plagued with rumors of rivalry between the respective factions of their sponsors. They knew they weren't supposed to credit idle gossip but week after week, month after month, it was difficult to ignore the intriguing tidbits told them by their soldiers and swains. As a result, there were collective moods or days when nothing seemed strong enough to combat anxiety. In a sense they were all doomed, weren't they? For if the National Socialists were permanently successful in their transformation of Germany and the world, there would come a time when they'd be too old or too weary to continue working. And then, they would have to go. Others had vanished. And if the Nazis lost their power who could say what would happen to them? Either way, they were frightfully vulnerable. It was only a question of time.

Herr Lorken did what he could to prevent liaisons from forming between the boys and their clients. Schedules were shifted, appointments rotated to discourage relationships. Lorken told them it was better this way. The boys should be free from concern about their clients; the men should be relieved from any feelings of attachment. The less personal, the better.

Sometimes it seemed more like a school or training camp than a brothel for soldiers on leave. When they were permitted to play out of doors, as on these fine summer days, they occupied themselves with relay races, tennis, nature walks, skimming stones in the pond, swimming, gymnastics or entertainment with the gardener's dog. And, because they all dressed alike, in white shirts, short blue pants and sandals, they often seemed more like cadets than courtesans.

On weekends, when the men arrived, the atmosphere changed. Friday was the great metamorphosis, the hinge of each week when the dormitories were transformed into the backstage area of a cabaret. Sports equipment was chucked aside in favor of rhinestone stockings and elaborate cosmetics.

At first, Michael found it bizarre, the idea of these sudden shifts from well-regimented boyhood to orgiastic enthusiasm. But they assured him it was fun. Once one learned to accept the game and to adhere to the guidelines, it would actually be enjoyable. Oh yes, yes, it wasn't what they'd been told as children. But nothing had turned out the way they'd imagined. So what if they lay with men? It was a lot more interesting than school or church! Besides, the champagne was good, the food was delicious and the men were not unkind. Some of them could be deliciously tender.

In any case, there was no alternative. They did what they were told to do and tried to be as pleasant as possible! And damn the rest! This was life and life was not so hard!

Michael was not so sure. He was torn between the natural modesty of his upbringing and the acclimatized decadence of the other boys. They were accustomed to sex; he was approaching it for the first time. And, while they were used to encounters with two or three or four people, he was frightened by the idea of physical contact. He found himself wondering what it would be like. The idea of physical contact intrigued him. But he had no idea as to how it would feel. He didn't even know what went on, not really.

Still, if he'd found it too disturbing or embarrassing, he had time. He'd see that it was better to accept it in the long run. But, if he didn't come around, if he couldn't or wouldn't there was only one way for him to go. No! It was better to give up any hope of chastity. There was no innocence here.

In time, they told him, he'd be allowed to join the others and attend the parties, but for the moment he'd have to live alone and observe and be patient. For it was a very exact progression between his position and Herr Lorken's.

Chapter Twelve

One evening as Michael lay on his narrow bed, the door opened. He looked up in surprise to see Helmut, the boy who had been there the longest, and who enjoyed the greatest prestige. He was the only one who dared address Herr Lorken as "Lorken" behind his back. Whenever the man had something to communicate to the boys as a group, he sent the message to them through Helmut. Consequently, the boy reveled in his status as the grand vizier of the dormitories.

Now, he stood in the door watching Michael very carefully.

"Do you like this room?" he asked.

Michael nodded.

"Of course, it's not one of the nicest ones," Helmut observed, picking an imaginary piece of lint from the sleeve of his dark blue sweater; Michael had noticed that he always wore the same one, in direct imitation of Herr Lorken. "The ones on the other side of the hall have a view of the gardens."

"It's fine," said Michael. His voice sounded rather stiff but there was something about Helmut which made him nervous.

"You shouldn't let it bother you."

"What?"

"Being all by yourself," Helmut observed, "but no one wants to live with you until you've proved that you can be trusted."

"I see."

The pause was uncomfortable. Michael examined his feet and wondered why Helmut had taken the time to come visit him.

Helmut seemed to divine his thoughts, for, when he spoke, it was along those lines. "I'm hearing rumors about you."

"Rumors? What sort of rumors?" asked Michael, looking up.

"Well, stories that you're somewhat *modest.*"

Michael flushed and regarded his feet again.

"Michael, I don't know what Lorken told you when you had your little breakfast with him but I'm here to say something for myself and all the others. We can't afford to take any risks. If you can overcome your hesitations, all well and good. But we're living on a highwire. And, if you are going to create any disturbances, it could be very bad for everyone."

"What do you want me to do?"

"Think about it and, if you decide you can't be sure of yourself, let me know and I'll speak to Lorken. Is that understood?"

Michael inclined his head but the full implication of Helmut's words didn't come to him until the older boy left the room and he was alone again. So! Helmut would speak to Herr Lorken about him! Somehow, the idea was repellent, the thought that those two would get together to determine his fate. Whatever his decision, Helmut would not hold sway over him. Herr Lorken was the master of this house. The boys with real potential watched him, studied him to see how he dressed and how he moved through each situation. The advice he gave on costume and cosmetics was almost as succinct as his explanation on how to defuse aggression, defray violence, satisfy an insatiable client, appease a petulant romantic or remain independent while appearing to succumb. That last was a very fine art, he stressed, one that might prove crucial.

One Wednesday afternoon some of the boys went out to play with the gardener's dog. Others accompanied Peter into the woods for a nature walk.

Michael felt better as soon as they entered the welcome coolness of the trees. For several days he'd attempted to adjust to his new environs, but it was too formal, too elegant to suit him. Here, at least, he might close his mind to recent weeks and pretend he was back home.

They followed a dirt road which ran into the trees from an area behind the forbidden barns and carriage houses. The road came to a fork; they meandered along the left lane where linden and silver birch crowded the smooth shoulders of the path. This way was hardly traveled at all; in the old days it had been used mainly by carts though none of the boys had any idea as to where they'd gone from here.

Felix said that this was the first time he'd ever been along this trail and he'd been in the palace for a long time. His assertion gave their outing a sense of adventure, of discovering the unknown. Even Michael shared in a sense of excitement as they continued on, walking deeper and deeper into the forest, choosing stout walking sticks, playing games of tag, hide-and-seek, and running ahead of the steady-paced Peter.

At first, Michael walked alone, happy to embrace the warm smells and enjoying the speckled green-gold light which mottled the dirt beneath his feet. High overhead, the sun was almost completely obscured by the leafy boughs of the tall trees. The air was moist and sweet.

After a while, Michael attempted to join in the games of the other boys. But, whether it was a lingering doubt in him, a look from Helmut or just a natural process which resulted in small bands he sensed he wasn't welcomed or wanted in their cliques. So, he walked alone.

"Do you like this?" asked a quiet voice.

Startled, Michael looked up to see Heinrich, a boy who lived almost directly across the hall from him.

Heinrich was about a year older than he, and taller, with sandy hair and gray eyes. Now as he regarded Michael, he seemed friendly but reserved, as if he too was ambivalent about the newcomer.

Michael was quick, almost too quick, to respond. This was the first time since he'd entered the palace that one of the boys had addressed him in a truly friendly way. The others were all following the example set by Helmut, that "wait and see" attitude. Yes, wait and see how Michael "worked" before making any commitment! Mindful of the hierarchy, the others had adopted an impassive, noncommittal air while Michael began his new career.

Heinrich was the most recent addition to Herr Lorken's stable, and as such, had a more tolerant attitude. It was rumored that he was having a hard time yielding to the men who demanded his company. Certain wags suggested that he wouldn't last long with that attitude. And Michael thought he understood. For Heinrich was one of the most beautiful of the adolescent residents. His eyes seemed incredulous and enticing at the same time; his body was lean, in the last smooth bloom of muscular boyhood.

"Yes, I like it," Michael responded. "I grew up on a farm. . . . We had woods behind our house."

"I didn't grow up in the country," said Heinrich.

"In a city?"

"No. A town. But there was a forest not too far from where we lived. When I was little . . ."

Michael listened as Heinrich told him the story of the wonderful fortress near the stream where he and his brothers had played. As he talked, the younger boy measured the road with even steps and long strokes of his staff. He tried to picture the house with stained-glass windows, the sickly grandfather who repaired clocks, the mother who practiced the clavichord, and the father, the cause of all this, with his membership in the Communist Party and his small printing press. Soldiers came. . . .

Heinrich paused; Michael sensed his pain and spoke quietly. "They came to our house too."

"When?"

"Two weeks ago."

"What did they do?"

"Never mind."

"I'm sorry."

"Don't be," the younger boy murmured.

"I shouldn't have asked."

"No, it's not that, really," said Michael. "It's just that I saw everything."

Sudden cries interrupted their conversation. Looking ahead they saw Peter ushering the boys through a gate in a high stone wall.

"What is it?" asked Heinrich.

"Let's go and see."

"Don't you want to talk?"

"Peter's waiting for us."

The man had come back to the road. They hurried to join the others and stepped through the gate. They emerged in a ruined enclosure.

Row upon row of grave markers lay before them, surrendering to lichen or the natural laws of gravity and decay. Many of the stones had already fallen; others leaned at precarious angles.

Row upon row of obelisks, crosses, mausoleums and simple rectangles encompassed succeeding generations of neighboring families. Here and there a tomb had been preserved or cleaned; one could see a spot where careful hands had picked moss from the stones. These memorials stood out among the pale green, gray or brown-stained tombs of the majority. And there, at the end of the long yard, close to the burned-out shell of an old church, was a series of newer graves marked with plain wood crosses.

"There aren't any names on those," observed Heinrich.

"It's odd. They're new."

It was true, Michael thought. They were freshly

painted and decorated with wilted flowers which could not have been very old.

"Someone cares enough to bring flowers," Michael said.

"Who cares about anyone?" Heinrich demanded, his voice sounding more bitter than before. It took Michael by surprise, and for a moment he couldn't think of anything to say.

"It's hard to care," he said at last.

"Tell me about it," said Heinrich, still bitter.

After a long pause Michael spoke again. "Heinrich?"

"What?"

"How does it feel?"

"How does *what* feel?"

"You know. . . ."

"No, I don't know."

"Well, working with the soldiers."

Heinrich turned away from him and looked up at the sky. There were fewer trees in the graveyard and it was easier to see the clouds accumulating. For a moment, Michael thought he would avoid the question but, when Heinrich turned to face him that disturbed look was gone from his face and his voice was less harsh.

"The others say they like it."

"But for you?" Michael persisted. "How is it for you?"

"For me, it's not good."

"But why? How?"

Heinrich stared at him for a long moment. "You haven't ever been with anyone?"

Michael lowered his eyes and looked away.

At the far end of the graveyard, Peter was leading their peers on an investigation of the ruined church. It was obvious there had been a catastrophe for the steeple towered above the charred beams of a decimated roof; inside they could see remnants of a blackened altar.

Heinrich shook his head and sighed. "It doesn't matter," he said. "For me it's painful because I resist."

"Why does that make it painful?" asked Michael, more frightened for himself than for his new-found friend.

"I don't like to do what they want. I don't give in."

"How should you give in?"

"Oh, I don't know! Helmut says you've got to relax, to let your body go to them. You've got to forget your thoughts. I suppose he's right. If I could forget everything, it might be tolerable. But I can't. I remember where I am and who they are and I get frightened, or angry and then, it hurts. Some of the men are so big, you know. Helmut says if I don't do better he'll talk to Herr Lorken about me."

"Helmut!" exclaimed Michael, with more than a trace of derision in his voice.

At once he regretted that tone. It seemed dangerous and wrong to reveal his animosity toward another member of the group.

"You don't like him, do you?"

Michael shook his head.

"Neither do I!" declared Heinrich.

"I hate the way he wears that blue sweater!"

"It's as if he's trying to imitate Herr Lorken!"

They laughed.

"It's so ridiculous!"

"He'd do anything if he thought Herr Lorken would approve!"

"Maybe we should tell him that Herr Lorken wants him to jump off the roof!"

Instinctively they lowered their voices. But even as they conversed in hushed tones, something was cemented between them.

"Helmut frightens me," Michael confessed.

"I think he wants to frighten everyone," said Heinrich. "When I arrived, he tried to intimidate me."

"Did he really?"

"He tried. But I'm stronger than him. Still . . ."

"What?"

"I don't care if I'm stronger!" Heinrich blurted out. "I don't care about anything! *I want to escape!*"

"You mean run away?" Michael asked.

"Yes!" Heinrich nodded emphatically. "I'm going to do it, too!"

"But how is it possible?"

Heinrich drew his breath and seemed ready to begin a detailed explanation of his plans when Peter emerged from the rectory, and looked down the long walk in their direction. When he called his voice sounded a bit agitated. And, when the two boys didn't answer his summons at once, he repeated it, this time with more authority.

The boys hurried toward him.

"We'll talk about it later," Heinrich whispered. "I'll come see you after dinner."

Michael nodded, and when they rejoined the others he pretended to be interested in their plan to have a relay race all the way back to the house. But, for the duration of the afternoon, he wondered if Heinrich was really serious about wanting to escape or if it was some sort of test.

Chapter Thirteen

Knut was seventeen; he was tall, dark and more hairy than most of the other boys. Helmut joked that he'd become more womanly to conceal his embarassment about that thick mat on his chest. But the other boys didn't dare tease him; Knut was a bully, a bully with a high-pitched, whining voice.

"All alone?" he cooed, peeping into Michael's dark room.

Michael nodded, not moving from where he lay. He'd been lying in bed staring up at the plain ceiling. It was curious, this part of the palace had none of the intricate plasterwork which was so evident in other rooms.

Knut pranced into the bedroom. "How do you like my new outfit?"

He wore a dark green doublet and tight hose; the front of the jacket was open to the navel, exposing his hairy chest. It was a strange combination. The slender legs in apple green tights and that powerful torso cinched in at the waist and bound with a wide leather belt.

"Isn't it divine?" he cooed, raising one hand to touch his earlobe.

Michael smiled an uncertain smile. Knut's effeminate manner upset him. He felt personally connected to the other boy's affectations. It might have been irrational, but he was fearful that, if he approved of the feminine voice and theatrical manner, then he too might become like Knut. He didn't wish to be rude but it was difficult to remain impartial as Knut displayed the precise tailoring of the velvet coat. Would he be like this in another few months? Oh, God, he hoped not!

"It's very nice," he allowed, uncertain as to whether he ought to say something else, something more extravagant or enthusiastic.

"I'm thrilled you approve," Knut said, turning to admire himself in the tall mirror on the door of the armoire. Knut scanned his reflection, leered at himself and came to perch on the edge of Michael's bed. For a moment he appeared to examine a seam on his left sleeve but, when he raised his head, it was clear he had something in mind. For his eyes were only half-opened. It occurred to Michael that Knut suddenly looked very, very sleepy.

"Do you like it here?"

Michael shrugged. "It's all right, I guess."

Knut's voice oozed understanding. "It's all so new, I imagine. . . . Of course, it's all so frightfully bizarre," he went on, "but of course, it doesn't have to be lonely. I mean, it can be very cozy here."

He reached out and turned off the light. Michael began to feel uncomfortable.

"Oh sometimes some of the soldiers can be brutes, but only a few, really. Most of them are just naughty boys. It's not hard to handle them. And anyway, that's no reason why we can't be nice to one another," he said, putting a heavily ringed hand on Michael's thigh. "No reason at all."

Michael disengaged himself as gently as possible, not wanting to be offensive, but afraid and more than a little queasy. It was a strange feeling in his stomach.

"I would like to be your friend," he murmured stiffly.

"Well! That's all I had in mind," Knut chuckled, patting the distant leg, allowing the hand to linger on the bare thigh. Michael didn't know what do to; the hand inched higher.

"Knut, please . . . don't," he whispered.

He was struggling for the right words, explanations for a simple "no, thank you" when Heinrich walked through the half-open door. Knut looked up, saw the new arrival and removed his hand abruptly. His voice was different now.

"Oh, I see! Our new *fraulein* has standards! Well, my dear," he cooed, pinching Michael's cheek just a little too hard, "we'll see how long you can retain your delicacy. Ha ha!"

"What's this?" Heinrich asked.

"Oh? Don't you know? We have a little virgin here," Knut snapped as he rose, and he turned at the door. "Come see the film that begins in fifteen minutes. *The Blue Angel* will show you what to expect from scruples. Goodbye darlings! See you in the library!"

And with that, he swept from the room.

Heinrich remained at the door. A shaft of light from the hall illuminated one side of his face. It made his gray eyes seem catlike. Michael thought he looked like a choirboy and was possessed of a sudden and totally irrational admiration for him.

"What's the matter with him?"

"I think he wanted to be . . . friendly," Michael replied softly.

"Oh," Heinrich grunted, coming over and sitting on the end of the bed. "How appetizing. I imagine you said no?"

"Yes." Michael nodded.

"I said the same thing when he visited me," said Heinrich. "For two days he wouldn't talk to me. Then, when he realized that I didn't care, he started to be friendly again."

For a moment Michael wanted to let the subject pass. But his curiosity and tension were an uneasy and recurrent source of doubt. The recent changes in his life, as well as his thoughts about touching himself, made him worry. At times he was afraid that if there was any stain on his sheets he would be punished. That Herr Lorken would take that as a sign that he wasn't interested in conforming to the rules. And yet, he didn't like to restrain himself or even think when he gave himself pleasure. Did this mean he was ill? Or crazy? Or different from the others in some terrible way? What would they do if they knew that he was frightened by the thought of being naked with another person? That he was afraid to even think about touching someone else? Or being touched? He hadn't ever seen his parents together, without clothes. The most he'd ever seen them do was to kiss and that was a fairly rare sight. So, how could he picture himself with a total stranger doing those things?

"Heinrich, may I ask you a question?"

"Of course."

"Is it different between people who know each other than it is with strangers?"

He'd said it! He'd managed to force the words out into open air. When the question was complete, he felt that he'd bitten the words from a larger question that remained coiled inside his throat.

"It's never happened to me," Heinrich replied. "I've only been with soldiers."

"Never with a friend?"

"You're my only friend."

Michael felt his face grow red and was thankful that Knut had turned off the small lamp. Heinrich continued speaking in a matter-of-fact way.

"I think with a friend it would be nice if there was, I mean, if both of them had some feeling."

"Feeling," Michael echoed, as if the word contained a mystery all its own. It was embarrassing to probe that possibility. He had to say something, to change the subject. "Tell me your plan, please?"

Heinrich rose and crossed the room. He peered out into the hall, closed the door and returned to the bed. When he was sitting in the same place, he spoke again, keeping his voice very low. "It won't be hard. We can go all the way through the woods on the road we took today! It comes out on the other side just sixteen or seventeen miles from the city!"

"Which city?" Michael asked, dumbfounded by the simplicity of Heinrich's plan and yet feeling rather foolish not to know the name of the nearest urban area.

"Munich!" Heinrich answered excitedly. "We can walk from the far end of the forest road. And, when we get there all we'll have to do is stay out of trouble. They won't ask any questions; they'll think we're just children so we won't need papers."

"But what do we do once we're there?" Michael asked, suspecting that Heinrich's plan sounded easier than it actually was.

"We can get on a train into Switzerland or anywhere else outside of Germany. They won't look for us here; they'll just get two others!"

"Do you really think we can do it?" Michael was afraid to hope and afraid not to.

"It'll be easy!"

"But the soldiers?"

"The only guards are at the front gates."

"And the night watchmen?"

"They don't patrol the woods," said Heinrich. "I doubt they've ever expected anyone to try to escape through here."

"But how do you know it isn't just miles and miles of forest?"

"Ah!" cried Heinrich, looking triumphant. "I knew you'd ask that!"

"Well?"

"I found out where we are! Can you guess how I did it?"

"No."

"Well, look at this place! It's very grand, yes? So, one day I went into the library downstairs and looked at all the books on art and architecture. There's one which used to belong to Herr Lorken on the great houses of the Hohenzollern. In it there are pictures of this one, with photographs of the front hall and the ballroom!"

"But how did that help?"

"Because," Heinrich continued, struggling to keep his voice low, "there is also a drawing which illustrates how each building fits into the gardens or the town. The map outlines the forest and points the way to Munich! You see! It's not really very far at all! We could be there in less than two days; if we leave late at night, we might get through the woods by dawn!"

"Two days!"

"Even less maybe!"

"We could be free. . . ."

"Yes, Michael, free!"

Michael thought it was too unlikely or too simple to be true, but Heinrich interrupted his doubtful thoughts. "It's best not to let anyone wonder if we're up to anything. From now on, we'd better not attract any attention to ourselves."

"Why are you saying this?"

"We should talk later. But right now, it's best if we watch the film."

They hurried toward the library. On their way down the stairs Michael heard voices. Just inside the front door, he saw two soldiers removing their gloves. One of them, a tall man with dark brown hair, saw him and pointed.

"I'll take that."

The old footman who'd greeted the car on Michael's first day motioned toward the yellow and gray room. "Won't you come this way? I'll send for Herr Lorken."

"I see what I want," the tall man insisted.

"Yes, of course," the footman demurred.

Michael shuddered and hurried after Heinrich.

"Don't worry," his friend assured him in a whisper. "They can't have you unless your picture's in the book. And we'll be gone before that happens if we . . ."

"Shhh," Michael admonished.

The green and gold library had been converted into a

cinema for the evening. A projector and a screen had been set up and cushions scattered around the floor. But the movie had barely begun when Michael saw a silhouette slip into the room, tap two boys on the shoulder and bid them to follow. Josef and someone else disappeared soundlessly.

"I adore the hat," someone remarked when Marlene Dietrich perched on a wooden chair to sing her sultry love song.

"Look how she's done her eyes! That's good!" put in another.

"That's just the lighting!"

"It is not!"

"Shhh!" cautioned Peter from the projector. "Talk later."

The room fell silent. They watched the decay of the schoolmaster and, at the end, when he staggered out onto the stage, seduced into becoming a buffoon by his passion for the glamorous chanteuse, most of the boys jeered at him. It was only when he crawled off to die that the room fell silent.

The boys came out into the hall. They climbed the stairs immediately, not wanting to linger on the first floor. But Michael and Heinrich remained in the library, eager to question Peter. He didn't discourage their questions.

"When will you show another film?"

"Oh, three or four days. Maybe we'll see Chaplin if Herr Lorken can arrange it," Peter said.

"*If!* You know he can!" exclaimed Heinrich.

Peter winked as he packed the projector into its black leather case. "I wouldn't doubt it. But it's not easy. You know that one I showed you last week? That one with Greta Garbo . . . ?"

"*Anna Christie?*"

"Yes, that one. It was very, very hard to borrow. It was sent down from the highest places in Berlin."

"From Hitler?"

"Never mind from where," Peter hedged.

"Herr Lorken told us he likes her very much," said Heinrich.

"So he does. . . ."

"Anyway, that film wasn't so great."

"You didn't like it?" asked Peter, as he took the screen down.

"Oh, it was boring," Heinrich declared, "and too serious."

Peter nodded and finished with the screen. He motioned for the boys to follow him as he walked out into the hall.

"Time for bed," he said. "Tell Josef and Udo that I'll show the film again tomorrow night so they won't have to miss it."

"All right," said Heinrich.

"Good night, Peter."

"Good night," the man replied, giving Michael a pat on the back.

The boys climbed the winding staircase. As they ascended the great blue spiral, the chandelier was extinguished, and they continued on their way in darkness. When they reached the landing, Heinrich stiffened and pulled Michael's sleeve, drawing him up against the wall. "Shhh!"

"What is it?" whispered Michael. Heinrich pressed a hand to his lips.

Someone had hurried into the hall from the long gallery which led to the suites reserved for visitors. From this angle it was difficult to determine who it was but the dark figure was moving toward the doors which led to the boys' dormitories. As the silhouette neared the top of the stairs, a voice broke the silence. "Josef!"

The silhouette froze.

The voice came again, out of that alcove on the far side of the rotunda. "You're not finished."

The silhouette remained in place.

"I said you're not finished."

The silhouette was strangely confident. "He told me he's satisfied."

"Go back for later."

Josef turned but didn't speak.

"I said, *go back for later!*"

"Herr Lorken, I . . ."

"Don't make me say it again."

Josef's sigh was audible from where the two boys stood on the staircase; he turned and melted back into the night. But long before his footsteps disappeared, the doors on the far side of the rotunda closed.

Heinrich and Michael's eyes met in the dark. "I'll go with you, Heinrich," Michael whispered.

Chapter Fourteen

It was a night of no moon. They had to feel their way along the narrow passage which led from the bottom of the back staircase through the kitchen and butler's pantry.

In the storerooms, terrified that even their breathing was clearly audible, they stuffed a pillowcase full of sausage and cheeses, fresh bread and fruit. While Heinrich commandeered a bottle of wine, Michael located a jar of lindenberry jam.

When they had enough for their journey, they turned, crept upstairs and hid their provisions in a chest of artificial furs.

The day passed uneventfully. Herr Lorken was off riding in the woods and Peter spent the afternoon working on one of the trucks near the barn. In the evening, when he went in for dinner, Michael saw the man examining an inventory book with a worried looking cook, but optimism and excitement overrode any apprehension. So what if one of the boys had stolen a bottle of wine? Surely it had happened before!

Peter said nothing to anyone during dinner, and as promised he set up the projector for a second showing of *The Blue Angel.* Many of the boys went down to see it for a second time, but Michael and Heinrich remained upstairs, hoping to get some rest before their departure.

As early as possible, they went to their respective rooms and got into bed. But it was difficult to fall asleep! And almost impossible to grasp the fact that, at this time on the next day, they would be far from the palace. Far from Nazi arms!

When Heinrich tapped him on the shoulder, Michael gasped. He was sure it was the soldiers who'd come . . .

"Shhh," Heinrich whispered.

Michael sat up, shook his head to clear it. He got out of bed, slipped into his clothes and took his sandals in hand. Heinrich already had their provisions in a small basket.

They collected their top blankets and, two minutes later, stepped out from the palace and raced across the lawns.

This time, he did not run into water! And this time, there were no dogs, and no spies to report their whereabouts! By the time anyone realized that they'd escaped, they'd be far away! When they'd reached the trees, Heinrich produced the flashlight he'd stolen from a cupboard in Peter's workshop. Cupping one palm over the bulb, he flicked it on and led Michael down the dirt road, deeper and deeper into the dark woods.

Michael concentrated on walking as fast as he possibly could. If they maintained a pace like this, they might reach the far side of the woods by morning; once there they might be able to stop a car and ride into the city. His parents had had friends in Munich! What were their names? Honegger? No, Hauptmann? No, well it wasn't important now! He'd be able to find someone to help! After all, if they could get away from this prison, they could find someone to give them shelter for a day or two.

They walked as quickly as they could for the first hour or two. But, it wasn't until they'd gone four or five miles that Michael's breathing came less constricted.

Heinrich removed his hand from the flashlight and a long beam sliced the pervasive darkness, indicating the road they followed to freedom. They smiled at one another with a sudden ferocious joy and gradually, very gradually began to shake off their nervousness.

"We did it!" Heinrich hissed.

"I didn't think we could," Michael whispered.

"I told you so!"

"Ssshh!"

"What?"

"Not so loud!"

"We're free, aren't we?"

"Yes, but it's still so scary!"

They walked toward the city in silence. Each had a great deal to think about. As the miles passed, Michael found himself wondering what he would do now. Of course, there was nothing to do but complete this journey, to keep walking through the cool hours just before sunrise. Now as they expected to find the main route in Munich behind each bend in the road, their thoughts were centered on the best excuses they might make for being without parents or the proper papers.

How could he get out of Germany? Even if he could stay in Munich without attracting attention or suspicion, how could he ever leave the country? Trains seemed to be the best solution. But was that something he could do alone? Would Heinrich really go with him, or if the situation deteriorated would the older boy strike out on his own? And, even if Heinrich and he were determined to make their escape together, how would they manage without money? Was there a way to cross the mountains into Switzerland without having to encounter the Nazis?

These and other questions ran through his mind as they walked. The only sounds were those of pebbles beneath their feet and the wind in the trees. It was no longer night but not all the stars had disappeared.

When Michael heard barking he tried to tell himself that it was a mistake or a memory. Perhaps they were almost at the road; perhaps these were the sounds of stray dogs, or guardians of a nearby hamlet.

Heinrich touched his arm and shook his head. But Michael jerked away and crouched a little as he half-screamed the words at his friend. *"We can run, Heinrich! Come on!"*

Heinrich didn't move.

They stood still, staring at one another in silence, until, with a bitter sigh, Heinrich reached out and pulled Michael toward him. For an instant they held one another but even the attempt at protection in one another's arms was a cruel and untenable illusion. They turned and looked back.

Michael told himself that it'd do no harm to run; at least there was some hope if he did. To stay here and wait was to give in. But his friend had said no and he would not go on without him. What good would it do in any case? The sounds were louder now, closer.

The black dogs bounded toward them. Later, Michael wondered if he'd actually been frightened at the time or if he'd been too weary for worry, in the moments before the Dobermans lunged, toppling them as they awaited orders to back off or kill.

They had to wait a long time for the car to arrive but it didn't make any difference; nothing made any difference. They were captives again. The dogs had had no difficulty in tracing an undisguised scent.

The Brown Shirts threw them back into the back seat of an automobile and motored back to the palace.

The driver drove up to the barn and stopped. The soldiers pulled the boys out and stood with their hands on their rifles. For a few minutes, Michael thought they were going to be shot but when Peter emerged from the barn, he allowed himself to hope.

Without a word, the white-faced Peter pushed Heinrich into the barn. Michael remained with the soldiers but, even from a distance he could hear the cries, the harsh words, the groans and sounds of blows. Then it was silent.

When Peter came out and seized him by the collar,

Michael tried to push him off. Peter took a firmer hold and started dragging him toward the barn but Michael punched him in the stomach and kicked his kneecaps.

"Let me go! I hate you!" he screamed.

Peter's first blow ended all resistance. Michael felt his head snap back violently as the broad hand fell, knocking him to the ground, stunning him.

Peter stood over him, holding him by the collar with one hand as his closed fist rose and fell again and again and again. He beat the boy until his cries were faint. The blows continued and, then, morning light was blotted out.

When he woke, he was slow to realize that it was still day. It was so hard to see! He had to force himself to try. One eye opened, very slowly. Light stabbed at the back of his eyeball; he closed the swollen lid and reached up to touch his face. Each movement was akin to stretching blistered flesh. His skin felt as if he'd been scalded.

The floor was cold; he felt wind in his face. He must be outside. He forced himself to squint and saw that he was, indeed, out of doors. In a cage, with a concrete floor and wire sides.

He managed to open both eyes. One seemed not to function too well. Pain, an electric circuit from fingertip to cheek to bruise to bone to brain, coursed through his head. Even the tears which spilled down his cheeks hurt; they were too hot, the salt aggravated his cuts and scratches.

Of all the pain, this was the worst! And from Peter! But why? Why? He leaned against the wire mesh and groaned.

And Heinrich? Was he still alive?

The boy forced himself to turn his head and look into the adjoining cages; the pens on either side were occupied by dogs. Involuntarily, Michael loosed a stream of urine. The warm fluid soaked through his pants before he realized he'd lost control. Forcing himself to stop wasn't easy. He didn't even know why he should try. Nothing made any difference. Nothing mattered.

Three cages away he could see his friend, lying face down. At first, Michael thought that Heinrich was dead but after a few minutes he saw slight movement. He lay down on the cement and tried to sleep but, this time, it was impossible. It was too cold, too hard. He lay a long time without dozing off. Once or twice he heard Heinrich groan. But it was late afternoon before the older boy awoke.

He and Michael regarded one another in silence. Heinrich's face was badly bruised and one eyelid was swollen shut. They didn't talk; there was nothing to say. But the dogs, aroused by the boys' conscious state, trotted up and down the long runs of the kennel, snarling and showing long yellow teeth. Each boy crawled to the center of his cage and avoided eye contact; the dogs grew quiet and growled only occasionally.

Just before sunset, Peter came and took a look at each of them. His attitude was sullen. Michael was astonished to realize that in some way Peter took it personally. Peter said nothing and walked back to the palace.

Fifteen minutes later a soldier came to feed the dogs. As the beasts devoured piles of meat from metal bowls, the boys watched, salivating in spite of themselves. Soon, they'll let us out, Michael promised himself. They didn't kill us. What good would it do to keep us here unless they plan to starve us to death?

The sun set with no sign of reprieve. Night came on, bringing with it the ugly fumes of dog droppings which hung about the pens. The boys were both hungry, but the only smell was the noxious odor of manure.

As the hours passed, the smell lessened. Curled up like the dogs, keeping their backs to the wind, the boys tried to sleep. But all night mosquitoes flew into their ears.

When the watchmen came to get fresh dogs for their patrol the noise disturbed Michael. It was still dark but, once awakened, he couldn't sleep.

He sat up and wrapped the thin blue coat even tighter about himself. It had to be nearly dawn, Michael thought. Light mist rose from the lawns; now he could discern the top of the barn, an uneven stone wall which ran toward a greenhouse and gardener's cottage.

There was something in the darkness! Something was nearby! The boy sat up. A silhouette moved in the mist. Soundless, perfectly silent. It was followed by another inky form. As they approached, Michael squinted as best as he could without hurting his swollen face. But as soon as he saw who it was, he drew back.

The figure paused about fifteen feet from the locked cages. In his great cape, he seemed like an ancient highwayman or an ivory-faced robber baron.

Michael forced himself to look back without blinking. But the price was pain, for his swollen face and stiffened limbs were alive with a steadily growing, familiar agony. He'd tried to escape. What was so terrible about that? He knew what they wanted him to do. He'd been told what to expect. So how could he be blamed for trying to run away? It wouldn't reflect on the other boys. He hadn't even started working so no one could care if he disappeared. What could they lose if he went away?

Peter approached and whispered something to the man. They spoke in low, audible voices, too quiet for the boys to hear. But the dogs woke and, alarmed by the intruders, barked until Peter commanded them to be still. His voice woke Heinrich who sat up in his cage.

That black figure stepped toward Heinrich's cage, still wordless. Heinrich's voice was hoarse as he stretched his upturned hands toward his master: "Please, please Herr Lorken."

The man's glance at Peter must have been a signal.

Peter unlocked Heinrich's cage and let the door swing open. As the boy pulled himself out of the cage, the dogs grew nervous and growled. Heinrich crawled on his hands and knees, and when he neared Herr Lorken, the battered boy lay down on the wet grass. Michael had to strain to hear the words for Heinrich's bloody face was half-hidden and the surrender wasn't loud.

"Forgive me . . . never . . . promise . . ."

With another glance at Peter, Herr Lorken indicated his acceptance of this disgraceful apology.

Peter pulled Heinrich to his feet. Heinrich groaned as Peter shoved him toward the house. Beaten, unable to resist, Heinrich stumbled away without looking back. But Michael could hear the sound of weeping. Herr Lorken returned.

Never, never, never, thought Michael. I'll starve before I beg forgiveness or kiss his boot! Let him go to hell where he belongs!

But the pale face which confronted him seemed to demand nothing. It occurred to him that Lorken was trying to convince him that there was really no chance of escape. That he would have to accept his new life or starve to death in the kennel. There would be no pardon, no forgiveness this time.

When Lorken turned and walked back to the palace, Michael was surprised to discover that his own cheeks were wet with tears.

At first the words were difficult but, as he began to speak, they were easier to say and believe, at least in part.

"I'm sorry, Herr Lorken. Please, let me out."

Lorken turned to Peter. "Feed him, put him to bed."

Lorken disappeared before Peter unlocked the cage.

Michael sat in the dining room and accepted a bowl of soup from a cook whose red face was not unkind. When he finished, he followed Peter upstairs to a warm bath. At first, the water hurt him, but as Michael surrendered to the heat, he felt his bruised muscles relax. Pain lessened its grip and it was easy to forget that he was naked with the same man who'd treated him so mercilessly just two days before. He bore Peter no malice; at last he understood the rationale; disobedience was treasonous. Escape was desertion. Both were intolerable. When Michael was dry, Peter collected his dirty clothes and started to leave the room, but he turned at the door.

"I am truly sorry to have hurt you," he said. "But what I did, I did for everyone." He paused, almost left the room and then looked into Michael's face without saying anything for a moment.

"My wife and children are at Dachau," he said in a quiet voice. "If I don't cooperate . . ."

He didn't finish the sentence. Michael nodded and, when Peter closed the door behind him, they had reached an understanding. He would not run away again.

Chapter Fifteen

Michael lay on his bed, staring at the ceiling. Outside, in the hall, he could hear voices. None of the other boys would come near his room. He'd broken a cardinal rule. Now, more than ever before, they mistrusted him. The only way he could win their confidence was to prove that he too could be an effective worker.

When Heinrich entered, neither spoke for a few minutes. Heinrich sat on the bed and stared at the floor. Finally, he spoke. "Are you all right?"

Michael nodded.

"I'm sorry. It was all my fault."

"I decided for myself," Michael said.

"But I got you into it. If it wasn't for me you . . ."

"I made my own decision," said Michael, more firmly than before.

They were silent again. They looked at one another carefully, examining, unconsciously comparing the cuts and scratches. Heinrich's eyes filled with tears.

"They've hurt you," he whispered.

"It's better now," Michael stammered, not wanting to think about his losses, not wanting to cry.

"I hate them! I hate them!" Heinrich cried, banging a fist into an open palm. "Do you know how I feel?"

Michael shook his head.

"I feel like I could kill them all and not think twice!"

"Heinrich, you don't mean that. . . ."

"Oh, yes, I do! After what they've done to me? I'd give anything to be able to kill even one of them! It'd be worth it!"

"Sshh!" Michael warned, one finger to his lips. "They'll hear you and then you *will* be replaced!"

"Replaced! Ha!"

Heinrich sounded brave but something must have frightened him. When he spoke again, his voice was cold and calm. "I don't care what happens to me. Do you understand that? I don't care anymore, Michael, and that frightens me more than anything they could do to me."

"But you've got to care, we have to . . ."

Heinrich reached out his hand and put it on Michael's shoulder. "Michael, turn off the light."

"Why?"

"Just because I asked," replied Heinrich. "Do it for me."

Michael reached out and switched off the lamp. The room was almost totally dark with the exception of a tiny shaft of light which came in from the hall.

Heinrich stretched out on the bed and pulled Michael down.

When Heinrich began stroking his arm, Michael closed his eyes. Despite the fact that his stomach felt tight, he told himself that sooner or later he had to know. And Heinrich was nice. He liked him . . . very much. . . .

But as the hand continued to caress his shoulders and chest and sides, he grew fearful that someone would walk in and discover them like this! Perhaps they should close the door! No, that wasn't necessary. This is what they were there for! Who would care?

He closed his eyes even tighter and told himself that he should relax and let Heinrich do everything. But the first thing which came to mind was an image of his father. He shook his head and accepted the soft kiss on his neck.

Was he supposed to just lie here or do whatever Heinrich did? Was he supposed to take off his clothes or wait for Heinrich to do that first? Yes, that would be better, Michael decided. Just do whatever Heinrich told him to do. After all, it was his first time so . . .

Heinrich pulled off his cotton jersey and lay against Michael. The younger boy put his arm around the smooth shoulder and was surprised by how good warm skin felt against his cheek. Yes, it wasn't so bad, now, was it?

He didn't feel especially excited, which didn't mean that he didn't like Heinrich or feel good about being with him but he didn't have the feeling he usually had when *he* touched himself down there and felt the warmth spreading through his thighs. That warmth which made him want to stop thinking and just touch and stroke. . . .

Maybe he was trying too hard to relax, he told himself as Heinrich stroked the inside of his thighs. He should stop worrying about how close Heinrich's hand came to his sex. But would the older boy feel rejected if he wasn't hard? Was he supposed to be?

"No . . ." he muttered.

Heinrich sat up at once. "What's the matter? Don't you like me?"

"Well, yes of course, I like you very much. It's not that." Michael had unconsciously lowered his voice.

"Then why are you so tense?"

"I don't know. This is so soon."

Heinrich didn't say anything. For a long moment the silence was uncomfortable for both of them. Then, the older boy stood up. In the darkness, it was impossible to see his face but he sounded sad when he spoke.

"It would have been so nice to be with a friend," he said. "But it's all right. Don't you be upset. I just wanted to love you."

He closed the door behind him and was gone.

Michael lay in his bed and wondered if he'd been right to send Heinrich away. His friend had wanted him; perhaps in some way he needed him. Wasn't it better to start off like that?

He unfastened his short pants and withdrew his sex. In the dark and safety of his bedroom, he began to stroke himself without worrying about what he should have done. It was like this, more and more in recent weeks, this desire to give himself pleasure.

Sometimes he pretended that he was able to have anyone he wanted, that he could drift throughout the world and take anyone who pleased him to his bed. There, they would roll across an endless terrain of soft flesh, nibbling, biting, pressing up against each other; they would not be afraid to touch or kiss or love each other.

But when he heard the knock at his door, he covered himself at once. Turning, to conceal his activity, he called "come in" and made sure he lay in such a way as to cause no suspicion.

Helmut marched in and stood over the bed. "So you got off with only a beating!"

Michael tried to sit up but the larger boy pushed him down and leaned over him. Close, too close. His words were a soft hiss.

"Michael, once before I told you about endangering us. Now I'm going to tell you again. And this is something just between us. Just our little secret. If you ever try that again, or anything like it, I'll see you're replaced. I can do it. I'll fix it so that you can't work even if you want to and that'll be that. You think it over. You can play with your life if you want, *but not with mine!* I want to live. Do you understand that? I want to live and get out of here! And so do the others! This is a team, Michael. If you can't do your part, we'll find someone who can."

Helmut turned and left, closing the door softly. Michael knew that Helmut was serious. He could do it and he would! Who was there to stop him? Michael didn't have any friends or allies. He was totally alone.

During the night, Michael was frightened by a nightmare. Dogs were chasing him through a black wood, coming closer and closer. . . .

He woke up screaming. The room was dark but he couldn't force himself to reach out and turn on the light. He was trembling; his whole body was shaking.

Someone knocked on his door. Michael was too frightened to answer. He tried to call out but he couldn't make any noises. The door opened and a tall shape moved into the black room.

"What is it?" Herr Lorken sounded almost gentle. But Michael couldn't talk. He was trembling again. The man reached out and turned on the lamp. "Can you talk?"

Michael shook his head. Lorken nodded. "Bad dream?"

Michael nodded and tried to clear his throat. There was a terrible feeling in his stomach. "I used to have bad dreams," said Lorken, picking at the sleeve of his black sweater. "I used to have them all the time."

"Really?" Michael stammered.

Lorken nodded and, folding his hands, continued. "All the time. At first, I used to try to ignore them; I thought that if I didn't pay any attention, they'd go away. But that's not how I got rid of them."

"It's not?" Michael was still shaking. Lorken noticed it but didn't say anything about it.

"No. Shall I tell you what happened? Yes, all right . . . Well, a friend of mine told me that she used to sleep as much as ten or eleven hours a day. I thought that was very lazy of her but she said 'No, it's not lazy at all. I'm an artist and I have to spend a lot of time in my subconscious, in my dreams. Because those are what I use to make my art.' And I thought about that and, the more I did, the more sense it made."

Lorken paused and saw that Michael was a bit calmer. And when he spoke, it was more to the point. "Michael, we all have bad dreams. Almost every person here, I mean, all the boys have had bad experiences. It's nothing to be ashamed of. Of course, you've been having a bad time recently and there hasn't been anyone to talk to or get help from. And that's not right. Tell me, is there any one of the boys whom you can be friends with or really trust?"

Michael shrugged and looked down.

"Then I'll tell you what: if you have bad dreams and want to talk about them, or if you feel like coming to my office during the afternoon and spending some time just looking at pictures books, you can."

"I can?"

Lorken nodded. "Yes. I know you must feel lost and frightened and uncertain about the future. All the other boys had those feelings when they first came. But, there's no reason for you to feel scared any more. You're here and no bad dreams can get you. There are a lot of people around you and we'll all help each other. It's just what I told you on that first day, remember?"

Michael nodded.

"Good. Do you feel any better?"

Michael nodded.

"All right, then. Shall I leave the lamp on?"

"No, but . . ."

"What?"

"Leave the door open so some light can come in."

"All right." Lorken paused at the door. "Michael, just remember, you are not alone." Lorken was gone.

In the days that followed, life continued as before. There seemed to be an air of forgiveness and understanding which originated with Herr Lorken. This was sensed, transmitted and acted upon by all the other boys until, by midweek, even Helmut had stopped giving Michael cold looks. His attempted escape was ostensibly forgotten and Heinrich and Michael were both restored to good graces. But when Heinrich went back to work, he and Michael began to drift apart in an imperceptible and mysterious way.

Chapter Sixteen

On Thursday afternoon, Peter led most of the boys outside for gymnastics and relay races. Michael elected to remain indoors. He still didn't feel comfortable at play with his peers. For the moment, tacit tolerance was enough.

Recently he'd been drawn to the library. It was pleasant to while away the hours looking at the beautiful picture books; they brought so much of the outside world into this restricted reality. There were wonderful albums of natural history, art, architecture, geography and oceanography.

Michael waited until the others had left for the playing fields and wandered out into the great hall. Descending the main staircase he turned in the direction of the library. Just as he was about to enter the green and gold room, he heard a sudden shout of laughter; it came from the direction of Lorken's office.

Michael tiptoed closer to the small room. Moving as quietly as possible, he crossed the marble floor of the hall of angels.

Lorken's study was an oval chamber adjacent to the library. In earlier times, it had been used as a writing room. Now Herr Lorken used it as his official arena. Beyond the gilt-paneled doors were his desk and filing cabinets and a great profusion of papers. It was all very official but, as the boy approached, it was obvious that Lorken was not working. Michael could hear him laughing; his odd, two-syllable laughter was unusually animated.

"Yes, it's very good! But are you sure you want it to be silver? I think red would be better. Or maybe *yellow!*"

Michael paused near the door and peered into the room. From where he'd positioned himself, he could see only a fraction of the office, just enough to pick out the head and shoulders of Karl—a ruddy fellow with black hair and hazel eyes.

There were papers littering the floor but Michael couldn't see Herr Lorken; he could only hear the mellifluous voice.

"Oh, it's funny! By far the best design you've come up with in months. Ever since that duck! Do you remember how . . ."

The voices dissolved into laughter again, but when it abated Michael thought Herr Lorken sounded more serious and perhaps a little more professional.

"There, that'll signify my unqualified approval for this! Now, why don't you take it up to the third floor?"

The thought that Karl might come out and discover that he was there, spying, was terrifying. Michael wanted to flee but he had to stay; he had to know just what was going on in that small room. He might find out who the real Lorken was.

Now he heard Karl, speaking more slowly than usual, his broad back swaying from side to side as he faced the invisible man.

"Do I have to go?"

"What? Oh, Karl! I . . ."

In that moment of silence, Michael tried to see into the office but Karl's back was in the way. And when the conversation resumed, the voices changed.

"What do I have to do . . ." Karl began, but Lorken cut in.

"You know I can't."

There was another sudden burst of laughter followed by another moment of silence. When Herr Lorken spoke again, he sounded even more determined. Still amused, but firm.

"Come now. Don't be foolish."

"That's what I want," insisted Karl.

"You're a child," Lorken began. And then he stopped. Michael craned his neck but it was impossible to see.

"Please, take your design to Herr Rosenwald; he'll get started on it right away and you'll have it in time for the weekend."

"But . . ." Karl began tragically.

"No, no! Please. It's enough."

"But you don't know how I feel about . . ."

"I know what's possible and what's out of the question," said Lorken in a firm voice. And then, more kindly, "Come, don't be so sad! I'll go up with you and help you choose a good color for that . . . absurd creation!"

Michael turned and hurried into the library. There wasn't time to run for the stairs without being observed.

Fortunately, they came out of the study and continued out into the hall without a backward glance. Looking over the arm of the chair where he'd taken refuge, Michael saw that while Herr Lorken appeared to be as calm as ever, Karl looked upset.

Michael had come to think of Lorken as something not quite human. A creature of silhouettes and silk. Something to be adorned rather than loved or desired. Hearing Karl's plea, he realized that the inmates of this fantastic prison might have their own private lives, regardless of the weekly stampede.

Sex had always been something fearful, a thing of darkness. Now for the first time, he began to think about it as something even more mysterious than light or dark, as an invisible transfer of power. Look how Karl had been humbled by his desire for Lorken! Look how Heinrich had drifted away from him! Was sex something one never did with a friend? Was it only an act between opponents? Two men couldn't have babies, so what did they do? Was it just a friendly thing like wrestling? Or was there something which made it more important?

These questions crossed and crisscrossed his mind, dead ending in a great sea of unresolved doubt. It was too confusing! Michael decided that he had to do something about it soon. At the very least, he could ask questions. Until now, when the other boys talked or joked about their encounters, he'd been too shy to admit his ignorance. He'd been afraid to invite ridicule or scorn. Now that had to change.

He walked out into the hall and started up the stairs. He hadn't even reached the landing when he saw Helmut and Albert coming down. They seemed excited.

". . . after he dies?" Albert exclaimed.

"Then it's Hitler and Roehm!" Helmut answered.

"Are you sure about this?"

"I was with my best source," Helmut boasted. "He's never given me wrong information."

Just then they saw Michael.

"Well, well, the endless virgin!"

Michael tried not to show any emotion as the boys joined him on the landing.

"Eavesdropping?" Albert inquired sweetly.

Michael didn't even look at Albert. He didn't like the swarthy-faced, curly-haired youth. Of all the boys in the place, Albert was one of the least attractive. But of course, some of the men found that appealing.

"You said someone is dying. . . ." Michael addressed himself to Helmut who smiled an artificial smile and pinched his cheek.

"Yes, my pet. So I did!"

"Who?"

"Can't you guess?"

Michael shook his head.

"It's the old man himself!"

Michael shrugged and looked bewildered.

"Hindenburg, you idiot! I presume you've heard of him!" Helmut bit the words off, but, for all his hectoring, he looked a little uneasy. "Do you know what that means?"

"No, I don't," Michael confessed.

"It means we are going to be even more important!" crowed Helmut before turning to Albert. "Come on, let's get away from him before we catch a case of modesty."

They laughed as they continued down the stairs, leaving Michael alone. He stared after them, and at that moment decided to go up to the house photographer. It was time to have his picture in the book.

Chapter Seventeen

On Thursday evening after dinner, Michael left his room and wandered out into the great hall. He sat on the top step of the winding staircase and gazed through the banister to the floor far below. Usually the soaring space impressed him but it was evening, the chandelier was dark and only a few sconces provided illumination. The hall of angels was a gloomy vault, the pastel cherubs and tapestries overwhelmed by shadows.

Across the marble cavern of columns and circular banisters was Herr Lorken's apartment. Michael wondered what his own chambers would be like. Based on his explorations in the library, and what was rumored in the dormitory, the boy pictured embroidered curtains hung with thick tassels, chests of tortoiseshell and gold or fantastic clocks where seconds were marked by a porcelain girl on a porcelain swing.

He knew what he was doing wrong; he knew it was against the rules even to think of such things. But despite his reservations Michael stood up and walked toward the tall double doors. They were recessed in an alcove. Paneled and capped with scrolls, they seemed to be maneuvered by long levers, like the handles of a pump.

He stood outside the door and tried to talk himself into courage. "Of course, I could say that I'd had a bad dream. He did say that if I wanted to see him, I could. Still he knows I know that no one's allowed in here. Of course, I could always say that I wanted to see him to talk and would he be in his office tomorrow? But what if he just says "yes" and closes the door? Then what? Well, then I'd just have to go away. But if he got angry? Or if he didn't get angry? It wouldn't look good to admit it was a lie. But what would I do if he's with someone? No, if he was he wouldn't answer the door. No one would, or would they? So there's nothing to lose except that he might be really angry at me for breaking the rules again. But those are only rules."

He knocked. Softly at first. Then, more boldly. No answer. He started to turn away.

"Michael!"

He wheeled around to see Herr Lorken standing in the door. For a brief instant they regarded one another. But Lorken stepped back, beckoning the boy to follow with a wave of his hand. "Come in."

Michael followed him in. Into a totally different world.

"I'm getting ready for a private evening but you can talk to me as I dress," the man said, tightening the belt of a long gold robe as he started for an alcove. Then, observing Michael's expression he added, "Well, take your time, I'll be in my dressing room."

Michael remained motionless as he stared at the sitting room. It was unlike any other room in the palace; there was no crystal, no carved mirrors, no ornamentation. The walls had been stripped of any paneling and each part of the room seemed to have been designed to be as simple as possible. In a sense it seemed furnished as if it was waiting for the finishing touches. But it was alive; it had its own atmosphere based on the interrelationship of three colors: black, pink and gray. Everything was one of those three shades: the gray rug, black lacquer piano, ebony end tables and two couches of flesh-colored silk. A glass vase was on the piano and held a full spray of roses; they too seemed gray in this light . . . their shadows corresponding exactly to shadows in the corners of the room where tall lamps threw light up to the ceiling from wide, fluted cones.

Michael had never seen such a room; it was almost severe. It was oddly inviting; the reflection of small silver boxes in the black tabletops and especially one painting above the black mantel of a geometric fireplace.

The painting showed a clown beside a pale red horse. Elongated and ethereal. The soft pinks, reddish browns and grays were contained by simple lines which flowed into one another, stretching the colors across the surface of the canvas as if they were a gentle cloud in need of redistribution. The lines of the face and circus stallion were delicate but just elemental enough to provide scaffolding for those pale hues.

It looked too simple but when he turned away, the boy couldn't quite remember where the lines had been. Almost, but not quite. He turned to the canvas again; the clown stood in his rose-colored tights, aloof and oddly angelic. Very gradually, Michael realized the painting was a portrait.

"Do you like it?" Lorken stood in the alcove watching him as he brushed his hair with a silver brush.

Michael nodded.

"So do I," Lorken confessed. He crossed the room and stood beside the boy and surveyed his image. "When I went to Paris for the first time, the painters adored me. Each had his vision of how I should be and demanded that I sit for them. I didn't have time for all that, I was busy. Only for one painter; only for Picasso. And these," said Lorken, crossing to the roses on the piano, "are *my* accomplishment. Beautiful, aren't they? Almost gray. I work on perfecting them in my greenhouse, it's one of my ambitions—to produce a smoky gray rose. But why don't you come and talk to me as I make up? I don't have much time but I did want to see you."

"Why?"

"To be sure you're all right." Frederich Lorken studied Michael. "Is there something on your mind?"

"No," the boy lied.

"Good. Then come with me. . . ."

Michael followed him away from the pale room, through the alcove toward the dressing room. Here again, he paused, dazzled by what he was seeing.

What was it? Sunlight on water? A prism held to flame? The boy couldn't decipher the effect. At one and the same time it seemed to be a spray of stars or an explosion of tiny fires creating an illusion of thousands of little candles, all darting and flaring up across walls and ceilings. It was a room of sudden incandescent runs of fire burnishing the walls. As the boy watched, the room seemed to flicker. Lorken was seated in a small chair facing a table which supported an enormous mirror. On either side of the golden glass was a candelabrum, a gilt-turbaned Moor holding aloft a pair of black candles. But the room was aglitter with tiny lights. Lorken smiled knowingly. "It's nice, isn't it?"

Michael nodded.

"It's done with little mirrors; they cover everything but they're not quite flat so, when the light hits them, they reflect into one another and so on and so on. Because the room is a barrel vault, the fire continues forever."

Michael took a chair beside a dressing table. Never, in his most farfetched dreams, had he supposed that such a room could exist! It was as if he was sitting inside a flame! And Herr Lorken had done it! Herr Lorken who sat in his golden robe, searching through a tortoiseshell box, changing his mind with a faint exhalation as he turned to a small leather case.

Michael watched him, almost hypnotized by this strange creature of flame and golden light. He was rubbing a salve into his skin, spreading a deep tint into his face; when he was sure it was applied evenly, he wiped his hands on a towel and turned to Michael. His face looked like pink mud.

"What do you think? Should I go down like this?"

Michael winced; Lorken examined his hands to be certain they were clean.

"I used to think it was so difficult!"

"What are you talking about, Herr Lorken?"

"Makeup! Before I started to sing or entertain, it mystified me. It's really simple. But oh, it used to require hours! Now, I think I could do it in my sleep. It's fun, actually. You just paint, using your face as the canvas."

He paused and glanced in the mirror. Now, he brought out a dark green jar, dipped a brush into it and drew dark lines across his lids and below his lower lashes. He paused, touched a finger to a brown salve, and rubbed it onto his lid, adding blue to one side and a dab of white to the center before turning to wipe his hands on the towel.

Next, he produced a leather box and opened it to reveal a shelf of little cakes, each a different shade of red. He selected one, tapped it with his forefinger and began working a berry color into his cheeks, rubbing slowly and with great care. As he did, his face seemed to change shape, becoming less angular. As Lorken darkened his lips he smiled at himself, but it was grotesque and sarcastic; a grimace.

"I want to look sweet tonight," he confided to Michael. "Repulsively sweet."

"But why, Herr Lorken?"

"Why, why, why? Because Herr Lorken is . . . Herr Lorken! Michael . . .?"

"Yes?"

"Would you mind if I asked you to call me by my first name?"

"Frederich?"

"Thank you."

"But . . ."

"Not in front of the others. Just between you and me. Is that all right with you?"

"Yes . . . I . . . yes, of course," the boy stammered. "But why?"

"Because," Frederich said as he touched up one spot

below his right cheekbone. "I like you and I don't want you to call me Herr anything!"

"You *like* me?"

"Yes," Frederich said. "I like you very much."

The painting was finished; Frederich had composed his even features into a pink-cheeked symphony. Not as dramatic as the other transformations Michael had witnessed. Although this face wasn't really a mask, as the others had been, it wasn't a human face. It was a new surface, exotic and ageless and somehow too perfect. Yes, that was it. With this face, Frederich severed any association with men, women or children. He'd made himself sort of an overgrown cherub and, while there was unquestionable beauty, there was something full blown about the way he looked.

Seeing the boy's stare, he turned and winked. "If anyone could want this, they deserve what they get!"

Frederich stood up and disappeared behind a folding screen which more or less divided the dressing room into two parts. The boy could hear him washing his hands.

"Hand me the coat inside the door to the closet, will you?" he asked.

Michael had some difficulty in finding the handle because the walls were covered with so many flames. Finally, he gave up and ran his hand along the two-dimensional fire until he discovered a tiny gold knob. He pulled at it and found himself staring into the darkness.

"Oh, Michael, how did you do that?" asked Frederich, peering over the screen.

"I don't know," the boy confessed.

"That's supposed to be a secret."

"Really?"

"Really!" Frederich echoed. "It's a private staircase which goes down into one of the pantries. In the old days, it was used by people who wanted to avoid . . . other people," he finished with significant emphasis. "Try again."

Michael closed the narrow door and discovered another knob. Behind him, he could hear Frederich brushing his teeth.

The closet doors were connected, like a hinged accordion mirror, or folding cards. They slid on a little track, one into another as they opened it wider and wider.

The closet itself was actually a good-sized room with deep shelves on one side and tall cubicles on the other. It contained a small storehouse of costumes.

There were racks and racks of every imaginable thing: velvet capes lined with fur, military uniforms trimmed with tassels and braid, coats of gold and silver foil, cloaks of sequin and sable. There were blue satin vests with amethyst buttons, glittering body stockings with glass beads, small, almost transparent leggings with dragons, mermaids and theater masks sewn onto flesh-colored crepe. There were shirts with metallic snake scales embroidered onto green satin, a matador's black suit of lights, tight white breeches and a Roman consul's uniform of black leather and golden eagles. There were top hats, tap shoes, tweed coats and masks. There were blue wigs spangled with gold coins, plumed headdresses crowned with exotic birds which spread feathered wings down to throat clasps of golden claws. Wreaths of silk flowers and lapis lay on velvet trays beside collars of ivory, ebony, jade, onyx and shell. Pearl-studded coats of gray silk, gloves stitched with black agate and carnelian. There were long scarves figured with silver or painted by hand. There were flowered robes from China with coral-eyed dragons twisting across flame-colored satin or silk the color of midnight. And, on the door, two favorite diadems; a silver wreath of laurel and a golden coronet.

Frederich came and stood beside Michael. The expression on his face was one of amusement as he watched the boy appraise his finery.

Michael turned and looked at him in surprise. "Why aren't there any dresses?"

Frederich laughed. "Because I'm not a woman," he answered lightly, tapping Michael's head.

"But there's everything else," the boy went on.

"I *am* everything else."

"Then I don't understand," Michael exclaimed. Somehow he'd expected to see a rack of woman's clothing in among the rest. But if it wasn't so, all his assumptions . . . well . . .

"It's just a question of fantasies," said Frederich as he reached into the closet and removed a blue velvet coat with silver epaulets. As he turned back to the folding screens, he said, "I never thought of myself as a woman. I always saw myself as . . . well, an androgyne, or a creature more than anything else. Specific gender has nothing to do with that."

"I don't understand what you mean," said Michael.

"No? Well, I'll try to explain. When I was in Berlin in the Glass Arcade, I wore things like this every night. They were the skin of my existence, the definitions of my world. At that time, for a great many reasons, I was involved in creating myself, making myself a work of art. But that process never involved becoming someone else, a woman, for example. It was more or less an exploration of my own dreamworld, of my own magnetic images."

"Then why don't you dress like this all the time?"

"Ah, there's the question!" Frederich exclaimed. "What can I say? It's not the time; it's not the place. Now I wear what I have to wear. It doesn't make any difference."

"It doesn't?"

"Not really," he replied. "Those things there are what's left of my Glass Arcade. Those costumes are just the ones which survived time and travel and needy friends. But," his voice brightened, "once upon a time, a long time ago, I had some really fantastic things."

The idea that what he had just seen were leftovers was a bit too much for Michael to grasp. Frederich laughed and continued his story. "The best, yes, the

best was a coat from a friend of mine named Josephine.
She gave me a coat made from leopard skins with a row
of clasps in front made from fangs! Now that was
sensational!"

He stepped out from behind the screen. In his blue
coat, white breeches and tall black boots, he looked
like a Prussian cavalry officer with the face of a
flustered virgin.

He frowned as he examined his reflection. Clearly,
he was not satisfied.

"You know, I've spent so much of my life in dreams,
I forget which is the real world. These things are part of
my profession but it's a different reality. I think I'd be
much more content at this point living every day in my
old black sweater."

"Don't you like to get dressed up?" asked Michael,
amazed that, in a way that seemed confidential and
spontaneous, Frederich would tell him anything about
his life or feelings. Frederich shook his head very
slightly and smiled a rueful smile.

"Once I saw costumes as very necessary, part of the
beautiful masquerade. The world seemed to be a
maleable parade which I could participate in, and
influence in some way. I thought I was part of
something which could reveal something about beauty,
something about the exquisite nature of a moment
taken from the day-to-day world, adorned, adored and
set apart. It may sound foolish now but that was an art
to me. That was something worth living for, to create
those moments. I was innocent then. Now it's as if I
have a sparkling nemesis which trails after me."

"You don't care?"

"It doesn't matter how I look or feel," Frederich
answered, placing a wreath of fat purple grapes on his
head. They sabotaged the military effect he'd created.
Now he seemed to be an impossible combination of a
wine king and lieutenant.

They were silent for a moment. Frederich examined
his reflection and touched the wreath. It was truly

ridiculous if one really considered it. He seemed pleased. "We're expecting someone very important," he confided. He paused and looked odd for an instant. "One of the higher-ups from Berlin. So tonight, I'm a Prussian Bacchus! Something like that. You know, once, long ago, we did a show where everything was silver, pale green and lilac. It was early spring and I was hopelessly in love with someone who adored me. We lit everything with soft lights and hung streams of flowers from the chandeliers at the Glass Arcade; there was a fountain of champagne and a silver and green jazz band which came up from . . . well, never mind, it was spring. . . ."

He opened a box and picked through a pile of trinkets. "In those days I was very much at the center of life in Berlin. Everyone talked about my cabaret and my tiger cubs and how I danced and sang and who I was with. But, in some ways, my life was not unlike yours."

"Like mine?" Michael was stunned by the comparison.

Frederich nodded. "In certain ways. I was young and impulsive and terribly independent. Like you. But it all happened so quickly. After a conventional childhood in a traditional family, I was swept away by events. Almost before I realized what was happening, I found myself at the center of an incredible circus, a glittering stage where people improvised their realities. At first, I was fascinated and somewhat frightened too. I was afraid that I wouldn't be good enough if I tried to participate. But then I learned, the circus makes room for all its true children. That was the turning point!"

Frederich found the object of his quest. A silver ring set with an enormous aquamarine.

"Someday you will remember I told you these things. You can tell all the others. Say, *Frederich Lorken told me he lived a long death without ideals and could only be destroyed by . . . love!* You tell them that!"

"Destroyed?" Michael asked.

"Yes, destroyed by love!" Frederich coughed and

added, "The real Trojan horse!" Then, after a moment he remarked, "The men are late."

Michael looked down as Frederich glanced at him. He didn't want to look stupid or confused but things were going so fast, he didn't know what to think. He'd come here to talk and, now, only a few minutes after he'd knocked at the door, everything was changing. He could call Herr Lorken by his first name; he'd been told a secret and, somehow, been taken into confidence by the very person he'd promised himself he'd never talk to, never trust or give in to. And, while one part of his heart was excited and eager for friendship and belonging, another part of him was reluctant to accept a truce.

Frederich opened a drawer in his dressing table and smiled a sly smile as he withdrew the little black jar. He unscrewed the top and dipped in. "Come closer," he urged.

Michael stepped to his side. Frederich's forefinger flew up from the jar and stroked his nose. Looking into the glass, Michael saw a silver streak, iridescent and luminous.

"Let me do some more. We have a little time!"

Michael surrendered to the able hands. And, in less than two minutes the deft fingers had smoothed more of the salve into his skin, tapping and dabbing at his face and neck.

Frederich spoke softly as he applied paint to the boy's ears and eyelids. "It's easy to put on and easy to wash off. Just a little water and it's gone. When you get good at it, you can do this very quickly. Don't worry though, because once it's on, it's on; even if you sweat it won't run or streak. You know," he paused to wipe his fingers, "I used to keep silver as a standby; it's always good, never out of place no matter where you go. And, if you need a quick touch-up or costume change, it's always an option. There are never any limits with silver."

He stood back to inspect his handiwork. "Excellent! Now, let me see if I've got something suitable for you to wear. You can't look so wonderful and remain in 'civilian clothes.' I've got a reputation to maintain!"

He disappeared into his closet. As Michael turned to examine himself in the mirror, he could hear Frederich speaking to him. "One Christmas, we filled the cabaret with artificial snow and had everyone painted silver with black plumes and red candles in the . . ."

Michael didn't hear the rest of the story. He was transfixed by his image. Until now, the world of sparkling colors and costumes had been distant, part of another world. Now, his future had welcomed him! He was initiated! Now, he was part of the exciting troupe! Now he wasn't just Michael Kurtz. He was something centuries old. The face that returned his stare was metallic, immobile, a mask. He had become a statue, precious and polished. He was a glimmering boy. He was beautiful!

Frederich reentered the dressing room, his arms filled with costumes. There were silver tunics, wonderful things! Turbans, boas, plumes, scarves, vests and sashes. There was even a coat of tiny links which felt like a second skin. But it was cold to the touch. Michael selected a pale green coat covered with silver cranes winging their way through a snowstorm. He put a wreath of silver stars on his head and searched the tall mirror. In the golden glass a dream creature smiled at him and waited for response.

He looked up at his mentor; the Wine King smiled. A bell rang. Frederich shook his head. "Ah! Why is it so soon? I have to go down. Why don't you show the others how you look? But they're not to come in here. This was special, something only for you. And, Michael?"

"Yes, Herr Lorken?"

"Frederich."

"Oh, yes. Frederich."

"That's better. Would you please tell Heinrich that he has an appointment with the colonel? Tell him to wait in the chapel. He knows what to do."

What was that note in his voice? Was Frederich sorry to end their time together? Michael looked up, hoping to decipher that tone, hoping for another secret. But Frederich's face revealed nothing.

"You look enchanting."

"Do I?"

"The others will be envious."

"I like this coat."

"Maybe we'll see about having it altered. But come now, it's time."

He offered his hand; Michael slipped his fingers into the outstretched palm and they left the room of dancing lights, through the soft pinks and grays, past the clown and that ethereal horse, out into the hall of the angels.

"I'll see you tomorrow," Frederich whispered.

Through the dim lights, Michael watched him hurry down the stairs to the men who awaited him. He hurried on; he didn't want to see Frederich with the soldiers! He ran for the dormitory but not fast enough to avoid hearing the laughter from down below.

In the back hall he made quite an impression. None of the other boys had ever been permitted to wear any of Herr Lorken's clothing, let alone visit his apartment. Some of the older boys gave him sidelong looks as if he'd usurped their rightful place. Knut, in particular, was quick to insinuate that there might be something "going on."

"How did you manage to convince him?" Knut asked. His tone was waggish and ingratiating.

Michael said nothing.

"Of course you realize that no one else has ever gotten a foot inside his apartment," Knut continued. "Did you get a tour of the whole place, or just the bedroom?"

"No, it wasn't like that! We just sat in Frederich's dressing . . ."

"Ho! Now it's *Frederich!*" Knut crowed.

"I meant . . ."

"We know what you meant!" the boy interjected,

"and we know what you said! Next I suppose you'll be moving in with him?"

Michael gave up trying to explain. But his silence didn't make much difference to Knut who came too close and squinted as he said: "Just be sure you don't press your luck at our expense!"

"What do you mean?" asked Michael.

"You know what I mean!" Knut snapped. "And you'd better hope no one tells Major Stauffer what's going on behind his back!"

"But nothing is . . ."

"Christian Stauffer could have us all replaced by making one telephone call," Knut warned, "so just don't go too far!"

"Knut, I . . ."

"Listen, Michael, either you're frightfully naive or just plain stupid. I don't know which is worse considering the situation. Open your eyes!"

Michael glanced at Knut with contempt and turned to push through the crowd which had gathered. But, to his surprise, he didn't have to force his way through the throng; the boys stepped aside in unconscious recognition of his new status.

Michael left the knot of his peers and ambled toward his room. But, just as he was about to leave the hall, he remembered his errand and went to deliver Frederich's message to Heinrich.

Chapter Eighteen

The voice that said "Come in" was faint. Michael opened the door and entered as quietly as possible. Heinrich had been asleep. He was naked; there was one candle burning on the small table beside his bed.

"You have an appointment in the chapel with the colonel," Michael informed him.

"I know," the sandy-haired boy answered. "I'm almost ready."

He stood up; Michael averted his eyes; nudity still embarrassed him. When he looked up, the slender youth had pulled on tight leather pants and was stooping to gather his boots. As Heinrich turned, Michael saw there were dark weals across his back.

"What's happened to you?" he cried in horror. "Who did that?"

Heinrich looked at him but didn't reply.

"I'll go tell Herr Lorken," Michael said. "You can't work like that!"

"Don't you dare!" Heinrich hissed. "Just get out of here!"

Michael came out of Heinrich's room dazed and upset. Some of the other boys were waiting to talk to him. Now that Herr Lorken had favored him, they were willing to follow suit.

"You know, you can get some good green velvet if you want a coat that'll fit you," said Hermann as Michael continued down the hall.

"Yes, yes."

"I'll be glad to go up with you and suggest some good material," the boy offered.

"Thank you, but not right now. I just want to be by myself."

"Why, sure," Hermann said, sounding a bit resentful.

Michael didn't care.

Something had gone sour with the evening! Maybe it was Frederich being with the soldiers, or Knut's warning or Heinrich's injuries or the loss of his friendship with the gray-eyed boy. Whatever the cause, he felt depressed. Everything was changing too quickly and there was no place he could feel secure.

He strolled out of the dormitory and into the main hall. From the front room, he could hear the sound of Frederich talking in a pleasant voice; at any other time, Michael would have stayed to eavesdrop.

He slipped into Frederich's apartment and closed the solid doors behind him; they were so tall and heavy that he had to apply himself to make them move. Now, he leaned against them for support and surveyed the room.

Gray and pink and black lacquer. This room was really Frederich, he decided. This soft, light and simple distribution of line and space. More than any other part of the palace, it reflected the man. All the other chambers had been designed; this one was inevitable. Anyway, it wasn't set up for soldiers and boys.

Soldiers and boys! Suddenly, he wanted to wash away the silver, to rid himself of this iridescence! Without the presence of Frederich, he felt himself prepared for another purpose. Well, wasn't that part of it? Part of the master plan?

He walked through the front room and into the chamber of glittering mirrors. It was so enchanting that he forgot his despair. He sat on a small chair and stared into the glass.

There he was, a silver angel in the dancing prism of

candles, golden glass and flame. This world of fantastic
jewels and masks and plumes and silver cranes led him
into reverie; the trance of glitter. But, in some way, it
had become his world as well. He loved the blue light,
the peacocks and sequins. They were pieces of a world
he'd always hoped he would find. In some way, they
were reprieve from the world of unyielding realities.
They were dreams. . . .

Michael stood up and removed his clothes. When he
was naked, he picked up one of the candlesticks and
danced with the black-a-moor, causing galaxies to
cascade and explode, extinguishing themselves as the
light changed the course and moved on yet another
sparkling run. He turned around and around, laying
waste to dying solar systems as he wheeled and gave
birth to a new universe only to grow bored with the
fixed order of things. He was the Lord of Light and
Darkness! Lord of Fire Almighty!

When, at last, he tired of his game, he replaced the
candlesticks and regarded himself in the golden glass.
Standing there, he seemed to be not one but two
people; the silver boy was archaic, a metal face from an
ancient frieze . . . but the lower half was human flesh.
Elongated and more muscular than before. The defini-
tion and new distribution of soft hair was evidence of
natural life changing from boy to manhood. He was
somewhere in between flesh and silver, partly a jade,
partly a virgin!

When he heard them come in, he panicked. He
scooped up his clothing and looked for a place to hide;
the closet was too dangerous, there was only one
relatively safe base: the small door to the dark staircase.

He closed the mirrored panel behind him, just an
instant before they entered the dressing room.

A shaft of light pierced the dark hall. Michael
pressed his eye to the aperture. Several of the reflective
mirrors were missing; this permitted him to see through
the door into the dressing room and on into whatever

lay beyond the closed doors. That was probably a bedroom. Michael had an unobstructed view of what was happening only six feet away.

Frederich was sitting at his dressing table, staring at his hands. He seemed withdrawn.

The other man stood at the door. He was blond with a handsome face. Handsome, but fearsome and hard, Michael thought. Gestapo. Yes, he was one of them, *really* one of them. If he hadn't been wearing that black uniform, he might have been attractive. As it was, there was something strange about his looks. He was beautiful in the way that dangerous animals were beautiful, with a look that made you wonder what they would do if they ever escaped. This man had that quality. He was frightening in his calm and measured fashion.

Michael tried to pick up the thread of the conversation. As the major talked, he toyed with a box of matches, lighting one after another, letting them burn down to his fingertips before extinguishing the flame. Each time it seemed that he'd be burned, but if he was, he showed no pain.

". . . which is where things are now. Von Papen went ahead with it."

"But why? *Why?*" asked Frederich.

"Your guess is as good as mine. Perhaps it has something to do with Roehm's efforts to consolidate the army under his own control. But whatever the reason, our old friend made a public speech last week calling for an end to Nazi terror and the restoration of a free press! Imagine!"

"But what will happen to him?" asked Frederich.

"What happens when Goering and Himmler oppose them?" asked the major. "They go down."

"But Christian, he's only saying what everyone is thinking!"

"You know that and I know that," replied the officer. "But as soon as Hindenburg dies, everything will change. Mark my words."

"That could be years from now."

"This time it's really the end."

"My God," said Frederich quietly, looking down at his hands. "After he's dead, what? What?"

"There are no certainties," Stauffer reflected. "But the old guard is gone. I don't know what reorganization will entail; that depends on the distribution of power between Roehm and Hitler. But I wouldn't worry if I were you. The Gestapo is sure to play an important role in the future, no matter what the bureaucrats decide."

"Yes, I'm sure of that," Frederich replied softly.

"And, as long as I have anything to say about it, you'll be safe."

"You never tire of reminding me," said Frederich. "Do you?"

"Well, let's just say that it's nice to be appreciated."

"Yes, Christian."

"With that in mind, perhaps you would be good enough to arrange a party for next week. Something unusual, special."

"Why is next week so important?"

"I thought I told you! The S.A. is on leave this month."

"But what has that got to do with me?"

"Well, as they're temporarily relieved of active duty, many of Roehm's inner circle will be joining him at Wiessee."

"So near?"

"They'll be staying at the Hanslbaur Hotel. We want to contain the situation. With your help, I'll have an easier time of it."

"I see."

"May I count on you?"

"Of course, Christian," said Frederich, sounding weary. "If you want an event, you shall have it."

"It would be very convenient," the officer remarked, staring at the match which burned close to his skin. "And it'd look good to Himmler. You know how he's always felt about you. So now, more than ever before, anything you can do to make the situation easier . . ."

Frederich raised his head and turned to face Stauffer. "What are you saying?"

The major shrugged. "Certain people have no patience with Roehm's . . . proclivities."

"Hah!" Frederich's tone was cynical.

"Of course, you don't have to worry for yourself."

"You've made that abundantly clear!"

"We made an agreement."

"You dictated terms."

The major leaned close to Frederich and spoke to him softly. "Don't make it hard on yourself, Frederich," he urged. "You've known for years that what's going on now is bigger than individual destiny. Go with it, Frederich! Don't question what you can't control or influence. Evolve with the times! Anticipate them!"

"Don't, Christian," Frederich began, but the officer hushed him up.

"I know how you feel. I've always known. But I'm saying this for your own good. You can't prevent certain inevitabilities. So you must do whatever you can to ensure your own survival."

"Survival becomes a debatable taste."

"My love, that is up to you. But, as long as you choose to remain among the living, I will continue to see you are comfortable. You know I wouldn't want to lose you."

"Don't be romantic, Christian."

"I'm never romantic. It's you who have sentimentalized everything. Sometimes I think it's my duty to instruct you in the realities of life."

"If that's so, you succeed magnificently."

"I hope so. I would hate to think I've failed you."

"Don't mock me."

"I wouldn't dream of it. After all, we understand each other."

"Yes, Christian."

The major smiled a strange smile and extinguished

another match. "You know, sometimes I think you care more for these boys than you admit."

"What makes you think that?"

"It's just a suspicion," the major insinuated.

"And what if it were true," riposted Frederich. "You heard your colonel. You heard him say what he liked! How could you bring him here, knowing what you knew?"

"I thought he'd amuse you!"

"Don't joke about something like that!" Frederich sounded angry. He pulled off his ring and tossed it on to the table as he spoke. The major's voice was smooth; he didn't seem ruffled by Frederich's anxiety.

"You take things too much to heart."

"Do I?"

"I think so."

"Sometimes I wonder."

"You know your boys are expendable. So what if something does happen?"

"Christian, don't talk like that!"

"It's for the cause, Frederich."

"Expendable! For the cause! Oh, I know what those words mean!"

The major lit a cigarette and shook the match out without letting it burn. "You're slipping."

"Yes, perhaps I am."

"Perhaps someone else should have this particular assignment," the major said softly.

"Find someone well qualified, Christian," Frederich retorted. "Someone comfortable with gargoyles!"

"What's the matter with you tonight? You seem so nervous. Has something happened to upset you?"

"What could possibly upset me *here?"*

"I thought you were glad to get away from Berlin."

"Perhaps I was, initially. Who wouldn't be glad to move away from Himmler?"

"And now?"

"Maybe I've changed."

The major didn't change his tone of voice but there

was a slight edge as he replied. "I know you're upset about what happened downstairs, but don't lose your head. If you go too far, you'll be responsible for an unfortunate situation."

"Which is . . .?"

"I might be forced to make a report about your attitude."

"Don't threaten me, Christian."

"Can't you understand that I'm saying this to help you? What you say to me in the privacy of your room is one thing. But as I say, you mustn't lose your head."

"What can they do to me that they haven't already done?"

"Well, let's just say that I would hate to lose you." Major Stauffer rested his hand on Frederich's shoulder.

"I thought we came to an understanding about that last week. Or else, tell me you've changed your mind again!"

"You sound bitter," the major suggested, unbuttoning the top button of his jacket.

"Can you blame me?" countered Frederich, removing his wreath and running fingers through his hair.

"Come, don't be like that. You know how I feel. . . ."

"Do I?" Frederich demanded. "Each week it's a new story. No, then yes, then no. Sometimes I think you and I have more to do with how things are between you and Freida and whether she's let you . . ."

But he never finished that sentence. With a small cry of pain, he was lifted to his feet. The major had one thumb pressed under his jaw just at the corner of the bone. Now, Frederich was backed into a wall of the glittering room as the white-faced major spoke. "If I say it's on, it's on. If I say it's off, it's off. I make the choice, not you. And if I change, I change. You forget our pact; I own you. You are my dog. When I want you, you'll come. When I say now, it's now. You've got a good life as things go, Frederich. Don't throw it off out of pride. If you go, they all go with you. So don't push too far. A little is fine, just to keep things fair. But not too much. I might lose patience and that could be very, very unfortunate."

Michael stayed long enough to see them kiss. But as the major pulled Frederich toward the closed doors on the far side of the alcove, he ran down the staircase, through the door at the bottom and out into the pantry; he ran, clutching his clothes to his breast as he shot by a startled page who called out for him to slow down. He ascended the staircase and vanished into the safety of the dormitory. He ran to his room and slammed the door behind him and threw himself on the bed, beating the pillows with closed fists until he was drained and depleted and temporarily deprived of hatred. He slept and stained his sheets with silver.

Chapter Nineteen

He was awakened by screams.

It was a warm night and the windows were open, as well as the door from the dormitory into the hall, which someone had left ajar. But, it was late and there were no other noises when Heinrich staggered out from the chapel and collapsed just outside the door.

Michael ran out into the dark rotunda; other boys followed but their elders urged them to return to their rooms. Michael ignored the arms that attempted to propel him out of the hall. He wanted to know what was going on!

He saw Frederich come running out of his apartment, racing toward the chapel in his golden robe. And, after a few minutes, he saw him reappear, leading a man into his apartment as he soothed him in a sympathetic voice.

"No . . . no. Such things happen all the time. You mustn't blame yourself. After all, he was so inexperienced. Please, calm yourself. Yes, this way . . . through here."

And they were gone. A light went on in the hall. Michael saw Peter and ducked back into the shadows. The lights went off and the hall was dark again. Whatever it was, it was over now.

After a night of bad dreams, Michael woke to hear that Major Stauffer had escorted the colonel back to Berlin. The boy hoped to see Frederich but he remained in his room.

It was a rainy day; all the boys were depressed. Each had different theories as to why Heinrich had died.

"He was crucified," Albert suggested. "There were holes in his hands."

"That's ridiculous," countered Josef. "Karl told me he saw the body. There wasn't a mark on it!"

"That's not true," said Karl. "I saw blood."

"There *was* blood," said Michael, participating in his first group discussion.

They all turned to listen to him; now that he was friends with Frederich, his slightest utterance might have significance. Without realizing what they were doing, all the boys, with the possible exception of Helmut, had promoted the new arrival.

"What else?"

"I don't know," Michael confessed. "But there was blood on the colonel."

"How do you know?" Helmut challenged.

"I was there. . . . I saw it myself," Michael replied.

"Any other surprises for us today?" the older boy taunted.

For a moment he wanted to let the matter pass but there was a certain amount of excitement at being the bearer of news, even if it wasn't good tidings. Without giving the matter much thought, Michael blurted: "Major Stauffer told Herr Lorken that he wants to have a special party next weekend."

They looked at him in amazement, astonished that he had such information.

"You're joking!" said Josef.

"No, I'm not," responded Michael. "It's because the S.A. is on leave; Roehm will be at Wiessee so Major Stauffer wants us to have a really good party."

"But they're not allowed to assemble for the whole month!" reasoned Karl.

"No, that's not it. They're not allowed to go on parade," corrected Albert.

"Or wear their uniforms," Johann added.

"They'll wear their uniforms if they come here!" Stephen asserted.

"What will you wear?" teased Knut. "That little gladiator outfit?"

"I'll think of something," Stephen promised. "Don't worry."

"Oh, I'm not, I'm not!" Knut shot back. "You always get by. . . ."

"Better than you!" Stephen interjected.

"Hah! That's what you think!"

"That's what I know! You looked awful in that African makeup last time."

"Awful? I suppose you think you . . ."

The argument that erupted took all of them by surprise. Whether they were conscious of it or not, they hadn't ever confronted one another in this way before. Suddenly each one of them was drawn in. Each became aware of longstanding grievances or private alliances which forced them to take sides and air unverbalized opinions about other boys, past times, former costumes and behavior. The impartial observer might have surmised that it was the combination of Heinrich's death, a knowledge of their own vulnerability as well as the surprise of Herr Lorken's unexpected patronage of a boy they'd collectively shunned. They were upset by the unexpected violence, and felt threatened by the reversal of their master's policy regarding the sanctity of his private apartment.

It was common knowledge that Heinrich wasn't the first to suffer such mistreatment. But until now, there had been no reason to dwell on such misfortunes. Suddenly, with a vengeance that startled all of them, they found themselves at the edge of an abyss, looking down into chaos. It was too frightening to remain exposed and vulnerable. And so they reacted with recriminations and blame and longstanding hostilities.

Death had claimed one of them. It might come again. In the interim, it seemed best to undergo certain rituals or secret rites to expel the ghosts, repel the phantoms and appease whatever gods might be responsible for their survival.

Michael was beset with worries. He wanted to see Frederich, to ask him what was going on and what would happen now. When he didn't appear, Michael wanted to go to him but it seemed wrong, too soon, too soon.

If Heinrich had been the first to die, then it might have happened to any of them. Including him! Sebastian said that there had been another one, a boy named Jules. And others!

The realization that such barbarity could go on, even with someone who liked him supervising operations, threatened to undermine the tenuous stability Michael had felt in recent days. Last night, before it happened, before he'd overheard Major Stauffer and Frederich, he'd let himself believe that all would be well. That he'd found a friend and could make sense of this world. He'd let himself think of Frederich as infallible, a magician who could accomplish anything. But, Frederich had spoken gently to the colonel, the one who'd hurt Heinrich. He was consoling Heinrich's murderer.

When Michael went to his bedroom, he had a surprise. There was a small package on his bed with the photographs taken by the resident photographer.

Because the pictures were for "official purposes" he'd been asked to pose in certain ways. But he was pleased as he sifted through the shots of himself in profile, full face and from oblique angles. In his white shirt and blue scarf, he looked like a cadet. But there was something else, something strange: the person who looked out from the photographs was strangely angular and very grave. Michael smiled at his own serious expression. Well, it was time! He selected what he considered the best picture and went down to the first floor. The front room was the only one he didn't like; he was inevitably reminded of Squatface and Otto. Still, it was where the album was to be found.

The boy sat on the couch and gazed at the pictures. Page after page of smiling, expectant faces. Beginning with Helmut and ending with a blank leaf where Heinrich's photograph had been.

It was most peculiar, he thought, as he examined the album. An ignorant person might think this was the yearbook of a school or seminary.

He slipped his photograph into the space vacated by Heinrich's.

Framed by the leather margins of the leaf, his image gazed up at him looking oddly vulnerable and far less confident than the other faces in the book. Well, he *was* less sure of himself! But he'd waited long enough. Whatever happened, he had to begin. He had to prove that he could belong and do what was expected!

At the end of the hall was a series of double doors which led into the largest and most wonderful room on the first floor. Michael slipped in, closing them behind him.

The ballroom was easily one hundred feet long sixty feet wide. All along one side there was a balcony supported by graceful, fluted columns. On the other side of the room, glass doors opened out onto the first of a series of terraces which descended to the gardens and lawns below. At the moment, the marbel goddesses stood empty handed. Someone had removed their smoke-stained torches. Between the glass doors which led from the great room to the terrace, mirrors in gilt frames reflected the balcony and great chandeliers

The room was composed of polished wood, parquet, crystal gilt and pastel panels illustrating the amorous escapades of courtiers, shepherdesses, minstrels and clowns. At the far end of the chamber, behind a profusion of ferns, was a dais.

Michael walked out into the center of the room; holding his arms at shoulder height, he turned and began to spin, beginning slowly but gradually increasing his speed until the ballroom was a carousel of gilt and glass, a kaleidescope of double doors, windows, potted palms, chandeliers, chairs, gilt, balconies, potted palms, chandeliers, angels, potted palms, frame, chairs, chandelier and glass; spinning around and around and around until he fell.

He kept his eyes open as he watched the chandeliers, pitching in a giddy sea, whirling this way and that in a drunken dizzy spin; he lay motionless until they were anchored to the ornate rosettes which held them in place.

It was raining. Michael rose and walked to the tall glass doors. From here, it was easy to see why he hadn't been able to observe the interior on the first night. The terraced gardens obscured the view from below.

He opened the doors and crossed the flagstone terrace but stopped short and stared at what he saw on the far side of the stone balustrade. On the gravel drive which bisected the gardens an old man sat in a yellow cart drawn by a brown horse. They were facing the woods but, despite a driving rain, they remained perfectly still. As the boy watched, he saw Peter approach the cart, converse with the gray-bearded man and disappear momentarily, only to return with another man who helped him haul a long crate.

Michael squinted as he leaned forward to get a better look. He realized that the box contained Heinrich.

Peter and his assistant slid the coffin into the back of the cart and the two strangers drove off, following the drive past the greenhouses, toward the woods. Peter watched them go, until, at last, he turned and walked back toward the palace. As he did, he looked up and saw Michael. Their eyes met for an instant. Peter went on his way, and moments later was gone.

The boy watched until the cart disappeared. Only then did he turn.

Michael slipped through the double doors and entered Frederich's apartment. When he reached the alcove between the deserted dressing room and the bed chamber, he paused. No one was permitted to enter Frederich's apartment, let alone walk into his bedroom, without permission. What if last night was only an exception? What if Frederich regretted letting him in? Still, he had to see him! He needed to!

He knocked. No answer. He knocked again. Still no answer. He took a deep breath and walked in.

The bedroom was carpeted with a pale gray rug and was furnished simply. There was only a low bed between two windows, fitted with rose panes, which cast a soft light into the large square room.

That was the furniture. But there was something else which made this chamber the equal of all the others.

The walls were not walls but circus mirrors which distorted each reflection; as the boy stood before the glass, he lost his head, grew an arm, fat ears, had his left leg swell to elephantine proportions which merged with the new stub of his left arm, swollen now and pointed at the top. He had a skinny head again, a pointed neck like Yellowface and two bead eyes, a round lump on his skull and a flat foot shrinking to a curvilinear thigh. He smiled and lost his cheeks to a corncob of bulging teeth which ate his ears and the tiny patch of hair atop his pinhead. He stood on tiptoe and Gothic flesh arched from pointed instep, squatted to bloat in pig-bellied corpulence. Each move distorted each shape, each shape cartooned each gesture. He turned away.

Frederich was asleep. Michael walked over to the low bed and stood, looking down at him. Suddenly he felt very, very foolish. Why had he come? What would he do if Frederich woke up and saw him? What would he do if he thought he was here to . . . do it or . . . wanted him or told him to . . .?

Michael turned to go but something caught his eye; he wheeled around and knelt to examine Frederich's face more carefully. In the rose light the man looked very calm. Not at all the fantastic creature of a Nazi cabaret. But there was a large bruise on his cheek, just below his left eye. It was swollen. Major Stauffer had hurt him!

Frederich hadn't been lying the day he told Michael that he too was a prisoner!

There was something sticking out from under the bed; he almost crushed it with his knee. It was a circular mirror of blue glass and a polished black box. He raised the lid; the box was filled with white powder and something which rolled off the mirror and fell to the carpeted floor. He picked it up and held it to the rose light . . . a silver straw. Michael shrugged. Was this another mysterious cosmetic?

Perhaps it was facial powder or some medicine or something to help him sleep? It made no sense, whatever it was. The boy replaced these objects and stole from the room.

When he returned to the dormitory, there was a dispute in progress. It was obvious that the situation had not improved with the passage of time.

The quarrel concerned the proper ownership of Heinrich's Harlequin costume. Alfred maintained that since he'd been Heinrich's companion on that night, it should belong to him. Knut countered that it had never been Heinrich's to begin with, that the ruff had been part of one of his old costumes so, by rights, it all should go to him. Especially now.

Knut's voice was clipped and sarcastic. "Look, you little fool . . ."

"Don't call me a fool!" Alfred raged.

"I will because you are!"

"You're the fool, Knut, because you don't even understand that he said I could have this after the last party!"

Knut gasped and looked about for allies. Seeing Michael standing among the others, he appealed to him for judgment.

"Michael, can you believe this?"

"Believe what?"

"I let Heinrich borrow my ruff and belt and tights. Not to keep but to borrow. And now this little *jew* says . . ."

But he never got a chance to complete the sentence before Alfred was upon him, punching and clawing and kicking.

The others went wild. At once, they formed a tight ring around the combatants, urging one and then the other. Whenever one of the two boys fell into the crowd, he was pushed back as the circle of whores shouted and rooted them on.

Michael was seized by a compulsion to see one of them win, anything that could be called a clear victory. He was eager for a physical verdict but the fight became a wrestling match and disintegrated into a static knot. When it was nothing more than a slow-moving pile, Michael turned away.

He entered his own room and lay on the bed. Outside, in the hall he could hear the exhortations, the hectoring and badgering. It was as if Heinrich had never existed except to provide an excuse for this ridiculous quarrel! Like ravenous white vultures, the boys clawed for their share of the spoils.

The following afternoon, Michael clattered down to the first floor. As he breezed into the library, assuring himself that his main objective was a book about mountains, he heard voices. He loitered at the alcove which led into the office. Frederich was just ending a conversation with Peter.

"Good. You'll keep a closer eye on them and how they're all getting along. That's all then. You may go . . . and Michael, come in and stop trying to hide out there."

How had he known? His back had been to the door!

Michael slipped into the room, half embarrassed and half suspicious. But Frederich's expression put him at ease. He motioned for Michael to sit down.

"Don't think I have eyes in the back of my head," he

explained. "But I heard your footsteps and guessed the rest."

Michael nodded. The bruises were still there. Frederich noticed the direction of the boy's glance and smiled but his voice was bitter. "Ah, yes. My love taps."

"What?"

"A friend and I had a . . . disagreement. He won as you see."

"Does that mean you aren't friends anymore?" Michael asked, amazed that he and Frederich were speaking as personal friends once again.

"I don't know," Frederich replied, standing up and going to the window. "I'm not in control of events, and the more decisions I make, the more decisions I regret. Can you understand that?"

Michael shook his head.

"It doesn't matter," said Frederich. Then, looking out at the bright day he said, "It seems a shame to stay inside on such a nice afternoon. Do you know how to ride a horse?"

The barn was sweet with the smells of oat hay, polished leather, liniment and alfalfa. As Michael stood with the small bay mare, Frederich disappeared in the direction of the greenhouses. He returned a few minutes later with a bouquet of gray roses.

Michael rode bareback on the small mare and Frederich was astride his tall gray gelding, holding the reins in his teeth and the roses under his arm as he adjusted his saddle.

It was a glorious day. The rains of the preceding twenty-four hours had left the sky bright blue and cloudless. As they approached the forest, Michael felt happy, truly happy for the first time in weeks. The day was warm and, for the first time, he imagined the rest of this summer as a succession of lazy days with little to do but drift. . . .

"Where are we going?" he asked Frederich.

"I don't know," the man replied. "But I do have to make a stop later on. Here, let's take this trail."

They turned off the old cart road and followed a narrow bridle path, the horses snorting and switching their long tails to shoo off flies which buzzed about their ears.

For ten minutes they rode in silence, enjoying the intermittent shadows of the forest, and bright patches of sun. Squinting, Michael looked up. Pressing his lashes almost completely together, he made a veil of tiny rainbows but lost the colors as they passed into the first heavily wooded area. As they rode deeper and deeper into the forest, passing through glade after glade, the colors darkened from jade to emerald, shadows deepened and bird calls seemed more ominous. Finally, it was silent and the only sound, aside from the wind in the boughs, was the neat clip-clop of shod hooves.

They crossed a trestle bridge and came upon a wide, unspoiled avenue. On each side pines reached up to a far distant sky.

"Do you feel like a gallop?" asked Frederich.

"I don't know the road," answered Michael.

"You don't have to worry," said Frederich. "It isn't used by anyone and there are no surprises, no holes. It's perfectly clear for the next two or three miles and almost entirely level. How about a race?"

Michael smiled and nodded. But a quick look at Frederich's mount made an even start out of the question, for the gelding was two hands taller than his mare.

"How much of a head start do I get?" he asked.

Frederich laughed his noiseless laughter but his eyes were bright as he said, "I'll count to thirty. After that, watch out!"

"You watch out," warned Michael, as he stroked his mare's firm back and tightened his knees very slightly.

Three days of a barn and a restrictive pasture had been unwelcome. The horse needed no further encouragement. At once she slipped from a walk to a brisk trot and, feeling Michael's knees press a bit tighter, extended her gait into a long and loping canter.

Gathering himself, Michael pressed both hands against her neck and let himself be rocked by this steady motion. She was ready for this, he thought to himself as he shook his head to dislodge the hair of her mane which had blown back in his face. More than ready! Indeed, she kept her head up and flicked one ear back to see if he wanted her to go faster!

Why not?

Michael gave an additional squeeze with his knees bunched up, offering as little resistance as possible to the wind. The little mare's long canter shifted from the rocking gait to a brisk gallop.

The only sounds he could hear were the sharp ring of her hooves on hard earth and the whistling of the wind. His eyes were useless now. Filled with tears and unable to focus, his vision registered only a moving blur of greens and grays and unexpected yellows. It was a liquid distortion of shadow and sun. But he was a small ball of human flesh crouched up on her shoulders. He was a sailor and together they were sailing the wind in perfect unison, pulling the earth as it circled the golden sun.

When he heard hooves approaching from behind, he assumed it was useless to urge her on to even greater speed. It was impossible for her to outdo her gallop. But as Frederich's mount came closer and closer, the mare put her ears back, extended her neck and increased her velocity until the wind was an audible scream.

Side by side, head to head, and stride for stride, they raced into the forest. Now there was no outside world! Nothing else! This was all union of horse and man, flesh and wind, wood and earth and spirit. They were one!

By the time they slowed to a canter, trot, and at last, a cakewalk, they had reached the end of the bridle path. Soon, they came out of the trees and crossed a meadow bordered by a long stone wall.

The horses were sweating; looking down, Michael felt a rush of love for the wet mare, a mixture of pride and curiosity. And although he had no idea as to what to think of true perfection, he felt he'd just experienced it for the first time.

The boy sighed and felt himself breathe with his entire being and, for an instant, his world was at peace.

They rode back in silence. Michael allowed his thoughts to drift and was surprised when Frederich interrupted his formless reverie.

"Let's stop here."

Looking about, Michael saw they were beside the wall which bordered the cemetery. Dismounting, they entered the sadly dilapidated graveyard. For a moment, Michael was confused, not comprehending why Frederich would want to come here. But as they approached the line of unmarked white crosses at the end of the enclosure, he understood.

There was a new grave in that row. Several of Frederich's roses had been decimated in the course of their wild ride, but most were intact. Frederich lay the flowers on Heinrich's grave. He paused a moment before the anonymous resting place with his head bowed. When he turned, his face was pale; he looked older.

"I will never forgive myself for what happened," he said, shaking his head and looking down at the ground.

"But what could you have done to stop it?" asked Michael.

"I don't know. But I should have been able to do something!"

"Don't . . ." Michael began. "Please."

Frederich hadn't heard him, or if he did, he ignored him.

"These others; two fell from the barn, Wilhelm had pneumonia but Erhart, and Jules, they were like Heinrich and . . ."

"But you didn't do it!"

"It's not that. It's because everyone goes on in their life doing whatever they want to do. For a while it's all very easy. Or it seems easy. You almost think you can have things your own way. And then suddenly, it changes and all those things you thought you controlled or managed fairly well get the upper hand and what you've thought of as your life turns out not to be yours but part of something less sensible, less rational."

"I don't know what you're talking about," Michael whispered.

"I'm being vague again. It's a chronic problem," said Frederich and smiled. But his smile faded as he said, "All right, I'll tell you about myself.

"Over two years ago, I made a 'mistake' as Major Stauffer would call it. I fell in love."

"Is that bad?"

"Love? Hardly!"

"Then why was it a mistake?"

"Because the person I loved was a wonderful, brave man who hated Hitler and Roehm and everything they stand for. At the beginning I didn't know that he was involved in politics. I knew he cared but I didn't know that he would try to do something about them. . . ."

"You mean stop them?"

Frederich nodded. "I was such a fool! I thought that because I was an artist I didn't have to pay attention to what was happening in Germany, to people in the streets which is where it all began, even to people in my own cabaret. At that time, they all came to the Glass Arcade. Hitler, Goering, Himmler . . . everyone you can imagine. Not because it was the grandest place to go but because there was something there, something you could see, something in the way the high life mingled with guttersnipes, and the costumes and the uniforms, the artistic and the military. It gave everyone a chance to glimpse the carnival which our society had become.

"But I was such a fool, so carried away with my own vision that I thought I could exert some kind of influence. I realize it must sound absurd in light of everything that's happened but at that time, before it all came crashing down around me, I truly believed that an artist was exempt from the social restrictions which affect other people.

"Can you understand what I am trying to say? I was blind, a stupid, stupid fool. That safety, that refuge, that special position *doesn't* exist! It's an illusion which allows others to take control of our lives. It's the thing that keeps us from seeing that what happens to someone else can happen to us all. I can't tell you how completely and utterly I was involved in the romantic illusion that I would be a part of an evolutionary experiment. My dreams have proved so banal in the light of everything which has followed. But, believe me when I say I was as hopeful and idealistic a dreamer as you could possibly imagine.

"When my lover asked me if he could use my cabaret and my motor car for political meetings I said yes. Of course. It was so that he could work against the Nazis. It was, or it seemed safe for me because I was always somewhere else, not involved. Ha! People got suspicious; he was betrayed. As soon as he was killed, murdered, they came after me! Perhaps some of his friends were tortured until they revealed the names of innocent people to save themselves. I don't know. They don't tell you what they know or who has denounced you. You're on a list; someone gave your name, reported you. That's enough for them. Particularly if they want to believe you guilty, or if they have some reason for wanting you out of the way.

"In my case he thought I would be useful working for them. The Glass Arcade was celebrated, or notorious, depending on one's view. He appropriated it and gave me a chance to save my life."

"Who?"

"Why, Major Stauffer, of course! He was the only one of my acquaintances who'd take the risk of befriending me. And do you know why?"

Michael shook his head.

"Because for years, ever since I first met him and his wife, ever since I'd first come to Berlin, he'd wanted me. Not out of love or admiration, but because in some demented way he feels that unless he has me in his pocket, he can't rest. I represent something to him, some concept, some sort of conquest. You see how ridiculous it is? He doesn't understand me or my art or anything I've tried to do. But because of who I was or what I was, he needs to feel that he controls my life.

"I wasn't interested in him. Ever. I think that only sharpened his interest. So he waited, and finally, when he had his chance, his big moment, he became my protector."

"What did he do?"

"He made a few telephone calls. I got a chance to explain myself to Hitler."

Frederich hunched his shoulders and leaned forward. "I think I died that day. Yes, that was the end of me. The end of my art, of my dream, of my desire to be part of a new world. The end of everything I'd lived for. Ever since, I've been waiting to live again hoping for something I could believe in as some kind of resistance. No matter how small. Something that would represent some act of defiance against them. I think I thought of it as another chance. But it never came. My compromise finished me."

Michael spoke very gently, hoping to shake him loose from the recollections which haunted him. "You're alive now."

Frederich nodded. "Yes, thanks to you."

"Me?"

"Don't look so surprised, Michael! From the first day you came here I knew that you'd fought them and that you'd continue to fight them until they ground you down! That's why I said what I said the other evening."

"What?"

"That of all the people in the palace, you were the only one who might understand me. Until you came I'd been numb. Part of Christian's collection, a trinket he fondles when he reviews his accomplishments. That house is his way of keeping me. Everyone on the staff with the exception of Peter is an informer. And Peter is obligated."

"I know. He told me about his brother."

Frederich nodded. "It's a very cozy arrangement, isn't it? And all the while Christian uses us to curry favor with Hitler or trade that for advancement with Roehm and God knows who else! In any case, he knows that no one can get to me."

"Except for me," said Michael.

Frederich smiled and looked like himself again. "Yes," he agreed. "Except for the worst rebel in the entire house."

"But that's why you liked me, isn't it?"

"I recognized a kindred spirit. Now let's go back."

As they walked toward their horses, Frederich seemed to regain his spirits. "Next weekend there's going to be a very big party. I want you to attend."

"But, I'm . . ."

"Not to participate. Not yet. You will be my personal escort. That way you'll be able to observe and I can protect you . . . to see everything is . . . manageable."

"But I don't have anything to wear! I don't know what to do!" Michael protested.

"In that order?" Frederich smiled a little mockingly. "Well, don't worry. You'll be with me and I'm sure we can dig up some old rags to cover your body."

Chapter Twenty

There was something amiss. Frederich's most recent visitor told him that Roehm was planning to meet with Hitler to discuss the future of his private army. Already there was considerable apprehension about that conference, only three days off. Although the General was said to be confident, others were not so sure. Roehm pooh-poohed such speculation. After all, hadn't he been instrumental to Hitler's career? Hadn't they walked side by side at Nuremburg? He had nothing to fear from Goering or Himmler. If they wanted a showdown, he'd give it to them!

Life in the villa went on as usual. Since Major Stauffer had requested it, there would be a large party for many of the Brown Shirts stationed nearby. Thousands were gathering on the shores of Lake Tegernsee; officers could drive in from Wiessee on Friday evening and stay until Saturday night or Sunday.

Frederich was preoccupied much of the time, arranging reservations, decorations, music and costumes. There had never been so many soldiers or civilians to entertain at one time and he spent the greater part of his days in his small office on the first floor. Thomas overheard him planning to have six people stationed in the balcony in the ballroom whose sole function would be to rain colored confetti onto the floor. Helmut let out that he was designing very special tapestries for the members of the elite Gestapo.

On Wednesday afternoon Michael finished the drawing he'd worked on for two days; he took it to the office and knocked. Frederich opened it and, without so much as a word of greeting, returned to his desk; he was occupied with his small mirror and black box. As the boy scrutinized him, he raised his head for a moment.

"Come in," he said reassuringly, "I'm indulging in a little vice."

"What is it?" asked the boy, staring down at the long lines of white powder on the blue glass.

"Ask me no questions," replied Frederich lightly as he inserted the silver straw into his nose and sucked a line into one nostril. He repeated the ritual with the other line.

"Is that a drawing for me?"

"Yes, a costume," Michael replied eagerly, handing over the sketch.

"Let's see. Ah, very nice!"

It was a cartoon of a shepherd with red tights and a full blouse of yellow cloth, belted at the waist with a black sash; there were sheepskin leggings and a soft black cap.

"It looks familiar," said Frederich.

"Don't you know what it is?" asked Michael, delighted by the praise and the man's confusion. Then, unable to restrain himself he blurted, "He's from the dome in the entrance hall!"

"Of course, now I remember!" Frederich responded, nodding his head. He was pale. Too pale and thin.

"It took me hours to decide, but whenever I'm lonely I go out and sit on the top step. And I always see him, the one who holds the lamb. We look the same; well, in a way. So, I'll be him!" he concluded triumphantly.

Frederich smiled and glanced down at the blue mirror. He initialed the drawing, reached for his box of white powder and said: "Take it up to Herr Rosenwald on the third floor. I told him not to work on anything else after you'd chosen your costume so it will be ready in plenty of time. But Michael," he cautioned, "remember that you are going to be my escort. If anyone annoys you, tell me."

Michael was already at the door. "All right!" he cried, and was gone.

As he climbed the great stairs, he looked up at the dome. From this angle he could see both the shepherd and the full-breasted shepherdess. He hadn't ever noticed it before, but while the lad looked happy, the girl looked wistful and sad.

At eight o'clock on Friday night, a full hour before the party was to begin, Michael donned his costume. The new clothes fit exactly. The red tights, furry leggings, yellow tunic, black sash and cap were perfect. He danced a delighted dance before the long mirror on his armoire and dashed out into the hall, past other rooms where boys were involved in their own intricate transformations.

Several glanced at him as he passed and nodded approval; perhaps they thought that tonight he'd begin working. He smiled appreciatively and returned compliments. Now there was a distinctly different attitude toward him, a palpable feeling of fraternity. At last!

Whenever the boys prepared for another evening, this sense of comradeship and solidarity was heightened by the forthcoming uncertainty and excitement. As they moved from room to room, arranging their costumes, borrowing or sharing cosmetics and advice, they looked more like a theater troupe than a group of sacrificial courtesans preparing for another flirtation with hazard.

Michael strode out into the great hall and stared up at the dome. He smiled at the similarity; Herr Rosenwald had reproduced the costume with flawless accuracy; even the leather straps which tied the leggings were identical. He *was* the boy on the dome!

He crossed to the heavy double doors in the alcove;

it no longer occurred to him that the suite was officially off limits.

He pushed the doors open and entered.

As Michael swaggered into the bedroom, Frederich smiled. "Let me look!"

Michael laughed aloud and spun several delighted circles in rapid succession. He wanted to jump, tumble and run, but forced himself to remain relatively still as Frederich examined his costume.

"You look wonderful, Michael!"

At last Michael felt that he really belonged to his life! At last he had a family! No matter how bizarre it might seem to an outsider he swore his allegiance to the tribe of sweet decadents and to the piper of this sensational folly.

Frederich was busy with his white powder. How strange he looked tonight! How forbidding and severe! He was wearing black hose, a black velvet doublet trimmed with jet beads. A wreath of dark red roses framed the austere face he'd selected.

It was more a lacquer or ceramic than a face. He'd coated his features with a thick white paint, broken only by dark lines outlining his eyes. Beneath his scarlet roses, he seemed tragic and proud, a jester mourning his fate.

As he watched his friend arrange the powder into long lines, Michael reviewed the costume and decided that it suited him. Perhaps it was the lack of extravagance, for this costume was not decorative or miraculous.

Frederich turned to the small mirror. The silver straw moved across the blue glass. Michael watched closely, hoping Frederich would sense his curiosity about the white powder. But the mask was immobile.

Frederich sat up, put the glass tray under his bed and winced as he gave a quick sniff. "Definitely not for children," he said, standing to go. "Let's see how the others have done."

They walked out into the hall; downstairs people were beginning to arrive. Though the great chandelier was dark Michael could see the periwigged footmen and pages taking hats and coats into the small cloak-room near the front doors.

Most of the arrivals were Brown Shirts, but there were S.S. officers, Gestapo and civilians as well. All seemed quite merry and congenial.

From time to time men glanced up to the dim chandelier, hoping it would light up to signify the beginning of the party. In this half-light, stewards carried trays of champagne through the hall.

From far away, Michael could hear sounds of musicians tuning their instruments. He had lingered to observe these preparations; Frederich had gone on. Now, Michael hurried after him and entered the dormitory. It had become a gallery of little whores, courtesans, miniature fauns, masked creatures and painted boys. There were Arabs in striped pants, small vests and red fez. There were Greek youths and Romans in white togas that offered little, if any, protection, against an exploratory hand. Minstrels and medieval pages put the final touches on their tunics and tights as sailors, acolytes and rhinestoned gladiators all plumed, made up, scented and oiled, prepared to enter the crystal pit.

Michael tagged after Frederich as he moved down the hall taking a few minutes with a clown, a ballerina, a ringmaster and a dancing bear. He pressed a small vial into the clown's hand. The white powder again?

There was no time to wonder; Frederich had turned his attention to a bevy of sequined ladies; a blue enchantress, a bride and another in black with glittering sleeves. They were joined by a pair of young woodsmen, their fair hair and suntanned legs set off by the *leiderhosen* and wreaths of flowers. A countess of sorts in a wide dress without a back of any kind tripped by on her way to rearrange an enormous plumed wig. Michael stared after the bare buttocks in amazement; the rear was completely exposed.

There were naked bodies painted with fish scales and one boy frescoed as a tiger, his body completely streaked with orange and black markings. Another was naked, his nude body covered with adhesive crystals. This living prism had accented the non-costume with blue circles around his eyes and sex.

Through it all, Frederich drifted, giving advice, straightening a seam, adjusting a sleeve, approving a color combination, adding a pin here, a plume there, selecting a belt, a cap, a different pair of gloves. For one he added a ribbon, for another he removed unnecessary ankle bells. Here he suggested bracelets; there, he removed a breastplate until, with a clap of his hands, he brought the hall to silence.

He spoke in a calm voice, as a gentle conductor addresses a well-trained student orchestra before a recital. His tone was firm, his manner appraising.

"Each of you knows what to do and how to behave. You know we are all here to help one another. We are all together, one family, one group. Tonight, no excessive drinking; Stephen, Wolfgang, that means you. Remember! No displays of temper, Knut, Alfred. We all know the way things are. Tonight there will be an unusual number of guests which means we can't afford to lose any of you.

"While I'm on the subject, I want to say a few words about Heinrich."

There was a total hush as soon as Frederich mentioned the boy. "Of course we all regret that such a tragic accident occurred. But, knowing what I know, I'm convinced that Heinrich resisted the colonel and brought destruction upon himself. As I've told you so many times, yield and survive. If you offer no resistance, if you are pliant, nothing can really hurt you! Nothing!

"Still, you can try other methods to protect yourself.

If you find yourself facing something unpredictable, something you fear and have no other options, no other way of escape, reverse the situation and become overly demonstrative, overly affectionate. At times, with certain sorts, too much passion can be as noxious as too little. Do you understand?"

There was general assent. Frederich nodded. "Most men are sweet fools," he said lightly. "Just pour a few drinks in them and tell them they're wonderful. Let them do the talking and you may find you have to pry them off their favorite topics and onto you!"

A few of the boys laughed.

"Now, let's go down and have a good time. I'm going to show Michael the ins and outs of the events tonight so I won't be available as usual. But I don't think any of you need much help. You're all looking splendid. You make me wish I was attractive!"

There was more laughter.

"You don't know what it's like to be so old and overlooked at soirees like these," Frederich lamented, exaggerating his despair even as he made mock of himself. "I spend hours and do the very best I can and no one even gives me a second look! As a matter of fact, I decided not to even bother attending any more of these primitive revels . . . Michael had to insist that I come or I'd have shut myself up in my room! I have a good idea as to what you boys are up to and I must say, I am shocked, *shocked!*"

They all laughed. Frederich winked and led them out into the hall. When they had assembled at the head of the staircase, the man pressed a switch on the wall; the great chandelier came to life. The music began.

Excitement was contagious as Frederich stepped back and bowed. Even Michael couldn't resist a cry of pleasure as the boys began their descent, winding through open space down to the men who waited far below.

There was a cheer as they all came down the stairs, as

a living tidal wave of velvet and satin and young flesh cascading toward the uniforms. As the boys rolled into the hall, infecting the air with laughter, soprano invaded the bass accompanied by a rush of jazz, popping corks, the clink of glass and the fizz of champagne.

The night was on!

Chapter Twenty-One

A band pumped out hot jazz; boys infiltrated each room. Clouds of smoke and green bottles foaming over with tiny bubbles were the first things Michael noticed.

An old man with an eye patch offered him a glass.

Frederich was greeting a fat man in a suit; he didn't see Michael take the goblet and drain it; it made him sneeze, this dry wine with a taste of bubbling grape. It tickled his nose. He tried again. Better.

He followed the dark jester, hiding in his shadows as soldiers came to chat, compliment, court or ogle the black-and-white-faced man wreathed in roses. Peeking out from the safety of Frederich's protective arm, Michael saw that the men were different with him. The officers didn't treat Frederich with the same air as they treated the boys. There was none of the pinching, leering or suggestive insinuations. Even to them it was clear that Frederich Lorken was more than just a pleasure vessel.

Michael, however, enjoyed no such preferential status. As they circled through the rooms, several of the men touched his cheek, smiled or pinched his red breeches. He masked his tension, ignored their suggestions and stole sips of champagne.

A soldier strolled by with a ballerina wearing his hat. Apache dancers were bounced on uniformed knees, bullfighters received tribute from Brown Shirt captains as everyone drank more and more and more.

It was all happening so quickly! More people entered the hall, far outnumbering the available boys; how many were there? Two hundred? Three hundred? The easy drunks gave up hope of young plunder and groped one another, the pages, the footmen. Even Peter was seized and pressed into a corner by a pie-eyed romantic.

Little cigarettes wrapped in black paper were passed from lip to lip, reddening eyes and lowering voices. Frederich indulged but rejected Michael's request that he be allowed to sample the rudely fashioned object. Michael *was* learning the ins and outs; he waited for his chance and stole a quick puff but the smoke burned his throat and he coughed until tears ran from his eyes. Frederich glanced at him and looked slightly exasperated.

"What am I going to do with you?" he whispered before a slightly greenish lieutenant asked where the nearest bathroom was. As Frederich gave the man directions, Michael stole some more champagne.

Frederich passed from room to room. In the blue salon an instrumental ensemble played chamber music. In the library, a band of men had gathered in a circle. At the center of this throng, a young cardinal was stripping off his scarlet robes. As he lay on the floor, men dribbled champagne onto his body. One of the officers, inspired by this spectacle, began removing his boots. By the time a nervous page had succeeded in worming his way through the crowd and advising Frederich of the situation, the officer was attempting to unfasten his belt. Frederich worked his way through the throng, and whispered to the man. A moment later, Michael saw two officers, and the cardinal, hurry toward the staircase. They were the first to disappear.

The party seemed to explode from room to room. As chambers filled with new arrivals, double doors opened to connecting salons where fresh buffets awaited anxious appetites. In the morning room, Klaus posed at the center of a fountain which sprayed champagne onto his body from six silver dolphins. He was wearing a green and gold fishtail which transformed him from boy to merman. As men shouted requests Klaus lolled in the carbonated basin and lapped wine into their glasses.

In some cases, men coaxed boys upstairs, but it was mostly the boys who'd made their selections for their evening. Michael saw several men crawling after youths who teased them on or helped them ascend, arm in arm. Some were already half-naked, others held bottles aloft as unopened supplies for the impending campaigns. A few stalwarts hoisted their trophies onto their shoulders and carried them up the staircase; Michael could hear delighted squeals of pleasure, spiced with hungry growls.

Frederich took his hand and they went down to the smoky den Michael had witnessed on his first night. In the blue gloom, men had stripped off uniforms and urged their favorites to join them on the wide divans. Pages in white robes had collected uniforms, folding and hanging them in an antechamber. Pipes passed by, tall silver pipes filled with wine or burning a thick tar. Boys in white muslin prepared a paste, rolling it on thin stems, cooking it over small lamps and presenting it to eager patrons. The air was infected with this heavy incense.

Even from inside, the room was outlandish. Twenty or thirty naked bodies under blue light, sucking on silver pipes, alternately revealed or obscured by the smoke which he now saw originated from a cube of dry ice mounted over a fan. Clouds of thick white mist billowed through the room, wrapping diaphanous tentacles about its occupants.

Buoyed by the champagne and proud to be with Frederich, Michael let the night seep through whatever was left of his adolescent inhibitions. What did it matter if all was uncertain and temporary? What did it matter if tonight was his initiation into sin or depravity? He was where he wanted to be, where he had to be, with the person he wanted to be with and the air was sweet with opium. So damn the rest!

Young boys and their amorous swains lay entwined

on soft pillows. The music of flute and drum was a warm and insistent continuity; yes, this was a cavern of sensation where the bodies lay in embrace, enmeshed limb to limb, leg to leg, young bodies pressed up against the flesh of their elders, reaching out for stems of passing pipes or stroking a muscular back, a thigh, a chest, a neck, a shoulder, cheek or lip. They might be swallowed up in a living compulsion but the only sounds the boy heard were soft moans or sighs of pleasure.

"Let's go up," Frederich whispered.

Upstairs the party was raging. A naked boy danced on a piano in the music room as an officer played the national anthem; S.S., S.A. and Gestapo alike wavered at boozy attention as Fritz marched, his cock bobbing to the austere beat. Petals from decimated flowers covered the rug.

The ballroom was apparently the main attraction; people came to compliment Frederich on how it looked. Ultimately, he and Michael worked their way through the throngs which congested the hall and entered that long room.

The walls were hung with black cloth, pocked with silver bones and skulls, the Gestapo insignia. The ceiling had also been draped with material so the six chandeliers hung in a pavilion of silver stars, scattered galaxies, skulls and crescent moons.

At the center of the ballroom, rising out of an island of silver palms, stood an enormous figure, a skeleton in a red mask. With a shining scythe in one hand, he presided over the dance, an incredible leer twisting the death head.

The Glass Arcade again! Michael felt he was really seeing Frederich; really seeing him for the first time. Now he understood this costume: the simple black, the white face, and wreath. For here, in the dark chamber, Frederich was indistinguishable from the pavilion. They were one and the same, an interior night couching the towering figure of death. His stark mask was no longer abstract or bewildering. This costume made more sense than any of the others he'd worn. It was his own uniform for damnation, his own theatrical demise. For here in this dark ballroom, beneath a rain of colored paper, the black and red uniforms of the Gestapo became costumes; the soldiers were transvestites in a military burlesque.

Someone grabbed him; he was swept out onto the floor! From a steadily lengthening distance, he saw Frederich looking after him, in alarm at first and then, acquiescent. Through the double lens of excitement and exhilaration and inebriation, he tried to make sense of where he was. But fine green eyes were smiling into his own.

"I can't dance," he blurted.

"Follow me," the soldier said.

At first he felt oafish but the step proved easy to imitate: one, two, three, one, two, three; he stumbled and almost fell but the man held him up; for a moment Michael felt self-conscious. Then, looking about, he realized that he didn't have to worry for the dance floor had become a vast collision course.

Pushing through a knot of intoxicated boys and enchanted fellow officers, the sweaty man led Michael out onto the terrace. He seized a bottle from a page and they drank. After Michael had had a few sips, the man took the bottle and poured the rest of the contents all over his own face.

Over their heads, a marble maiden raised her torch to the sky. To their left, a soldier relieved himself over the balustrade. A golden arc rained into the cool night but Michael couldn't even pretend to be surprised. He had just seen everything. The world had become a carousel, and though it might slow down, he told himself he would never see it as he used to, before. No, there had been a moment where it blurred and ran together. There was nothing left to shock. So, he let the man embrace him, allowing the thick hand to explore his chest and smooth stomach as their lips met.

Michael tried to jerk away but the man forced his hand against the front of his dark pants. As the boy tried to extricate himself, he could feel the flesh swell; the soldier smiled and wiped his sweaty face with the sleeve of his free arm. Then he opened his pants, directing Michael's hand to enter the unbuttoned flap. Michael tried to pull back.

And Frederich was there. Frederich whom he hadn't seen in, how long had it been? Fifteen minutes? Twenty? A half hour?

He was laughing and waving a bottle at the soldier who trailed after him. "The last drink in the world," he claimed and turned to face Michael's abductor. "Ah! So you're the one who stole the babe from the nursery!" said Frederich, smiling in approval as he threw one arm around the man's shoulders. "But listen, *mein Herr,* there's something you should know about this *innocent.*"

He whispered into the soldier's ear. Michael looked up at the storm trooper and then at Frederich; his friend was still whispering. The boy tried to hear but the words were too confusing; he was dizzy. He was sweating.

". . . who had the infection . . . still carries it . . . any of the others, I assure you . . ."

The big hand fell from Michael's shoulder; the man looked at him with disgust as Frederich finished his explanation with a helpful expression. The soldier pushed the boy away and stumbled back into the ballroom.

"Well, so much for him!" Frederich pronounced and muttered, "We'll probably all face medical examinations in the morning."

Michael had no idea what had happened; he weaved a bit and reached for Frederich; the arm he found was firm.

Frederich looked into his face. "Are you all right?"

Michael tried to nod, but his head bounced on his neck.

"How much have you had to drink?" asked Frederich.

Michael grinned and shrugged.

"You'd better come with me."

Frederich kept a firm hold of Michael's hand as they passed through smoke-filled chambers where men and boys stood or sat or danced or lay in embrace on couches, chairs or on the floor. Just as they were about to attempt the stairs the music stopped; people grew quiet as someone called Frederich's name. He turned toward the yellow and gray sitting room and muttered, "Oh, no!"

Michael felt sick; he sat down and tried to keep his eyes open. If he closed them, he'd fall forward. No, it was better to hold onto the banister. Eyes open. That's right.

There were two men standing just ten feet away. One seemed vaguely familiar but Michael couldn't recall who he was. His eyes felt so heavy. He closed them again. Why did Frederich seem so tense? Why were the soldiers standing at attention? Why weren't they laughing? It was a wonderful party . . . a wonderful, wonderful party!

"Frederich Lorken!"

"Colonel! How good to see you again!"

Michael squinted and looked up. Oh, yes! The colonel! He was the one with Heinrich the night of the accident. But why was he here again? Heinrich was already dead.

He approached Frederich with another man. Michael closed his eyes again; thinking was too difficult.

"It was all taken care of," Frederich was saying. "Those things happen from time to time. But I'm glad you could come tonight! As you see, things have progressed!"

"Yes, General Roehm . . . may I present Frederich Lorken? I'm sure you know him by reputation."

The general's voice was very strange. "I remember Herr Lorken from the days of the Glass Arcade."

Frederich laughed but there was something unfamiliar about his laughter. It was almost out of place in the quiet hall. "It seems I'll never live those days down. Even though I've left Berlin and moved to the country, where, as you see, I pursue a quiet life, there are still rumors of outrageous behavior in my youth!"

The colonel chuckled; the general did not.

"We've been reviewing your photograph album."

Michael wished he was able to stand; he'd take Frederich by the hand and lead him away from these men, away from the crowds of quiet men upstairs where they could be alone. But, of course, he had to wait and be patient. He kept his eyes closed as the colonel spoke. How long could it possibly be before they'd just go away? They were ruining Frederich's party!

"This one looks familiar. . . ."

"Oh, I don't think so," Frederich replied. "He's a newcomer."

"He looks a little tired."

"I'm afraid they never limit themselves voluntarily; he's the first casualty of the evening."

"Ah, this is his first adventure into your Glass Arcade?" the colonel inquired.

"Yes, and as you see he's been overwhelmed by it," Frederich sighed. "I estimate five glasses of champagne, but God only knows how much he stole when I wasn't looking! Next time he'll know better!"

The colonel pursued the matter. "He seems too young to drink."

"Yes," Frederich said rather hastily. "He's too inexperienced and . . ."

"Inexperienced, you say?" Roehm interjected.

"Unfortunately, totally," Frederich stammered. There was no doubt about it, Michael thought to himself, clutching the banister as his stomach threatened to pitch forward. Something was upsetting his friend! Frederich was trying to pretend that everything was all right but it wasn't true; the boy knew it wasn't true. Maybe he should have some more champagne! That might help!

"Gentlemen, I must ask your indulgence. This boy has had so much to drink, I'm afraid he'll be ill. Please excuse us. I'll be down in a few minutes."

"Herr Lorken," the general said softly and with great precision. "You will please take him to *my* room."

"Your room?"

"Yes, the colonel has kindly consented to let me have use of his favorite chamber. It is called the chapel, I believe."

Frederich's words came out in a jumble. "Well, but I . . . you . . . there isn't . . ."

"And I think I'll have this boy. Of course, you did say he's not been initiated?"

"No. Not at all. He . . ." Frederich began.

"Well, perhaps I'll teach him a few things," the general hissed. "He looks as if he needs a lesson or two!"

The colonel giggled and muttered something to his friend about discipline but Frederich didn't laugh. Well, he should have some more champagne, Michael thought, yawning. Yes, a lot more! He tried to open his eyes but they were too heavy.

"General," Frederich said, his voice sounding strained. "He's so new, so green. Let me acquaint you with one of our best boys. A man of your rank and stature . . ."

"No!" The voice was clipped, brusque.

Frederich was off balance. "Sir, you know me from a long time ago, so perhaps you know my reputation. Usually, I maintain a professional distance. It's my prerogative as director of this institution to refuse any invitations. But this boy is nothing! I can't allow a man of your greatness to go away from here with a poor impression. Why don't you give *me* an opportunity? Surely our country's commander, the master of our army deserves the very best. This child couldn't possibly satisfy a man of the world like you!"

"I appreciate your gesture," the general countered, his voice a shade softer, "but this evening I will have him. No other. Now, you will go sober him up and prepare him to obey my instructions. Oh, and Herr Lorken . . .?"

"Yes?"

"There's a black case in the back of my car. Have it taken up to the chapel."

"Of course."

"And Herr Lorken?"

"Yes, General?"

"Deliver him in something befitting a youth of the Third Reich."

Chapter Twenty-Two

The coffee was black; he didn't like coffee. But the cup came up to his lips again and again. At first he refused but the shock of a cold towel on his back and the unwelcome caffeine brought him to his senses. Frederich was leaning over him; they were in his living room.

Looking down, Michael saw that he was almost naked; his body was wrapped in a thick towel. He smiled, nestled into the cozy couch and tried to close his eyes. He'd dreamed that he'd been sick but Frederich had taken care of him and washed him off and now . . .

"No!" The voice was sharp.

Frederich shook him until he opened his eyes. The coffee came again and he drank. He sat up and stretched and tried to prove that he was sober.

"Michael, listen to me!"

Michael inclined his head; Frederich nodded and stood up. "Do you feel all right?"

"What happened?" Michael asked.

"You drank too much and got sick. I washed you off and let you sleep but now, you've got to wake up and listen."

Why did Frederich seem so agitated as he paced the room? As he moved, he seemed almost lost in his wonderful room. But he was mesmerizing. Michael watched the smooth steps and the quick turns, the tap of fingertips on his thighs.

"Did you insert your photograph in the album downstairs?"

The boy nodded. Frederich looked desperate.

"But why? How could you do such a thing without asking me?"

"I want to belong. I . . ."

"Good God!"

"Was it wrong?"

"I can't. . . . Yes, it was. No, no . . ."

"What's the matter?"

"I've got to tell you something, Michael. Try not to hate me."

"I don't hate you."

"Not now," Frederich admitted. "But you might . . . later."

He stood for a moment, looking out a window, gazing down to the front of the house where sounds of the party persisted; there were people spilling down from the hall into the roundabout onto the lawns.

Frederich sighed and shrugged before turning around. "An extremely powerful man wants you. He saw your picture in the album and then he saw you with me. You're the one he wants. No one else. I can't possibly stop it. . . ."

"Oh."

"I tried. Please believe that! I even offered myself! But he wants *you*, Michael!"

Frederich came and knelt before Michael. Looking into his eyes, Michael forgot the mask and the severe paint. The eyes were alive but they were not the cool, remote eyes of Frederich Lorken as he attended to the house, its occupants or clientele.

He's trying to warn me, Michael thought. He's trying to tell me that it's going to be bad.

Suddenly he remembered Heinrich's words and understood why the dead boy wanted to share himself with a friend. It would make doing what he had to do easier. And more bearable. As it was he'd missed that opportunity. Sex was to be another form of violence and he would be its victim.

"You've got to go to him," Frederich was saying. "You've got to make him believe that you're actually enjoying it. No matter what he forces you to do, it's not only for yourself but for all of us."

"I know."

"Please, believe! I had nothing to do with this!"

"I do."

"I don't want it to happen," cried Frederich, making both his hands into fists. "But no one in Germany has any power over him. And yet, somehow, *you* have to survive. So, yield, Michael: yield and survive!"

"I understand." He paused for a moment. "Should I go now?"

Frederich nodded; Michael stood up and let the towel fall from his body. For an instant he was embarrassed, but it was too late for that! Innocence was over!

"I'm ready."

Frederich turned and gathered a pile of dark clothes from a chair beside a fireplace. He pulled a pair of leather pants out. "Try these," he offered.

Michael slipped into them; they were so small! He had to force them up his legs and struggle to close the zipper. But, once on, they felt like his own skin.

"The coat," said Frederich softly. "Boots." They were the right size. Frederich stepped back and nodded. Then, his manner changed and he looked away.

"You are beautiful this way. Now go, and forgive me."

"I do. I *do*."

Frederich turned away. "He's in the chapel. You know where it is? Down the first gallery to the first hall on the right. It's the heavy wooden door at the end. Go to him quickly; he's been waiting."

He opened the doors to the hall and stepped back, allowing the boy to pass. Michael turned but Frederich shook his head, avoiding meeting his eyes and slamming the heavy doors.

The party was back in full force; music and the sounds of euphoric chatter floated up the great stairwell. He went to the marble banister and looked down.

Two people were stumbling up the stairs: a fat old man in a gray wig and a young boy in an S.S. officer's cap. They were laughing and dragging a hanging from the ballroom. Trailed by the tapestry of black satin and Death's-head skulls, they ascended, paused for a moment to embrace and continued.

The old man looked up and saw Michael.

"Oh, look at that one!" he enthused. "Let's capture him!"

His companion followed his glance and Michael recognized Johann, a slender youth with large brown eyes who lived in the same hall as he. Johann was very quiet, very withdrawn; he preferred to spend most of his time alone or playing with the gardener's dog. Now, in the S.S. cap he looked totally different, a jaded angel.

"You won't have the strength for him after I get through with you," he assured the old man, grabbing the wrinkled buttocks. The old man giggled and shrieked: "Rape, rape!"

They laughed; Michael turned and walked away from the stairwell down the gallery, turning into the first hall. It was darker. . . .

At the end of the hall, there was a heavy wooden door studded with enormous nails. There was a small window in the door, covered with bars. It was closed. On either side of this entrance were fat, black candles impaled on long spikes.

For a moment, Michael turned to run. But what would happen if he did? The others? Frederich? No, it was too late: escape was out of the question. He'd put his picture in the book of his own accord. He was part of the fraternity for better or worse. Perhaps it was better to have it end than to begin. He knocked on the door. From inside he heard General Roehm's voice: "Come in, Michael!"

Michael stood at the door, letting his eyes adjust to the darkness.

"Come here," the voice commanded.

The chapel! What a sinister room! The original murals and windows had been painted black; the great space was a chamber of shadows where inky angels festooned with dark garlands hung suspended. And at the end of the eerie vault on an altar beneath soaring arches was a large double bed draped with dark velvet.

Looming over the wide bed was an enormous crucifix; wreathed with silver thorns, the darkened savior raised hopeless eyes to a pervasive night sky. Blood seemed to drip from his open wounds onto the bed, the same bed where Heinrich had died.

In shadowy alcoves around this chamber there were other statues. As Michael's eyes adjusted to the darkness, he could see a woman with a bleeding heart and a saint bound to a stake, his body pierced with arrows. Interspersed with these religious artifacts were familiar icons of the Third Reich: swastikas on golden poles, flags, banners, iron crosses and an enormous photograph of Hitler and Roehm at Nuremberg, their arms raised in salute.

All along one wall were implements of torture: a black gallows, whips and chains, dark hoods, an ax, block and Iron Maiden, that infamous coffin with six inch spikes on the inside lid.

"I said, come here!" the master of Germany snapped.

In a dark chair beside a table of black candles the general was waiting. In his hands he held a whip.

Michael stood before him and looked into his eyes. He hadn't been able to focus in the hall. Now he could see clearly the pockmarked face, muddy eyes and bulbous nose. The thin lips scarred with a bright red weal which pulled the lower lip down toward the double chin. He reminded the boy of Squatface; involuntarily Michael shuddered.

The general grimaced; he pointed to a chair opposite his own. "Sit there."

Michael obeyed.

"That's right. Now don't be frightened," the man cooed in a false and soothing voice. "I see you noticed my scar. That is a souvenir from Verdun. I was decorated for bravery. That is how I began my career. Now," he paused for a moment to wet his upper lip, "let's have a look at you. In leather, I see. Have you ever worn anything like this before?"

His throat was dry; Michael shook his head and managed to say no.

"And did I understand that tonight is the first night you've ever been downstairs to one of Herr Lorken's parties?" the general asked, narrowing his eyes. Although his voice was soft, there was something troubling about those flat, bottomless eyes.

Michael nodded.

"And I am the first one to enjoy your company?" the man asked, tapping his leather boots with the whip he held.

Michael flushed and looked down and managed to say yes.

"In that case I must respect this great responsibility. I must try to teach you something about sex. And, in exchange, there are some things you will have to do to satisfy me. Is that understood?"

The boy nodded. As he did, he remembered Frederich's words. *Yield and survive.*

Roehm smiled; as he did, his unpleasant face looked even worse. "On the bed you will find a large case. Please bring it here but be careful. If you drop it, I will be very, very upset!"

As Michael carried the heavy black box back to the general, he noticed the man adding another taper to the many-armed candelabrum. With added light, the room became more visible as a web of wrought-iron dragons and demons.

The general turned. His skin seemed horrible in the

candlelight; it was an uneven terrain of craters and blemishes. "Before we begin, would you like some champagne?" he asked.

Michael nodded. Champagne would help. Maybe, if he drank too much he'd get sick again or fall asleep! Maybe he could escape what had happened to Heinrich! He looked over at the bed as the general poured the champagne, half expecting to see blood flow across the slate floor.

They drank in silence.

After two glasses the man discarded his goblet and picked up the braided whip. "Now we are ready," he said, examining his nails for a moment. "I want you to do everything I say, on command. I will say things once and once only. There will be no repetitions! So, you will follow my orders or face the consequences. If you fail to obey an order, I will strike you with this whip. If you fail to correct the mistake, I will strike you a second time. And so on until you get it right! Is that completely understood?"

Michael had to urinate but it was too late to ask to be excused. He inclined his head to signify that he had heard the instructions. The general stood up. "Undo my coat."

Michael forced his trembling fingers to undo the buttons, beginning at the top and working his way down.

"Help me out of it."

The coat fell to the floor.

"Remove the shirt."

When the dark tie and shirt lay on the floor and the flabby-chested body was revealed, the general spoke again. "Undo my pants."

The belt and buttons were loosened; the man sat down and extended a leg.

"Boots . . ."

One after another, the tall leather boots slipped into the boy's arms.

"The pants . . ."

When the dark trousers lay among the other articles, Michael looked up. The general sipped his champagne slowly. "Turn around."

Michael did as he was told.

"Take off your coat . . . very, very slowly."

Michael unzipped the leather jacket and slipped out of it, allowing it to fall. Behind him, there were strange rustling sounds; the man's voice was sporadic, his breath ragged.

"Now, the boots. Don't turn. I don't want to hurt you, boy."

The boots came off.

"Now, your pants, slowly, slower. . . . Don't make me use force. I don't want to be angry with you!"

The general laughed, a strange and expectant laughter. Michael unfastened his pants and eased out of them, pulling off the tight hide as slowly as possible. Behind him, he heard the man muttering, "Good, ah, very good, excellent . . . slower, slow."

It was finished; he stood naked with his back to the man. And gradually became aware of a hand or a forefinger touching his back. Very lightly, it traced the line from the delicate heel up the inside of the leg and thigh, across his smooth buttocks and up the small of his back, shoulder blades and neck. . . .

The man was mumbling. Incoherently at first, but more and more comprehensible. It was a low, almost musical chant: "You will like me little boy and we will have a very good time! Don't talk! Don't talk! Just let me do everything! I have it all planned as you will see! It's all in my mind! That's why they made me a general! Ha ha. I am above all the others! All the others know it, too—all the rest of the men with their stupid plans! Just stay like that!! Stand still! Stay as you are! Now, close your eyes and turn, yes, turn around and face me!"

Michael turned.

"All right. You can open your eyes."

He did so.

The general was sitting in that tall chair, staring at him, alert and watchful. "Now give me a kiss, here, on the scar. Don't be afraid! And now, we'll really begin! Are you ready?"

Michael forced himself to nod. The general pointed at the case and looked at the boy for a moment.

Whatever happens, I must not show fear, Michael thought. Whatever he has inside that box, I must not let him know I'm afraid.

The general's voice was soft, almost a whisper. It was obvious that he was pleased with the way things were going. "My friend the colonel told me all about this place and all the wonderful young boys. So, I thought I'd bring them something to make this night even more special. And, of all the boys, I chose you. Do you know why?"

Michael shook his head.

"Because your picture is in the book, and you weren't smiling! And I want you to be happy like the others! Now, I want you to open the box. Just tear off the paper. That's right! Now, open the lid and tell me what you see."

Michael looked down. "Packages."

The general nodded. "That's right, packages. Now, you take one and give me one to open. It doesn't matter which you choose because we'll open all of them together before we do it. All right."

The boy held his small parcel and looked into the man's face.

"Now, slowly, let's unwrap them together. Very, very carefully. Good."

Michael trembled as he peeled off the tissue paper. He tried to control himself but it was useless now. The wrapping paper lay on the floor.

In his hand, he held a delicate metal band—parallel blades bound by crossbars. From each end, thin needles emerged. Michael stared at the object in dismay; he looked to the man who held a similar object. The general's face was eager, trying to peer into the boy's thoughts. But all was doubt.

"Do you understand?"

Michael shook his head.

"Give it to me!"

Michael handed over the metal webbing; the general took it from him and said, "Open another package."

A third piece, similar to the others, lay on the rug. The man hissed as he fit the pieces together into an arc of wire ribbons, one unified section.

"Try one of the larger ones," he suggested.

Michael selected the largest parcel which lay beneath the top layer. He unwrapped it slowly, with a growing sense of dread; the urge to urinate was practically unbearable.

It was a black box with electric wires. On the top there was a dial and a series of numbers. He tried not to shake as he looked up, more frightened than before.

"Take another one!"

He ripped the tissue off, faster this time, and stared amazed as Roehm laughed and laughed and laughed until the saliva ran down his double chin, making the scar look like blood.

In his hands, Michael held a bright red caboose.

Champagne and electric trains!

They set up a circular track, plugged in the black transformer and he was free to play as he liked, any way he wished! He was free to drink as much as he wanted! But he was still more relieved with the toy than with the available alcohol. Sensing Michael's relief Roehm refilled the tall glasses.

They made the train travel circles, faster and faster, backing up or negotiating severe angles until it tipped and fell from the track. They constructed new routes, designed bridges at precarious angles and created chasms between pieces of furniture or plinths of tall boots.

As they played, Roehm's pleasure seemed to multiply rather than decrease. He muttered, "Strategy, strategy," and stroked himself and occasionally patted the boy's bare bottom. Once he even sighed and called Michael "my child." But, for the most part, he confined his attentions to the game at hand, designing strategic positions, ramps, tunnels, mountain passes and explaining to Michael the difficulties and mathematical risks inherent in accompanying a cargo of champagne across a battlefield.

Hours passed.

The train ran beneath furniture, across dark velvet and beneath the feet of the inky Christ. Across slate and velvet until, at last, the general announced the game was over.

Somewhat reluctantly, Michael helped the man repack the marvelous toy. Once again, the minutes lengthened and, across the morbid room the double bed seemed to wait, wide and expectant. Now it was only a question of time

But the general yawned again and picked up the small leather coat and held it out for the boy. Disbelieving, Michael slipped it on.

The general zipped up the front and picked up the tight leggings. For a moment he seemed to hesitate, looking at Michael and then down at the black leather pants. But, speaking as if he was a concerned grandparent helping a small child off to his first day of school, he urged, "Now put your leg through here. Good. We don't want to be late, do we? We don't want the teacher to have to thrash us? No! That would hurt! That would hurt very much!"

When Michael was fully dressed, the man had the boy sit on his lap. Now it will start, Michael thought to himself. Now, it will begin. *Yield and survive!*

But Roehm stared into his eyes for a long moment. And when he spoke again, his voice had changed. It was brusque again. Cold. He was the soldier. "All right, Michael, we've had our little game but I want you to make me a promise. Just one thing."

Michael nodded, bewildered by the sudden change in the man's attitude and confused by the fingers which gripped his arm. They were too hard! Now, the general's face was very near. "My child, don't ever tell anyone what happened in this room tonight!"

Michael nodded and the fingers relaxed a bit.

"If you do, I'll find out," the man hissed, "and I'll be very angry. I'll come back. Do you know what happened to that other boy, last week?"

"Heinrich?"

"Poor little Heinrich! Do you know what happened?"

Michael nodded and looked away from the face; it was terrible now, murky-eyed, frightful.

"All right, then, you promise." The fingers tightened on his arm again. "I'll know if you tell anyone. Even one person. Not Herr Lorken. Not anyone!"

"I understand. I promise!"

The fingers released him and the voice was impersonal. "Maneuvers are finished. You are dismissed!"

Chapter Twenty-Three

Michael walked out into the passage, down the dim gallery and out into the central hall. There were a few lights coming from the first floor; far away someone was playing the piano.

The black cloth with crescent moons and bones had been abandoned on the staircase; the floor below was littered with confetti, flowers, bits of costumes, uniforms and empty bottles.

Two Brown Shirts were sleeping on the stairs; a third was unconscious on the floor beside the first step. The chandelier was dark.

Michael stood for a moment, looking over the banister, staring out into the baroque gloom. And gradually, as he began to feel, he felt relief. But his legs were weak. They felt hollow; he almost lost his balance.

He turned toward the double doors, pushed them open and entered.

The alcove was in shadows; the dressing room was dark. He knocked on the other door. Frederich opened it.

He seemed unsteady, pale. For the first time, Michael saw him look shaky and uncertain. He'd washed away his mask. Now he seemed almost ordinary in the blue robe.

"Are you all right? Come in!"

Michael entered and glanced at the bed; it was empty. Although the lights were dim, he could see two

bottles beside a pillow on the floor. One was over-
turned; the other stood beside a glass and that blue
mirror. He glanced at Frederich who was still standing
by the door, staring at him.

"Michael, what happened?"

"Don't ask me that."

"What do you mean, 'Don't ask me that?' " Frederich demanded angrily. "What the hell does that
mean?"

"Just what I said," Michael replied, feeling weary
but oddly excited by the anxiety in Frederich's voice.
"Just don't ask."

"I can't believe you're serious!"

"I'm alive. Isn't that enough?"

"No! It's not enough!"

Frederich approached him and peered into his eyes.
He's drunk, Michael surmised. And he's probably been
using the white powder.

"For the past three hours I've been waiting for you to
come out of that horrible room! Every awful thought
has occurred to me and now you waltz in and tell me
not to think about it! Are you mad?"

"I promised him I wouldn't discuss it. Please don't
force me."

Frederich seized his arm. In the mirrors, a blue
gargoyle mushroomed from a waif and loomed over
him. But, in reality, it was an unsteady creature who
held his sleeve.

"What are you talking about? Don't force you? What
about me? I've been waiting, not knowing anything,
hating myself, blaming myself!"

"You shouldn't have . . ." Michael began.

"Wait a minute," Frederich interrupted, looking at
him more closely. "You're all right, aren't you?"

"I told you I was."

"He didn't, I mean you aren't . . ."

"Frederich, I . . ."

"He didn't touch you, did he?"

Michael didn't answer.

"Did he? Well, did he?"

Michael pulled his arm away; in the mirror, his shoulder and chest were inflated; the blue gargoyle became an azure pyramid. But Frederich grabbed him again and forced him to turn, to face those dark eyes. "Well, here's to you and your selfishness!" cried Frederich. The slap landed squarely on his jaw and stunned him for a moment.

He stared at Frederich's anguished face as he touched his cheek. Frederich looked half wild as Michael raised his own hand, drew back his arm and slapped him back, as hard as he possibly could. In the glass, the blue shape reappeared. Frederich rose, and it disappeared.

They glared at each other in silence; Frederich shook his head and turned away. Michael's eyes filled with tears. The mirror was obscured; he closed his eyes. They'd hurt each other again!

He hadn't thought of resisting Frederich since his second attempt to escape. Then, he'd been warring against the outside world. Now the battle was internal. Now, they were both too tired to care about the generals, the Gestapo, the spies on the staff or what had gone on in the chapel. They stumbled toward each other with open arms.

"Oh, Michael, Michael, I'm sorry," Frederich whispered, as he cradled the blond head against his shoulder. "I didn't mean to do that."

"It's not your fault," Michael said, tightening his arms around the slender waist.

"I know, but it is, it's . . ."

Frederich tried to pull away from the hug but Michael pulled him closer. "Michael, I . . . don't . . ."

They kissed; they kissed again and let tongues soften dry lips. Holding one another, leather against satin, they merged in the mirror and parted.

Frederich held him at arm's length and smiled his

faint smile. For the last time, he looked somewhat distracted but, when he unzipped the leather jacket, he looked shy for the first time.

"Don't stop," the boy begged. "Please, don't. Just love me."

Warm and cool, they fell onto the bed, disappearing from the mirror. Warm and cool, they ended the carnival and surrendered. Night reversed destiny and the real night began, erasing the impossible roles they'd played by day. And so it was, with occasional words and frequent kisses, they welded their lives into present tenses.

Michael woke first; it was light; his head hurt too much to move.

He turned and looked at Frederich who was still fast asleep. There was confetti in his hair. Michael smiled and snuggled into the soft pillows.

The mirrors had reflected first love. All night pale dragons and hydras had done loving battle in a ruptured landscape. Twin serpent kisses had blossomed into trees of life, sucked light from the room, thrown back fire and erupted.

But his head was pounding. Michael forced himself out of bed and staggered into the bathroom, hoping to find something in the medicine chest above the sink. All the pills were in small silver boxes or vials; nothing was marked or labeled. Michael groaned; leaning on the black sink for a moment, he turned and stumbled out into the living room.

For the first time, he enjoyed his nudity. For the first time he was actually glad to be naked and had no fear whatsoever about being seen or discovered. If what he'd found out last night was any indication of why grown-ups put such a store in sex, he had no reason to remain uninitiated or virginal.

There were noises outside. Michael pressed his face to the window and looked down.

Almost all the cars had disappeared! Now, as he

watched, he saw several officers emerge from the palace, hurry across the courtyard, enter automobiles and drive away. But today was only Saturday! They were expected to stay another day.

Another man came out of the palace and beckoned for a driver to bring his car. Squinting, Michael saw he had one of the boys with him! Who was beneath that wide hat? Stephen? Erich? It wasn't possible to recognize the youth from this distance.

Whatever it was, it was all very strange. Michael leaned against the window and decided that he didn't want to know. Somehow, it was all the soldier's problem; let him work it out.

So he sat on the windowsill and looked out at the lawns, the formal gardens and the long line of trees bordering the level playing field. This orderly enclosure of stone within the great ring of trees had become his world. All that had gone before had led him to the man who slept. All loss had come to a new home, a new beginning and love.

Now when he thought of his parents, their bloody death, he didn't have to feel so alone. There was something alive in his life. Death had been replaced if not erased, and though he swore he would never forget or forgive the agony of those days, there was a new reason to participate in the present day.

There was a silver box on a table near the window. Michael lifted the lid and saw some cigarettes; he picked one. Out of curiosity, he lit it and puffed smoke against the windowpane.

The cars were all gone and it was silent in the courtyard. Hundreds of years ago, it would have been like this, he thought. The clouds sprayed out and billowed back toward him, curling around his head.

He glanced at the room. The three colors were especially good for morning and perfect for cloudy days. No wonder Frederich rarely appeared before noon! Naturally he'd prefer to pass his early hours in this room. It was so soft, so timeless.

Frederich!

Michael smiled as he puffed on the black cigarette and blew another cloud against the glass. He thought of the preceding evening and hugged himself. He'd been so awkward, so unaware until Frederich revealed the simplicity of pleasure.

This wasn't something they could take away. It would never be denied again, the forthcoming days would only enrich what had begun last night.

The cigarette made him dizzy. Michael stubbed it out and looked around. He stood up, stretched, stroked his abdomen, walked into the dressing room, lit a candle and gazed into the golden glass.

His face was changing. Everything was changing. How was it possible that in only a few short weeks all would have such a different aspect? He had been brutalized, savaged, lost everything but come back with something new. What was that? Was it love? No, he'd had that before the soldiers came. Was it because of Frederich and who he was? No, well, maybe.

Still, the face in the golden glass was altered. More like his father's, perhaps. His dark blue eyes looked darker now and his pale hair was growing in darker at the roots.

He opened the top drawer in search of the pot of silver paint. But he found something different. He stared at it in astonishment. Then, he reached in and pulled it out. A loaded pistol, a deadly weapon! Why?

After a long moment, he put it back; whatever it was, he didn't want to know why.

Michael blew out the candle and stood in the darkness. He was frightened suddenly, and uncertain. What was the pistol for? Did Frederich care about him; was he worried for their safety?

After the night before, Michael didn't feel that he required protection or assistance. He'd handled General Roehm, hadn't he? And he was the most dangerous of all!

The thought occurred to him that if Roehm had

wanted to do the things that had happened to Heinrich to him, he'd have been helpless to prevent it, helpless to refuse, and obligated to . . .

He turned at the sound of Frederich's yawn and walked into the bedroom. Frederich was sitting up, ashen faced and bleary eyes. His hair was a mess, and he looked totally scattered, but Michael smiled and leaped onto the bed.

"Ooooh! My head!" he protested as Michael embraced him.

"My head too!" Michael chimed in enthusiastically.

"You're really here, aren't you?" asked Frederich, wiping sleep from his eyes.

"Uh-huh!"

"I didn't know if I'd dreamed everything or if . . ."

"It happened!" Michael avowed. Frederich curled up, trying to protect himself from Michael's tickling, trying not to laugh, trying not to let Michael ambush him again.

"Are you one of those people who are cheerful in the morning?" Frederich asked from his protective shell. "They are the very worst and I won't stand for it!"

"Oh, yes, you will!" insisted Michael, attempting to wedge his hand through the man's outer defenses. "I'll make you!"

"Let's truce," offered Frederich, looking out from the rumpled covers with a mysterious expression in his eye. "If you don't abuse me so early in the day, I'll . . ."

"You'll what?" Michael demanded, certain there was nothing he could possibly find more tempting than conquest.

"I'll give you something for your headache," Frederich suggested. "Otherwise, you'll have to suffer alone!"

"All right," allowed Michael, after mulling it over for a minute. "But that doesn't hold for this afternoon."

"Oh, I'll think of something else by then," Frederich

assured him. "But, for the moment, let's take care of these headaches."

He stood up, put on his robe and stumbled toward the bathroom.

"Did you have a good time last night?" asked Michael.

"I must have." Frederich appeared with some blue tablets and a glass of water. He offered two to Michael. "Here. The mysteries of the West."

"What is it?"

"Reprieve," Frederich said. "Just take them."

Michael swallowed the pills as Frederich crawled back into bed and buried his head in the pillows. He took the half-empty glass back to the bathroom and emerged to see Frederich talking on the phone. "No, in my room. Two cups. Coffee and . . ." He raised a brow in Michael's direction. "Do you want coffee, tea or chocolate?"

"Just coffee," answered Michael, feeling very grown up.

"Just coffee," chorused Frederich, winking at him. "And rolls and Peter, tell everyone to stay away. I have a headache until this evening. What? *What?*"

Frederich stared at the telephone for several minutes and when he finally said "thank you" and hung up, he seemed shaken. "Peter says they're all gone. *Everyone.*"

"I know."

"You do?"

"I saw them from the living room. They were all in a hurry."

"But why?"

"I don't know. But Peter says there was trouble in town."

"What kind of trouble?"

"He didn't know; there are rumors of some dispute between Hitler and Roehm."

"Can't you keep me with you?" asked Michael, thinking to himself, *Say yes, oh please say yes!*

"I don't know Michael," Frederich answered, as he reached for the blue mirror and black box. "I don't know where I'll be if I'm not here."

They were silent as Frederich spooned some powder out onto the mirror. Michael wanted to talk but he didn't know what to say to change the man's mind or extract a promise from him.

"Whatever happens," said Frederich, as if divining his thoughts, "I'll do whatever I can to help you. That's a promise."

"But I want to be with you," Michael said.

"I realize that."

Frederich put the silver straw to his nose and inhaled two white lines, smiled and replaced the mirror beneath the bed.

"Don't you want to be with me?"

"Of course. If it's possible."

"But I thought . . ." the boy stammered.

"What?"

"I thought you cared about me!"

"I do! You know that, don't you?"

"I thought I did."

"I do care for you. A great deal."

"Then if you love me, why don't you keep me with you?"

Frederich held out his arms. "Come here," he said. Michael crawled into his embrace and felt himself expanding to receive the gentle strokes of the hand on his hair. Frederich's voice was gentle and reassuring. "I know how you must feel. You've been through a bad time and now you and I have what we have. And there's nothing in the world that could make me want to leave you."

"Then why would you?"

"Because there are times when the best thing for us to do for someone else is to stay away or leave them alone, or even go away. Can you understand that?"

"No," Michael said truthfully, tightening his arms around Frederich, thinking that if he held on with all his strength, his friend would have to keep him and not throw him out into a world of soldiers and their plans.

"All right, I'll try to explain it another way," Frederich began.

"Do you love me?"

"Michael, love is something very . . ."

"Do you love me? Yes or no?" the boy interjected.

Frederich sighed. "It's so odd, isn't it? How little we know what effect we have on other people! I was certain you'd known how I felt about you almost from the beginning."

"I didn't and I still don't!"

"Isn't that remarkable?" asked Frederich. "Well, it's official."

"Then if that's true, why would you ever leave me?" asked Michael, not wanting to cry but feeling there was no guarantee of tomorrow in the way the man said the words.

"Michael, I've got to do what's best for you, to keep you safe from harm."

"But I don't care about myself!"

"Ah, now that is foolishness," Frederich remonstrated. "Don't you realize that I'll always have you with me? Wherever I am, you'll always be a part of . . ." He continued talking until the boy was calm.

They lay together. It was so quiet, Michael could hear both hearts beat. A knock on the door alarmed him; he wanted to jump up and hide but Frederich soothed his fears.

"It's only Peter with our coffee. Don't worry; he won't say anything." And louder, then, "Come in!"

The door opened; Christian Stauffer stood in the door with a tray.

Chapter Twenty-Four

For a moment no one spoke; Michael felt Frederich's hand squeeze his own to give him courage. But his eyes remained fixed on the black-uniformed soldier at the door.

"I trust I'm not intruding," the major said, with exaggerated courtesy.

"Don't just stand there looking self-righteous, Christian. Come in. I want my coffee," replied Frederich smoothly.

The major entered, leaving the doors to the alcove open. As he set the tray down on the end of the bed, his armband was reflected in the mirror; an enormous swastika ballooned over the goosedown quilts. Michael and Frederich were little pinpricks in the fun-house glass.

"Two cups!" the major exclaimed. "I saw Peter on the way up the stairs with one tray and two cups. He told me it was for my colonel but I saw him not twenty minutes ago. He was having breakfast, in town! Isn't it fascinating?"

Frederich said nothing. The major turned to Michael and snarled, "Go on! You get out of here!"

As Michael dressed, his chest and shoulders were burly in the mirror; he had an enormous phallus and tiny legs. His forehead was cut off and his waist disappeared.

The room was silent; Frederich rose and poured a cup of coffee.

As he zipped up the leather jacket, Michael was

aware of the major's eyes on him; the stare was oppressive but, when he reached the door, he turned and blurted out, "I'm not sorry!"

Then he ran. He ran out into the hall and down the great staircase where two footmen were sweeping up the last of the debris from the night before. Several of the major's lieutenants were coming in from outside.

He ran past the blue salon, the pale music room, the grand dining hall with its twenty-four court portraits, into the back hall, the first pantry on the right and through the hidden door, concealed behind a set of shelves. Up the carpeted stairs, up to the narrow door with the little hole.

He could see across the alcove, into the bedroom where the major stood. His back was to the door. Frederich was invisible.

Michael took a deep breath and slipped into the dressing room; he crossed the chamber and concealed himself behind the folding screen. From this vantage point, he had an unobstructed view into the bedroom, only ten or eleven feet away.

The major's voice was audible: ". . . until four A.M. at the Hotel Hanslbaur. Even Hitler was there to preside over the end of poor General Roehm. It didn't require too much of his time to wipe up the gutter rats. So, they're all gone: Roehm, Heins, all the others. The Gestapo shot them as they returned from your party, which I'm told was marvelous. The ones who left last night, as well as the ones who left this morning . . . all dead. You see what I mean when I say the game is over. I managed to intercede on your behalf as I promised I would; I came to tell you that I've gotten orders for this house to be closed and for the residents to be taken to Berlin for reassignment. And look what I find!"

Frederich's voice was cool and absolutely self-confident. "Are you going to give me a chance to explain?"

"Of course you can explain! But then you'll die."

Frederich's voice was steady. "It's more complicated than it appears."

"I heard what he said. I think he loves you."

"Of course he loves me!"

"So you admit it! How unexpectedly candid!"

"They always love me when they first arrive! Oh, Christian, don't be so boring! I've never told you these things because I didn't want to disturb you but many times boys have come in here to sleep. Sometimes, it's because they've had a fight with one of the others, like Josef. Sometimes it's nightmares or problems with the soldiers. Can't you see? I'm not only the curator of this museum, I'm the only person, with the conceivable exception of Peter, whom they regard as family. Don't laugh. It's true!"

"I'm not laughing at you," the major said good-naturedly. "I was remembering something else."

"They're just boys," Frederich continued reasonably. "They are hardly more than children, chosen for appearance, forced into this life and induced to make whatever adjustments might be necessary. But they're human, they need warmth and care. And tenderness too. Not just what they receive from the soldiers. Especially if they're going to try and satisfy the clientele. Michael's just another example of what I mean. Christian, before they brought him here, he saw his family butchered. Schüller sent him to me. On the way he was brutalized. After he arrived he was seriously ill. All this in the past month, mind you! Of course he comes to me for comfort. You don't seriously think that there's anything more to it than that, do you? That a fourteen-year-old boy could be your rival? Really, Christian, use your head!

"Michael has been going through severe trauma. I saw that if he was ever to be a good worker, he was going to have to have some stability. Otherwise he'd never be any use to anyone. It was my job to see that he performed his work well. So now, as in the past, if it meant giving him a little personal attention, I accepted it as part of my responsibility. Not to do so would have been negligent. But I'm glad you came along when you did. He was becoming maudlin and sentimental. And you know how I feel about such things! I suppose it's one of the hazards of associating with the very immature."

There was a long pause in the bedroom. Michael wondered if Frederich was telling the truth. Was he only another commodity to be soothed and prepared for the soldiers to use up? Did Frederich lie as easily to him as he did to the major, *if* all that was a lie? His words sounded completely convincing but when the officer spoke, his tone was skeptical.

"You always were a bad liar, Frederich. Even back in Berlin when you had to explain your association with Max . . ."

"Christian, don't . . ."

"The lie was obvious. Hitler knew it too; he thought you might very well become an agent if you weren't already working for his enemies!"

"That's ridiculous!"

"Is it? I don't think so. You've always been a bad liar. Even in bed."

Through the crack between the panels of the folding screen, Michael saw Frederich's reflection in one of the distorted mirrors. He smiled so his eyes and mouth became two parallel wrinkles, as if his face had been folded into strips.

"So, it's really the end then?"

"Yes, it's really the end," said the major.

"After all this time and so many false starts?" asked Frederich as he stood up and walked toward his bathroom, a thin blue line slicing a mirror in half.

"I'm afraid so. What are you doing?"

Frederich had disappeared but Michael could hear sounds of water as he stepped out from behind the screen and crept toward the dressing table.

In the mirror, in the bedroom, the major faced a

moving blur of dark shapes slipping into silvery blurs as Michael opened the drawer and pocketed the loaded gun. If he had turned and looked across the alcove, Stauffer would have deciphered those liquid shapes. But he was preoccupied and remained with his back to the dressing room.

"If I'm going to die, I might as well look my best," said Frederich.

"Vain to the end, aren't you?"

"A clean face requires no defense," replied Frederich. "You'll give me a minute?"

"Of course. And I think we'll have that boy up here to complete the scenario. What was his name?"

For the first time, Frederich sounded sharp. "Michael? Oh, Christian, no!"

"Ah, *Michael*. Thank you!"

As Michael crept back to his hiding place behind the screen, Frederich came out of the bathroom; his face was clean and his hair was combed but he looked like a bug-eyed fish as he tugged at the major's sleeve, his white eyes bulging.

"But I told you he's nothing to me. Less than nothing!"

"Less than nothing? In that case, why so alarmed, Frederich? Why so emotional? You should be happy to lose one and not all of them! You should thank me for making arrangements to see that your troops will be spared!"

"But he's only a child!"

"Not from what I saw . . ."

"Please, punish me if you must but don't hurt him! He's been hurt enough. He can't be blamed!"

"I don't think so." The major sounded more determined. "Now, where is your telephone?"

"Christian, please don't!"

"I'm afraid I must. It appeals to my Wagnerian sense of justice. Ah, there's the telephone. I'll let *you* invite him to join us."

"Never!" Frederich snapped.

"Very well, then. I'll do it myself. Surely you don't want to die alone!"

Frederich said nothing. But the mirror revealed a hollow-cheeked urchin with yellow skin, turning away from a swastika blimp.

"Where does he live? Which room?" The major had the house telephone in his hand and was leaning against the mirror, only two feet from the bedroom door. His request was ignored.

"Very well then, I'll ask Peter. He'll know."

He dialed the telephone. In the mirror the spinning dial was the revolving roulette, the wheel, shot with wiggly numbers.

Frederich's voice was ragged. "Christian, for the last time, leave Michael out of it! He's not involved!"

"Nonsense! And let you die without your lover? How heartless! You know I'm incurably romantic. I want to see both of you stretched out, side by side. Perhaps with some of your gray roses in hand . . ." Then, speaking into the receiver, he said, "Hello, Peter? Oh, is he there? Yes, this is Major Stauffer. Ask him to come to the phone immediately. Thank you."

In the pause, he whispered to Frederich. "They're calling him. He's been attending to the trucks."

Frederich tried to push past the major, but the man stopped him. "Christian, let me pass!"

"Why?"

"I need something from my dressing room."

The major pushed Frederich back into the bedroom. In the mirror, Frederich's shoulders shriveled and his head got pointed. "You stay where I can see you. I'll be off the telephone in a minute and then you'll get what you need."

"Hello, Peter? This is Major Stauffer. I'm in Herr Lorken's room and I want you to locate one of the boys for us. Yes, his name is Michael and . . ."

Michael aimed for the heart and pulled the trigger. The shot was so loud it made all of them jump. He knocked the screen and tipped it. It fell with a crash.

In the glass, red eels shot across a reef and laced tentacles around Frederich's neck. The wounded man dropped the phone and stared at Michael, amazement on his face. He looked from Michael to Frederich to Michael, grew fins in the glass, spit up a red fount and stained his swastika as the black sank to the floor and he fell, eyes rolling back in his head.

Frederich ran from the alcove to the living room, locked the heavy doors and returned to Michael. He hung up the telephone as an unconscious gesture and turned to Michael.

The telephone rang at once; Frederich ignored it. He took the pistol from Michael and shook him by the shoulder. But Michael was still staring at the dead man. Blood was oozing out of his mouth. Frederich pushed him into the bedroom and took him by the shoulders. The gun was near his head; he could smell powder as Frederich spoke.

"Michael, please listen carefully. There's not much time. You see? It's come even sooner than we thought."

The faces in the glass didn't even belong to him or his friend. There were blobs of skin and bone, mats of hair, squishing in one direction and then the next.

The telephone continued to ring. Frederich went on. "Now, you've got to go down the back stairs and get to your room. Above all, you know nothing. *No matter what happens!* Do you promise?"

No matter what happens . . . These words echoed in Michael's head from another time! Maybe dogs would come out of the glass, out of the dark shapes, into the blood on the rug and the bodies. Maybe this was the film repeating with guns and soon, too soon, soldiers would come for him. . . .

"Michael, do you promise? Say you promise!"

Frederich was shaking him so hard his head snapped back and forth on his neck. Oh yes, this world again! This man with the white face! Frederich!

"Yes, Frederich . . ." His voice sounded flat.

"Good, what else?"

Frederich ran into the dressing room and Michael turned to watch him. There was no distortion. Just the clear sight of the man rooting through a drawer and pulling out a blue velvet bag. Michael followed him instinctively, dulled somehow to the rest, conscious only of how far he was from Frederich and cognizant that he had to stand as close as possible to him. He had to be with him now.

He crossed the alcove, stepping over the major's corpse without looking down, but, as he did, there was knocking at the living-room doors; the telephone was still ringing. . . .

Frederich turned. "They're here! Michael, there's jewelry in that bag! It's extremely valuable. Take it. Sell it. Do whatever you can with the money, only save yourself!"

"But you?" the boy began, his mind just beginning to surface from the shock of killing, barely a minute ago.

Frederich cut in. "I think I can save you *if you go now!*"

The pounding was louder. Soldiers called out, demanding that the doors be opened. Receiving no answer, they began smashing at the solid wood.

"The Gestapo. Subtle, aren't they?" Frederich smiled his vanishing smile.

Michael couldn't move; if he took a step away from his lover, he'd have lost everything again. No! He had to stay here. He had to fight for Frederich! He could use the gun and kill more soldiers! He could shoot them or they could run for the trees or get horses or . . .

"Frederich, listen, I . . ."

"No, you listen to me! And remember that, at last, I escaped!"

"Yes, that's it. . . ."

"That in the end, I was saved! Think of me sometimes and be glad. But live, Michael, live!"

The living-room doors were giving way; Michael's eyes filled with tears. He was losing hold again. He was

falling   backward,   being   erased,   reduced   to
nothing. . . .

"I love you Frederich!" he sobbed.

"Yes," Frederich murmured. "Kiss?"

They kissed; Michael threw his arms around Frederich, trying to hold him up but Frederich broke away,
pushed him into the hidden hall and slammed the door.

Michael ran, but just as he reached the bottom of the
stairs and opened the door to the pantry, he heard the
shot.

Chapter Twenty-Five

He was blank; all was numb. He moved through the next half hour as if it was no more than a dream.

He did what he was told to do. When they told him to sit, he sat. When they said line up, he lined up. No one cared who he was or which room he had. He was no one again; he had nothing; he was one of the ones who was left. That was all.

The man in charge said that they would go back to Berlin as planned. The trucks were ready.

He sat in the hall with the others. Some were frightened; a few were crying. But he sat still without moving, without talking, staring straight ahead. All he could do was follow orders. There was no reason not to. He was dead. Let the others ask questions or say they'd be shot or tortured. Michael was gone; Michael had no thoughts. Michael was unable to think or feel or reason or anything.

Peter came down the stairs with the lieutenant. He saw Michael and blinked, looked down and then up at the man who asked him questions, the man in the black uniform.

"And that's all you heard?" the man asked.

"Major Stauffer said Herr Lorken had shot himself and that he was going to do the same."

"A suicide pact," the lieutenant mused.

Peter said nothing.

"Well," the lieutenant exclaimed. "I don't think this will get much attention considering what happened last night. But I can't understand it myself."

"The major was an unusual man," Peter suggested.

"He was very quiet this morning," the lieutenant admitted. "But who could have guessed this?"

Peter shrugged and looked dumbfounded. The lieutenant waved his hand and the boys filed out of the palace, one by one. As Michael passed, Peter turned away.

Transport vans with open backs had been brought up to the front steps. The boys climbed in dutifully but Michael lingered, wanting to be the last one in.

It was easy. All the others were already moving on, forward to the future, whatever it was. Only he looked back, again and again trying to memorize the urns, the statues, hoping for a glimpse of his beloved at the window, hoping and giving up hope.

He was successful; he was the last one in the truck.

The convoy was ready to go when the small group of officers came out of the palace; Peter emerged with them but remained at the top of the stairs as they descended, got into the motor car and moved off.

The trucks followed.

As the van moved down the long drive, Michael remained unable to cry. Unable to feel anything. He couldn't talk. All was nothing as the trucks drove through the forest to the tall gates and the outside world.

PART IV
1964

Chapter Twenty-Six

Michael wept; for the first time in his adult life, he wept without shame or reservation. Scott sat still for a long time, until at last he reached out and took Michael into his arms.

The touch of his hand was reassuring. Michael could let himself accept the gentleness but he avoided meeting Scott's eyes. He was afraid of what he'd find in them. Perhaps blame? Michael felt he deserved it.

His eyes filled with tears again and he looked down as they splashed from his face onto his bare chest. He wasn't aware of how long they sat like that or how irregular his breath had become but, finally, he sensed that he could sit up and breathe without difficulty. He stole a glance at the grim, red-eyed boy and tried to form a wry smile.

"I'm still shaking."

"Just be still; it'll pass," Scott said quietly.

"Can you get me a cigarette?"

The boy crossed the room and returned with Michael's coat. Michael reached into his pocket and withdrew his silver case. He lit one but shook the match so slowly it took five shakes to extinguish the flame. Scott watched the operation without any expression. When Michael lay back on the bed staring up at the ceiling, the boy leaned forward. "You've never told anyone what happened?" he asked.

Michael shook his head.

"Not ever? Not even your wife?"

"Especially not her."

"Jesus."

"I was too afraid."

"Afraid of what?"

"Afraid to trust her, or anyone else."

"But you told me . . .?"

"You and I and the way we met. I mean . . ."

"I understand. But can I say something?"

Michael nodded and Scott continued.

"I can't understand why you've never shared these things before."

"I don't know. It's just that . . ."

"It's just that what?"

"I always felt so guilty."

"You, guilty?"

Michael nodded; Scott frowned.

"But nothing that happened was your fault!"

"They all died because of me!"

"Wait a minute," Scott protested. "Who? Frederich? Your parents? They didn't die because of you. They died trying to save you!"

"What difference does it make?" asked Michael. "Everyone I ever cared about was murdered. I was there. I couldn't do anything about it. I didn't help."

"It's every difference in the world! Don't you see! They knew what they were doing! Your parents . . . and Frederich! You weren't responsible."

"If I hadn't been in his room, Frederich wouldn't have . . ."

"Wouldn't have had to kill himself?"

Michael nodded. Scott shook his head.

"Michael, even if they'd have let him live, he'd have been taken back to Berlin and reassigned. From what you told me the major wanted to save him."

"Frederich would never have worked for the Nazis!"

"Wasn't that what he was doing when you met him?" asked Scott quietly.

"But that was different!"

"I agree with you but you yourself told me, he died with his ideals!"

"That's what he said but . . ."

"But what?"

"I don't know if he meant it."

"Why not? He said it. You heard him."

Michael pressed the flats of both hands against the bed.

"It came so soon after the other murders. It happened so soon after. And I can't remember too much of what happened. I know I was sick but they didn't put me away. They took care of me."

"Who?"

"I don't know. It was a long time, and when I was better, and even after I ran away and got out of Germany, I never could think about it. For so long I wanted to but, when I did I'd feel confused again. I was so frightened all the time, but it seemed right in some way. It seemed fair. That I was being punished. Even if I was wrong, it was so easy to think it all happened because of me. That it was my fault, my shame."

There was a knock at the door. Scott jumped off the bed, wrapped a towel around himself and answered it. The girl was there with the laundry.

"How much was it?"

"Three dollars," the girl replied.

Scott reached into his leather coat and produced a wallet. He pressed some bills into the girl's hand and accepted the clothes. "Thank you very much."

"Thank you," she said, and was gone.

Scott put his clothes on top of the bureau and brought the clean shirt over to Michael. "Here."

As Michael put on his shirt, Scott yawned. Michael glanced at the bleary-eyed boy and smiled.

"And now?" Scott began.

"What?"

"What are you feeling?"

Michael tucked his shirt into his pants and sat on the bed. He picked up one shoe and held it in his hands.

"I feel like I've been trying to balance it out ever since I was there. In so many ways, I've been trying to escape. That hardness, that need to survive became my major consideration. Everything I did was to be sure I wouldn't ever suffer like that again. Or that I wouldn't bring disaster into any other lives. I had to prove myself. I think I've spent twenty years trying to show myself that I could protect somebody."

"You protected your wife and kids. That's important. I mean it's been hard for you a lot of the time, I bet. You've given them protection and love."

"And love. Of course. But I could never be soft with them. I could never let them know that inside me, the man, there was that child who'd lost everything, everyone, who felt responsible for so much death."

"What do you feel now?"

"I'm not sure of this," said Michael. "But I feel as if I don't have to run anymore. That, if I tell the whole truth, it won't mean death or disaster."

"Is that the answer?"

"Maybe not the whole one. But it's a big part of it," said Michael as he picked up his coat. "I think I know how it's going to help."

Scott nodded. "I think you're right."

"I hope so," said Michael. He glanced toward the window. "It's getting dark."

"Which direction are you driving?"

"South. Home. Will you be all right?"

"Man, I didn't ever expect to get this far today!"

"Neither did I," Michael said.